C0035 88328

libraries | **Parkhead Library**
64 Tollcross Road
Glasgow G31 4XA
Phone: 0141 276 1530

This book is due for return on or before the last date shown below. It may be renewed by telephone, personal application, fax or post, quoting this date, author, title and the book number.

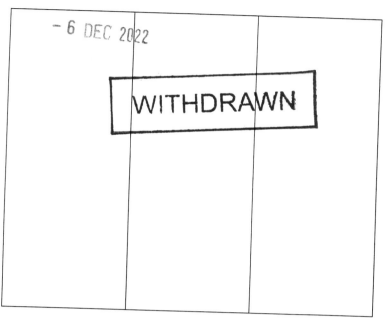

- 6 DEC 2022

WITHDRAWN

Glasgow
CITY COUNCIL

RULES, REGS AND ROTTEN EGGS

H. R. F. KEATING

THORNDIKE
WINDSOR
PARAGON

This Large Print edition is published by Thorndike Press, Waterville, Maine, USA and by BBC Audiobooks Ltd, Bath, England.

Thorndike Press, a part of Gale, Cengage Learning.

The text of this Large Print edition is unabridged.

Other aspects of the book may vary from the original edition.

Set in 16 pt. Plantin.

Printed on permanent paper.

LIBRARY OF CONGRESS CATALOGING-IN-PUBLICATION DATA

Keating, H. R. F. (Henry Reymond Fitzwalter), 1926–
  Rules, regs and rotten eggs / by H.R.F. Keating.
    p. cm. — (Thorndike Press large print mystery)
  ISBN-13: 978-1-4104-0909-6 (alk. paper)
  ISBN-10: 1-4104-0909-0 (alk. paper)
  1. Martens, Harriet (Fictitious character)—Fiction. 2. Policewomen—England—Fiction. 3. Politicians—Crimes against—Fiction. 4. Fox hunting—Fiction. 5. Large type books.
  I. Title.
  PR6061.E26R78 2008b
  823'.914—dc22
                                       2008020784

BRITISH LIBRARY CATALOGUING-IN-PUBLICATION DATA AVAILABLE

Published in 2008 in the U.S. by arrangement with St. Martin's Press, LLC.

Published in 2009 in the U.K. by arrangement with Allison & Busby Ltd.

U.K. Hardcover: 978 1 405 64436 5 (Windsor Large Print)
U.K. Softcover: 978 1 405 64437 2 (Paragon Camden Large Print)

Printed in the United States of America
1 2 3 4 5 6 7 12 11 10 09 08

Rules, Regs and Rotten Eggs

CHAPTER ONE

Detective Superintendent Harriet Martens spat out her bottled-up rage.

'I'm going to resign from this bloody job.'

'Oh, yes?' said her husband, sitting beside her in the car he had just brought to a seatbelt-tightening stop.

'*Oh, yes?* Is that all you can say when I tell you I'm going to quit the job I've had ever since I was fit to have a job? That I'm going to forget the belief I've always had that being a detective is something worth devoting one's whole life to? *Oh, yes?* Is that your only reaction?'

For a second or two John sat thinking, his features under the waning light of the September evening seemingly settled into their customary calm.

'Well,' he said at last, 'it's really a question of what's made you explode like that. Was it just momentary fury because that huge crowd in the square down there is mysteriously blocking our way? Or was it the sudden coming to a head of a long-nurtured feeling?'

'Both.'

John laughed.

'I suppose it's no use pointing out to you that the two statements are logically at odds.'

'All right, John Piddock, part-time Professor of Logic, let me say I don't feel they are at odds.'

'Very well, Mrs Piddock, licensed husband critic, I concede that perhaps my claim wasn't completely correct. But, all the same, a sudden announcement like that does call for some explanation.'

'Well,' Harriet answered, her flare of rage diminishing, 'I suppose actually it was both things at once that made me come out with it. You've got to admit that appalling lunch we've just endured was enough to make anyone think about quitting a job when you've virtually been ordered to go to it. And —'

'No, wait a minute. That lunch wasn't altogether awful.'

'Oh, come on. Would you yourself have liked to find you'd been dragooned into going all the way out to that dreadful inglenooky cottage just to meet a writer —

forgotten his name already, thank goodness — who *absolutely had* to find out about a senior woman police officer's life. And kept me there all bloody afternoon.'

'But you didn't have to arrive so set on being frosty.'

'Justifiably frosty, let me remind you. The wife had given the most appalling directions for finding the place, and, what's more, she distinctly said *One-ish,* and we were there by twenty-past. Or only a bit later. There wasn't any need for those chilly looks.'

'Except that, apparently, she was certain they'd said twelve-thirty, and her soufflé starter was pretty well a puddle by the time she brought it in.'

'Her fault for expecting us to keep to that stuffy *Never later than a quarter of an hour* etiquette.'

'*Etiquette?* I haven't heard anybody actually say that word for . . . at least twenty years.'

'OK, OK, I haven't either. I'm not even sure I know what exactly it means. But —'

John, the dictionary devotee, broke in.

'It's something like, quote, conventionally accepted standards of proper social behaviour. Came across it the other day and looked it up. But, note, it's very probably etiquette to give a full explanation for any sudden life-changing announcement.'

'Oh, that. Yes. Well, I suppose I should explain. A bit.'

'Even quite a lot?'

'All right. But it's not altogether easy.'

'Try. The only way.'

'Pig.'

She sighed.

'But, well . . . Well, I suppose it's really all to do with the new ACC.'

'The Assistant Chief Constable (Crime), chap at the head of the CID?'

'As you ought to know by this time. Right, the fact is the man's doing nothing but make life difficult for me.'

'But you used to get on very well with his predecessor, didn't you?'

'I did. I certainly did. Which only increases my feeling that this man is deliberately picking on me. I think he got it into his head at the start that I'm not the detective I used to be. He'd been told about the terrorist bomb that killed Graham, and simply decided I'd still be affected. But that dull weight has gone. Gone altogether. You know it has. I am not what I was in the months after that happened.'

'You're not. Without any doubt. Time has done the trick, as incidentally it's done for me, more or less.'

10

'Thank you. And, now I come to think of it, yes, it was in fact probably the ACC who decided I was fit for nothing more arduous than going off to Inglenooky Cottage to talk to that idiot writer.'

'If he did, and I don't think for a moment it would have entered his mind —'

'You don't know him, John. You don't. He's a typical example of someone who's risen up the ranks by sticking firmly to the regulations and the rules, as if he's climbing some sort of rope-ladder. And in the end he's got to a place that's simply too high for him. Oh, I know that as a graduate entrant myself, I'd be accused of being an intellectual snob if I said this to anyone but you. Yet it's true. I tell you, the ACC, stuck there above, is pigheaded from the neck up.'

'All right, that does happen, but —'

'No. It's the prospect of working under him all the way to my retirement date that's made me seriously contemplate just now turning the job in. So there's your answer.'

'If you are that serious about it, I think we'd better make our way home, sit down with a quiet drink and discuss it all.'

Harriet looked down again at the market square ahead. It was a seething black sea of shoulder-to-shoulder, heaving and swaying people.

'Hardly possible to drive through that,' she said. 'I can see why you braked so suddenly.'

'Right, not exactly according to the Highway Code. But I didn't expect to come over the crest and find it.'

'What are they all doing there?' Harriet demanded. 'On an ordinary Tuesday evening, for heaven's sake? I've had a bloody awful time, and I want to get home.'

'I suppose,' John said, with a puff of a sigh, 'I'll have to see if I can get round somehow. Do you know this place? What is it? Gralethorpe, did the sign say?'

'Yes, I do know Gralethorpe, as a matter of fact. Been out here a couple of times. On inquiries.'

'Very well, give your ignorant husband the benefit of your knowledge.'

'Sorry, can't really be much help. I was only here for an hour or so each time. Talked to a nice old lady once.' A wry laugh. 'Went to her door wanting information, all ready to pretend I was from the Council. Then, the moment she appeared, apple-cheeked and innocent but with a look sharp as a pecking bird, I found myself dropping the pretence and producing the plain truth. *Police officer on your doorstep.* And, no fuss, she simply told me everything I'd needed to find out. And gave me a very good tea, too.'

'Ancient rules of hospitality. I like that. And I quite like the Hard Detective being taught a lesson.'

Harriet bristled.

'Look, I've warned you often enough about giving me that stupid media label. There's a house rule about not ever mentioning it.'

'So there is. Grovelling apologies. And I think I can see, now that the street-lamps are coming on, what that crowd's there for. It's a flavour-of-the month anti-hunting protest. You can see the banners, *End Blood Sports.*'

'Ah, right. And I know something about it, actually. Piece of paper landed on my desk last week. There's a politician of some sort, ex-MP I think, who feels he's got a right to speak up for hunting wherever he can. In fact he's probably that chap on the platform over there, all dressed up in the proper gear. And, yes, I remember the name. Rather an odd one. Roughouse. Something Roughouse.'

'Spelt with only one *h?* If it is, I can tell you something about Robert Roughouse. I've read a book by him, travel book. He went out of his way to mention that Roughouse is an old Northumbrian name, deriv-

13

ing from an ancient keep or castle.'

'Thank you, Mr Encyclopedia. But, as I was saying, apparently Roughouse insists on addressing any anti-hunting rally he hears of, and won't be warned that he may get more than he bargains for. People can be pretty aggressive in a mining town like Gralethorpe. At weekends they like to go walking out in the open. They don't much care for toffs riding roughshod — or, actually, extremely well-shod — all over the countryside.'

She looked once more at the square below.

'But my piece of bumph doesn't seem to have been read by any Gralethorpe police officer. Not a uniform in sight. Should be. I wouldn't be surprised if there's trouble before long. Those are pretty angry yells now.'

'You could be right. Brave of Robert Roughouse really to come here and face that, though I suppose he's got as much right as that crowd has to have his say. And there is, actually, a good deal to be said for foxhunting.'

'How d'you know? Confess. Ever been up on a horse? Ever?'

'Well, no. Got me there. But listen. Listen to what he's telling the crowd, now he's got hold of a mike. *You cannot just end 400 years of history, 400 years of courage and daring over the fences. That, in the end, is what keeps Britain great.* He's got a point, you know.'

'I suppose he may have. But what I want is my supper. Or, in fact, after wading through that sodden soufflé pretending hard for manners' sake, what I really want is to postpone that heavy discussion you're planning till tomorrow and flop in front of some mindless telly till it's time for bed.'

'Then we'll be off. If you can tell me how to weave our way through the back streets.'

'Certainly time I tried to. Specially as I think someone up there on the platform's just switched off Roughhouse's mike.'

'There speaks the cynical Hard — the cynical police officer. More likely, if his mike is off, it's someone saving him from the anger of the mob.'

'Oh, but, look. Look. No one's saving him now. Those are rotten eggs beginning to fly.'

'You're right. They are. Dozens of them, too. Brown, white, and I dare say speckled.'

They sat on, looking at the ever-growing bombardment.

'But how do you know the eggs are rotten?' John said after a little. 'Evidence of the smell? At this distance?'

'Oh, all right. Most likely straight from

the supermarket, today's bargain offer. But by age-old tradition they ought to be rotten.'

'Know what you mean. The conventional missile. But, rotten or farm-fresh, I still wouldn't like to be Robert Roughouse up there in his nice red coat. Or *pink,* that's what you have to say. Pink, despite the evidence of your eyes.'

Any question of getting home temporarily forgotten, they stayed watching in fascination.

'Wow, look, at that one,' John exclaimed. 'Almost purple in this light. May really be rotten. And sailing straight towards —'

Then, as the dark missile struck the wall only just behind Robert Roughouse, there came an odd sharp noise like a thick stick snapping.

And Roughouse, right arm raised, finger pointing high, pitched forward and lay face-down and unmoving.

CHAPTER TWO

So Harriet never got her mindless flop in front of the TV. She knew, with no other police presence at the scene, that it was her duty to do what she could to investigate, though already she could see dozens of the potential witnesses quietly slipping away. Telling John he might as well make his way home as best he could, she grabbed the heavy torch they kept in the car and ran across to the town hall and the victim outside it.

The inert body had been turned on its back with a rolled-up raincoat pushed under the head. Shouting *Police officer. I am a police officer,* she told the people clustered round to move aside and knelt down. At once she saw that whatever it had been that had exploded just behind Roughouse it had not killed him. But it was plain he had been appallingly injured. Blood was pumping out from a dozen wounds or more. Judging by the quota of victims she had seen over the years criss-crossed with savage cuts, it looked as if he could well be in imminent danger of death.

'A doctor?' she called back to the onlookers standing round. 'Has anybody called a doctor?'

Voices from the dark assured her that one had been summoned. She saw now from the pieces of shrapnel all around that what had seemed to be a purple egg hurled straight at the gesticulating figure on the platform must in fact have been a small bomb or grenade.

So, attempted murder. And, probably, before long plain murder itself.

She took out her dedicated police mobile and spoke to Headquarters. A few sharp words, and she had an assurance that an ambulance from one of the Birchester hospitals would be sent with all speed and a strong contingent of Gralethorpe officers would be urgently ordered to the square. Finally, she had it established that she should take immediate charge as Senior Investigating Officer.

Putting the mobile away, she realised a man was kneeling at Roughouse's other side. Little of him bar a thatch of tumbled blond hair was visible in the patchy light as he bent with his ear close to Roughouse's face.

'You know him?' she asked, penetratingly enough to make the man look up.

'Yes,' he answered, blinking in the beam of her torch. 'Old friend. Since school and all that. Why I'm here, actually. Old Rob had heard something like that egg bombardment might happen, and I thought . . .'

His voice faded away at the reminder of how any idea of protecting his schooldays friend had proved out of the question, and he went back, with a new urgency, to dabbing an already sodden handkerchief at the still flowing blood.

And, yes, Harriet said to herself, what in my torch beam I saw glinting just at the top of his cheek must have been a tear.

She waited until he seemed to be a little less distressed, and then asked his name. But, with the people round now arguing loudly among themselves about what exactly had happened, she failed more than once to make out what he was saying. Eventually he fished out a card from one of his pockets and pushed it over to her.

However, as the minutes went slowly by while they waited for doctor or ambulance, she did manage to extract a few more thimblefuls of information. Roughouse, she learnt, was rather more than a simple politician, and rather less. Once holder of a Conservative seat, he had decided 'the way ahead' was to form a break-away organisation.

'Do you know about the Innovation Party?'

Harriet quickly agreed she did, though that was barely true, a matter of glanced-at headlines. Details would be easy enough to come by when she wanted them.

'Typical Rob,' her informant went on in the same jabbed-out snippets. 'Always going by his own — what? — code of honour. Yes, that.'

Harriet, thinking of the way Robert Roughouse had defied the increasingly ugly crowd, decided *his own code of honour,* outmoded phrase though it might be, had got it pretty well right.

'Before that, all set to be an MFH.'

For a moment Harriet was totally baffled.

'MFH?'

'Master of Foxhounds.'

Then, after a little, came an added comment.

'Tough job. But better to be in that than in politics. Poor Rob.'

The *poor* set up a new train of thought in Harriet. As soon as she could she asked another question.

'Doesn't being a Master of Foxhounds mean you have to be really very well off?'

The pale-haired head briefly looked up.

'Didn't mean *poor* as in cash-strapped. But, yes, you do have to be pretty rich to have your own pack.'

He bent his ear closer to the blood-stained face once more.

'Not quite the done thing to say *rich* nowadays,' he brought out as he raised himself up again. 'Or not unless you put a *filthy* in front of it. But, as it happens, we all are rich, Rob's close friends. Same school, enormous fees.'

Harriet thought momentarily how people from such schools still obey that rule of *the done thing.* The wisps of tissue paper laid on their lives, piece after piece, year after year after year, till they became a cement-hard casing.

With a jerk, as bright headlights dazzlingly blinded her, she realised the ambulance had arrived, and brought herself back to the immediate present.

When Roughouse had gone on his way to Birchester's St Oswald's Hospital, ambulance bell clanging out, Harriet saw that a party of uniformed officers was coming hurriedly into the square.

Right, Gralethorpe to the rescue at long last. And that man leading them, looking harassed and out-of-temper, should be a DI.

But, before I see him, must have another word with HQ. At St Oswald's there'll probably not be any stronger police presence than a single bedside detective. And it must be possible that whoever tried to kill Roughouse will make another attempt if, watching from somewhere in the dark here, they've seen that ambulance leaving and have realised their attempt failed.

When she met the Gralethorpe DI, sullen and grudging, she hammered out with him a plan for questioning such curiosity-filled protesters as still remained in the square. One by one then they had them brought under two of the street-lamps to have names and addresses taken and be asked if they had seen 'anything suspicious'. A question which, Harriet knew, was highly unlikely to be answered in any half-useful way.

Even when, some half hour later, forensic officers from Birchester arrived with another contingent of detectives she felt no lift of hopefulness. What chance was there that anyone in that crowd concentrating on the figure of Robert Roughouse would have noticed someone take a single backward pace and throw something with all their power? Throw an egg that was neither white nor brown nor speckled but dull purplish metal?

At last the square was empty of every possible witness. Stretching and yawning, Harriet allowed to enter her head thoughts of home. She longed simply to perform those necessities of existence that hold the world together, the ordinary bedtime tasks of brushing teeth, taking off make-up, putting dirty clothes into the laundry basket.

She began looking to see if there was anyone near the cars whom she could ask to give her a lift back to Birchester.

But then, from the deeper darkness at the foot of the old Methodist chapel facing the town hall, she saw emerge a curious-looking individual. Shuffling purposefully, head jutting forward tortoise-like under a jammed-on shapeless soft hat, he was plainly making straight towards the lamp she was standing under.

'You're a police officer,' came a yapped-out assertion as he got nearer. 'The one in charge, it looked to me.'

An inner groan of dismay.

'Yes, I am the senior investigating officer

here. Is there something I can do for you?'

'Pidgeon, Percival. Not Percy. Never, never Percy. Always Percival Pidgeon.'

Harriet suppressed, in her barely controlled weary mind, a faintly hysterical laugh.

'And there's something you want to tell me?' she asked, striving for calm authority. 'Something about the missile that injured the Hunt speaker?'

'Of course.'

She got a quick assessing glance.

'You know I am armigerous?'

This was altogether too much. It was all she could do to bring out a reply even marginally polite.

'I'm sorry. I don't understand.'

'I am armigerous. Entitled to bear heraldic insignia. Do you know nothing?'

She battened down the temper beginning to swell up.

'Yes,' the old man went on. 'With canting arms and a pigeon or dove presenting.'

'Very well, Mr Pidgeon,' Harriet brought herself to answer, just coming to terms with the heraldic jargon. 'But I am afraid I don't quite understand the relevance of what you've told me.'

'It implies, surely to goodness, that I am a properly responsible person. Why else should I have given you the information?'

Harriet buckled to once more.

'So, what is it, as a responsible person, that you want to inform me of? It's getting very late and — and, frankly, I'd like to be on my way.'

However calm I'm managing to be, she said to herself, when I do get home I'll have the right — it's in the unprinted book of rules — to be as irritable with John as I like. Spouse's privilege.

'I suppose the fact will be of some interest to you that the object sent towards that Hunt gentleman did not come from anyone in the crowd he was addressing.'

A cantankerous glare.

'Not from the crowd? What exactly do you mean?'

'I mean what I said.'

But can this absurd old man really be telling me that the purple egg was not thrown by someone in the crowd? Should I just send him off home, here and now?

She decided to make one more effort to get straight what it was he had claimed.

'Let me be clear. You're saying the missile was not thrown by anyone in the crowd here in the square?'

Percival Pidgeon's turn now to suppress anger, something he seemed to be all but failing to do.

'I cannot have put it more plainly, even to make myself clear to a woman police officer.'

Harriet ignored the emphasised *woman*.

'Very well,' she said. 'If that egg-like object was not thrown by somebody in the crowd, how did it come to strike the wall within a few inches of Robert Roughouse's head?'

'There can be only one answer to that.'

Then a provoking silence.

Harriet stood there for an instant or two more looking at the old man. Then she settled for what she had thought about him from the beginning, that she had been waylaid by an obsessed idiot living by conventions altogether unconnected to the real world.

'Well, thank you for your assistance,' she said.

She turned and set off towards the Birchester cars.

But she had gone no more than three or four yards when a new thought entered her numbed brain. A totally unaccountable one. Abruptly she had remembered telling John about the old lady she had once interviewed in Gralethorpe — Miss Abigail Something? — who, bird-sharp, had promptly seen through her attempt to pass herself off as a Council official but had then told her everything she had wanted to know. She had even, it came back now, confessed over tea to a years-ago love life outside the bounds of propriety.

A lesson to me, as John pointed out. When there's something that has to be brought to light, you abandon lofty notions.

She swung round to Percival Pidgeon, still standing, a rigidly angry post, under the lamp where he had produced his unlikely claim.

'Mr Pidgeon, I'm afraid I was a little abrupt just now. Tell me, please, why is it you think that object was not thrown from somewhere in the crowd down here?'

And he gave her an answer.

'Plain enough, isn't it? Because, from up there outside the chapel, I heard a sound like a fowling-piece being fired.'

'A shot from up there?'

'That's what I said, and that's what I heard. A small report, very like a shotgun's. I may be eighty-two years of age but I've still got my hearing. We Pidgeons have always been noted for our acute ears. Down the generations.'

Momentarily the weird notion came into Harriet's head of a set of different heraldic arms for the old man to flaunt. Not a pigeon or dove *presenting,* but a pair of ears *flappant.*

'I heard what I did, say what you like,' he snapped at her now. 'I was on the point of going up to investigate when that shout of horror from the crowd made me turn to look in the other direction.'

But, Harriet thought, if he's right, Mr Never-Percy Pidgeon, he may actually have heard something like a small mortar firing that grenade. And will the person who . . . ? But, no, they'll have raced off as soon as they saw Pidgeon beginning to head towards where they were hiding.

'Why didn't you tell me this at the start?' she asked, speaking in her flare of excitement more sharply than was sensible.

'Would you have listened?' Percival Pidgeon shot back. 'You police are all the same. Go by your set rules, never think that something may be different from what you've been taught to expect.'

Harriet accepted the rebuke, unjust though it might be.

'Very well, Mr Pidgeon,' she said, 'shall we go up there and see what we can find?'

She directed the beam of her torch towards the dark mass of the chapel.

Percival Pidgeon trotted off ahead, almost too rapidly for her to keep up. They mounted one of the paired flights of stone steps leading to the wide balcony in front of the chapel doors. And there, at once, they saw what looked as if it must be, precisely, the device that had shot out the missile which had so terribly injured Robert Roughouse.

'Stop. Don't touch,' she shouted, as the old man, grinning ferociously, bent down towards it.

He jumped back upright.

'There may be fingerprints,' Harriet said. 'Because, you know, this discovery of yours means only one thing. The grenade that almost killed Mr Roughouse was not thrown by some anti-hunting idiot who scarcely knew what he was doing. I haven't the least notion why there should have been a deliberate attempt on Roughouse's life. But one there was. It was an assassination. And it only just failed in its object.'

CHAPTER THREE

At home not long before dawn Harriet, in her utter tiredness, was every bit as out of temper as she had thought she might be. Teeth unbrushed, clothes tossed in a jumbled heap on the chair, pants and creased shirt simply dropped on the floor, she turned at last to the bed. For a moment she thought of letting rip her bad temper and accidentally-on-purpose jolting John awake. But she managed, just, to restrain herself and set her alarm for a precise 8 a.m.

The moment it was practical in the morning she was going to phone her bête-noire the ACC, and tell him that Percival Pidgeon's evidence clearly pointed to an attempted assassination. Then she would make sure the investigation stayed in her own hands.

To Hell with thoughts of resignation. There's a task here I can bring to a result, if anyone can. And I mean to make sure I get it.

When she made her call, however, she found she had walked into a battle. The ACC, early informed of the events at Gralethorpe, had come to the conclusion that the attack on Robert Roughouse must be the work of Animal Rights activists. He told her brusquely he intended to pass the investigation to the national team set up specifically to combat such militants.

For a brief moment she tried to make a fair assessment of this theory. But, however far outside the rule of law she knew Animal Rights extremists felt themselves entitled to be, she could not see them going as far as deliberate assassination.

Nothing for it then but to tell him about the grenade-hurling mechanism Percival Pidgeon had heard being fired. I can only hope it will convince him he's got it wrong.

But, even before she began putting forward this evidence, she was struck by a sharply miserable thought. Did the ACC hit on passing the investigation on simply because he wanted to take the case away from me without having to produce any arguments to show I'm not the detective I once was?

All right, put it to the test.

31

'Sir,' she said, 'I discovered last night that the bomb that all but killed Mr Roughouse was not thrown by somebody in the crowd in the square at Gralethorpe. It was propelled from the chapel opposite the town hall using a sophisticated mortar-like device.'

Will he even listen?

But, yes, there's a trace of puzzlement at the other end.

'Sir,' she went on rapidly, 'surely this indicates the attack was nothing less than a purposefully attempted assassination. Sir, the device is still where I left it, ready for our own Scene of Crime people to make their daylight assessment.'

'This contraption of yours,' the ACC said at last. 'Did you take steps to see it was properly protected? Or has it been left where anybody could come across it?'

Does he really think I wouldn't have taken that obvious precaution? Or is he simply implying it's something any other senior officer would have done but that I am all too likely to have omitted?

'Yes, sir,' she said, in as even a tone as she could manage. 'I made sure the device would be guarded all night and into today by officers from Gralethorpe. It's there, untouched, to be examined as soon as practical.'

'But . . .'

And then a silence.

'Yes, sir? *But* you were going to say?'

Abruptly then the ACC caved in.

'Very well, Mrs Martens. Since you believe the case is most likely to be resolved in Birchester, you had better take charge of it. Set up an incident room at Waterloo Gardens PS, let me know what personnel you think you'll need — it shouldn't be all that many, unless Roughouse dies and it becomes a murder case — and carry on from there.'

Which was precisely what she had wanted. Not that it did not immediately occur to her that an investigation that was unlikely to produce any early result might suit the ACC's book rather better than not giving it to her at all.

If I fail over this, won't he have a perfect excuse to get an inefficient officer posted to Traffic, or to anywhere outside the CID?

Scarcely half an hour after she arrived at her own office at Waterloo Gardens there came a perfunctory knock on her door and she discovered she had been allocated as a 'bag carrier', whether wanted or not, one Detective Sergeant Woodcock, an officer she

33

had, as it happened, never worked with before. But she knew about him. From his unswerving determination not to do anything requiring more work than bullying answers out of hapless witnesses he was called by almost everyone 'Bolshy Bill'.

At once she wondered whether Bolshy Bill's sudden arrival was the ACC's revenge for the way she had stopped him shovelling off to distant London an inquiry likely to be nothing but heavy trouble. Or am I being too sensitive, she promptly asked herself. John would tell me I am. But, no, I don't think so. Or, anyhow, not much.

She gave Woodcock a long look. A pale, freckled face stared back at her, blue-grey eyes flicking this way and that. He was wearing, as she recalled now that he invariably did, a grimy black-and-white dogstooth-check sports coat with under it a hideously bright shirt. A red-splotched tie was pulled down by a long inch from its top button. The whole outfit, it seemed, designed to offend every convention, particularly the long-in-print unspecific directive that plainclothes officers should *at all times dress with due respect for public standards.*

Ah, well . . .

She set to putting this dubious assistant in the picture.

'OK,' she concluded. 'I'm off quite shortly to St Ozzie's to find out how well Robert Roughouse got through the night. I need to talk to him, of course, as soon as he's in any way fit. No point in you accompanying me, though. Instead, I'd like you, yes, to do this. Get on the Net and find out as much as you can about Roughouse. Political career, financial circumstances, marital state, address — I think, in fact, he may have a house somewhere in our area — anything and everything you can dig up. All right?'

'Ma'am.'

Monosyllable acknowledgement somehow made to carry the message *Idiot detective superintendent tasking me with idiot inquiries.*

Harriet left him to them and turned to considering the incident room the ACC had instructed her to set up. One thing had already occurred to her. If the personnel needed were to be as few as, plainly, the ACC thought they should be, then it was important to have someone in charge she could absolutely rely on.

And, damn it, she thought, I know the very man. All right, it's been a long time since I worked with DS Hapgood, but I haven't forgotten that, in strong contrast to foisted-on-me Bolshy, he's not only extremely efficient but that he's not called

'Happy' Hapgood for nothing. His ever-ready geniality, if I can get hold of him, will make sure any outfit he organises will run perfectly smoothly. The essential background mechanism, the filing and cross-filing, the logging and assessing, will go like clockwork and, more important, every man and woman on the team will be willing to work full-out at every hour that's needed.

I must get him if I can. In no time at all Happy will organise to the full whatever incident room I get allocated, do everything that's needed, check the VDUs are in working order, make sure enough phones are connected, see to it that whiteboards and corkboards are cleared of the detritus of their last use, all ready for newly scrawled reminders, newly taken photographs. Whatever's needed.

She reached for her phone, and rang B Division where, she supposed, DS Hapgood must still be posted.

He was. And, thank goodness, it appeared not engaged with anything too important not to be put aside.

Right, a word with Happy and then a quick wrestle with the people in Admin and the barriers of regulations which I'll be told stand in the way of any transfer.

■ ■ ■ ■

It was only when, some twenty minutes later, that Happy Hapgood himself poked his head through her door that doubts came winging across her mind. Oh God, she thought, Happy's suddenly old. That neatly pointed little beard I remember has gone grey-white, the hair above it is a yet whiter halo. It really has been a long time since I actually saw him. Will he still . . . ?

'Happy,' she said. 'Good to see you again. How are things?'

'Fine, fine. Just done my thirty, you know. Three weeks' leave, starting next Monday, and then it's feet up for ever.'

No, she thought with a jolt of dismay. No. He's here to tell me I'm not getting him. And I really must have him. There's no one else who'll take all the paperwork off my hands in the way he used to. God's sake, I need to be free actively to investigate if I'm to get anywhere. I need to.

Panicking thoughts rioted through her mind.

But try . . .

'I suppose, Happy,' she ventured, 'you couldn't put off your feet-up life just for a week or two, or a bit more? I've been tasked with the bomb attack on that man Robert Roughouse — you've heard about it? — and I must have someone in my incident room who really knows what they're about.'

Happy shook his white-topped head.

'Can't be done, ma'am. Can't be. Retirement paperwork's all but gone through. Much as I'd like working with you one last time, nice end to it all, it's just not possible.'

Harriet sighed, all but groaned.

'Well, if you're aboard that unstoppable train, I suppose —'

She broke off.

Into her mind had come, unbidden, a favourite story of John's, usually trotted out at dinner parties when somebody complained they had bumped up against implacable bureaucracy, whether merely some lowly individual's intransigence or the full weight of official might.

Years ago in Delhi, negotiating for Majestic Insurance with the Ministry of External Affairs, John had lunched a junior diplomat at a particularly good restaurant, if one haze-thick in the customary Indian way with cigarette smoke. As they finished the meal, the young man dropped on the table a packet of Gold-flake, still in its British wrapping.

'Mr Piddock,' he had said, 'I wonder could

you do me a favour?'

'If I can.'

'Would you offer me a cigarette from that packet there?'

'But . . .'

'You see, I've taken a vow not ever to smoke again, and a vow must be kept or what's the use of making it. But I have allowed myself a period of grace during which a cigarette does not count — if it's one that's offered to me.'

John, even as he had held out the packet — so he would end the story — had seen how by going to an influential uncle the young diplomat had mentioned he could circumvent the obstacle threatening his whole negotiation.

'Listen, Happy, I have an idea.'

'Ma'am?'

'What if I have a word with my friend, Mrs Maltravers, in Admin? She might, you know, find some complication in your retirement paperwork that would delay it for some time, and . . .'

'That'd please me, all right. Please me, no end.'

Arriving at St. Oswald's, where she herself had once spent long sedated days poisoned to the point of being at death's door, Harriet found a shock awaited her. When she asked at Reception who could tell her about Robert Roughouse's condition, at once had come the answer 'Not here any more.'

'Not here? What do you mean? You — You aren't saying he's died?'

'Wouldn't ever go roundabout that way to break bad news,' the man at the counter replied. 'Not the number of times I've been left to tell it. No, your Mr Roughouse has been taken off to somewhere his friends think better than St Ozzie's.'

'Where? Where? And what friends?'

'Where's he gone? To that Masterton Clinic out beyond Boreham, I was told. But who those friends of his were is more than I know. Three of them came, my mate said when I arrived for duty. Here before six. Straight up to the Night Admin Officer they went. And, next thing the chap here at reception knew, the lift was bringing down someone on a stretcher and taking them straight out to a private ambulance. Only then did somebody say it was that fellow as was shot or something last night.'

'What about the police officer I arranged to be on duty down here? Didn't he show up? And if he did, didn't he ask questions? Where is he? Is he still here?'

'There was a cop here, so my mate said.

But, when your Mr Roughhouse was put in that private ambulance, he took himself off.'

'Right,' Harriet said. 'I'd better have a word upstairs. I take it the Administrator himself is in by now?'

'Oh, yes. Since before nine, matter of fact.'

Questions began shooting up in her mind.

Three men coming with a hired ambulance to St Ozzie's even before it was fully light? What could that mean? Has Roughouse been taken away, not by any friends but by the very man who shot that grenade at him? The man and a couple of his accomplices? Did he never get anywhere near that redoubt for the rich, the Masterton Clinic? Has he been driven off somewhere and killed? Surely that can't be what's happened. A St Oswald's administrator, even a night deputy, can't have been that easy to hoodwink. But, all the same, is there behind that dawn descent here something more than a wealthy man being removed to where he'll get luxury treatment? Would, in fact, any clinic offer better treatment than Birchester's biggest and best hospital? Or can it be simply that the men who whisked him away were only taking him to somewhere safer from any chance infection than a big public hospital? Or — Is this it? — were they wanting to keep him safe, not from infection, but from an enemy wanting to finish the job? Do these friends of his, if that's what they were, know a lot more than I do about who wants him dead? Or are they simply anxious to protect him from the intrusive media? But why should that require such hurried, and risky, action?

Questions, questions. And no answers.

She found Mr Green, the Administrator, sitting happily sipping at his mid-morning coffee. Barely introducing herself, she asked point-blank why a seriously ill patient had been allowed to be taken away in such unusual circumstances.

Mr Green looked abruptly unhappy.

'Yes,' he said, 'I know what you mean. But —' He shifted in his seat. 'But — well, my night-time colleague, who incidentally got me out of my bed to answer the phone, told me the people who were there with him were very insistent. Mr Roughouse, they said, had to be protected from any intrusion.'

'Protected from what sort of intrusion? Did they tell him?'

'*Intrusion* was all they said, insisted on.'

'And did you say he would be perfectly well protected from that here at St Oswald's?'

'Yes, yes. Of course I did. But — well, my

colleague said they were persuasive, the visitors. Very persuasive.'

'You're not — You're not telling me he was offered some sort of inducement?'

'Good heavens, no. I would have immediately . . . No. No, eventually I told him to use his own judgment. After all, I couldn't, at the end of the phone, at that hour of the morning, make any reasoned decision myself. So in the end he let them take Mr Roughouse. He told me, when I came in, that they were . . . It's difficult to explain really. They seemed to act, he said, as if there was no question but that he would agree to — to whatever they asked.'

Harriet felt pure astonishment. Could anyone, could any three visitors, really act in that high-handed way? At once an answer came to her. Yes, they could — if they had the arrogance of the really wealthy.

And didn't Roughouse's friend *from school and all that* tell me last night that all his friends were — unutterable word — *rich?*

'And — And one of the people who came,' Mr Green plunged on, 'was actually a member of the medical profession. Quite a well-known surgeon, Mr Jackson Edgeworth. And he did give my colleague his assurance that the short ambulance trip to the Masterton Clinic could not possibly aggravate the patient's condition. I don't know . . . should I, all the same, have withheld my agreement?'

'No,' Harriet said, feeling a flicker of sympathy. 'No, I think I can understand how you came to agree as you did.'

'Thank you. And after all Mr Roughouse did arrive safely at the Masterton. I rang them from home myself, and they told me he had arrived and his condition was — er — stable.'

Condition stable. Does this mean he'll be able to talk? Right, off to the Masterton straight away. Wait. No, collect Bolshy Bill first. The Masterton, as I recall, is well used to 'protecting' anyone admitted to it. Over the years more than one film star caught up in some media brou-haha has taken refuge there for treatment for 'a nervous condition'. It might be no bad thing to arrive at the citadel, as it were, mob-handed.

'Bloody Masterton Clinic,' Bolshy grunted as, half an hour later, he brought their car to a halt just inside its ornate gates. 'Clinic for the masters, ask me.'

Yes, Harriet thought, a useful weapon sitting here beside me.

She sat looking at the house ahead. It seemed, from her line of vision taking in its

44

front and part of one side, to be a mansion from the Victorian era. Ponderous in uncompromising dark brick, half-masked by a heavy growth of dull green ivy, it sat there proclaiming *I'm here and I'm staying.* Only incongruous glass entrance doors and clean-as-clean white paintwork showed its purpose had altered.

Yet best perhaps to keep Bolshy in reserve should its defences prove as formidable as they looked.

She tasked him with using his mobile to continue his inquiries into Roughouse's background.

'I mustn't be too long,' she added as she set off. 'When I came to collect you I found a message from the ACC. He wants me to report as soon as I can.'

'Ma'am,' Bolshy acknowledged.

Had there, though, been a touch of *I know about you and the ACC* behind the brief word? Or, damn it, am I being absurdly touchy?

Mounting the steps to those out-of-keeping heavy glass doors, she found they swung open at a single easy push. At the far end of a spacious entrance hall she saw, half-hidden on the reception desk by a massive bowl of glowing bronze chrysanthemums, a young smartly dressed black woman. She crossed over towards her, each step echoing out on the decoratively patterned tiled floor.

To her surprise, the girl seemed not to hear. Even when she was near enough to read a neat plastic triangular name-plate saying *Tonelle,* the girl did not so much as look up. Only from directly in front of the desk was it apparent she was deeply absorbed by the crossword in her newspaper.

At a crisp *Good morning* she gave a sudden start and pushed the paper, in a welter of rustling pages, down to her knees.

Some rule against slovenly newspaper-reading while on duty?

'Oh. Oh. Yes? Yes, may I help you?'

'Greater Birchester Police, Detective Superintendent Martens. I believe you have as a newly arrived patient, a Mr Robert Roughouse. I'd like to see him.'

A rather too hastily summoned-up extra smile appeared on the ebony-black face looking up at her.

'I'm sorry, but we have a strict regulation that no visitors are allowed without prior notice.'

Harriet was hardly going to be stopped by this.

'Right,' she said, 'I'm giving you notice now that I wish to see Mr Roughouse as soon as possible.'

A tiny flash of a grin came back to her at this attempt to get round the imposed regulation.

But no dice.

'I don't think the Administrator, Mrs Fishlock, would quite accept that.'

Second administrator today, Harriet thought. And will she . . . ?

'Shall I try seeing her?'

She had been tempted to add something like *Unless, of course, she has to have prior notice too.* But that would have been rather unfair on young Tonelle whose duty it must be, when not defying the edict against the sloppy reading of newspapers, to defend to the last the privacy of the clinic's clients.

Peering a little further forward to satisfy her curiosity about the rapidly concealed paper, Harriet saw it was the *Guardian.*

Well, well. So the Masterton employs receptionists of a good deal higher than average intellect. Able not only to tackle the *Guardian* crossword but also to deal effectively with any awkward inquiries from the local media. And, as it seems, the police.

'You want Mrs Fishlock? I'll ring through. But I can't guarantee she'll let you see Mr Roughhouse.' Another half-mischievous flicker of a grin on the generous, and generously reddened, lips. 'She's a bit of a dragon, actually.'

'Is she? Well, thanks for letting me know.'

When Mrs Fishlock's secretary ushered Harriet though the door into her office — *Mrs Sylvia Fishlock, Administrator* the plaque on the door proclaimed — she saw at once what Tonelle had meant by *dragon.*

Sylvia Fishlock was a lady of fifty or so, slim almost to viciousness, with a long, sharply downwards-lined face and greenish eyes glittering behind rimless glasses.

'Detective Sergeant — er — Martens, didn't Reception say?'

Tonelle on the phone had been more accurate, and perfectly clear.

'Detective Superintendent,' Harriet corrected her, flatly.

'Oh, yes.' A tiny pause. 'I'm sorry.'

But not, Harriet registered, very sorry.

'And you are wanting to see one of our patients? I must say this is very irregular.'

'It's Mr Robert Roughouse, who, I understand, was admitted here early this morning.'

'That would be quite impossible.' The immediate answer.

'Oh, and why is that?'

A sharp come-and-gone smile.

'Our Medical Superintendent informed me, only a few minutes ago as a matter of fact, that Mr Roughouse has not yet recovered consciousness. And, as there is some question of the necessity for a minor operation in the area of the head, he is unlikely to be in a fit state to receive visitors for some time to come.'

Then she made her mistake.

'Not even a visit from a senior police officer,' she added.

Open war then. But not, actually, at this moment defeat.

'I perfectly understand. And of course I'm satisfied.'

As soon as she saw that Mrs Fishlock seemed satisfied in her turn, Harriet began to get up from the low chair she had been directed to.

'Oh, and by the way,' she said, almost at the door, 'Who was it who brought Mr Roughouse here in that private ambulance?'

And, nice to see, a flicker of dismay behind the glinting glasses.

Then something that might be a gulp of recovery.

'I am afraid I am unable to say.'

'Unable? Does that mean you don't know? Or is it that the Clinic's rules forbid you to say?'

For a moment she thought she had Mrs Fishlock at a disadvantage. If not on the ropes. But she was a tougher fighter than that.

'I can only repeat that I am unable to say.'

Harriet thought for an instant.

Can I ask who made the Clinic's rules, and whether they are the sort that can be observed or not according to circumstances?

But at once she decided her war had to be won by other means. Means perhaps not within some Geneva Convention's curious code of what, in any international conflict, is or is not permissible. War as a sort of game.

For a moment into her head there came a picture of a favourite childhood pursuit, *Dover Patrol.* Little cardboard warships advanced dice-throw by dice-throw on their tin stands. By virtue of their blank, red or blue backs, each one sea-mist shrouded.

'Well, thank you for your assistance,' she said to Mrs Fishlock, keeping out of her voice even the least trace of sarcasm.

Down below on her way out, something tickled at the back of her mind as Tonelle, unauthorised *Guardian* now altogether hidden away, gave her a friendly *told-you-so* grin. But what that tickle of thought was she could not, hurrying off, put her finger on.

Getting into the car beside Bolshy, ignoring in the interests of a good relationship the throat-tickling smell of the cheroots he was notorious for smoking, she told him briefly of her lack of success. In return, she received, hardly to her surprise, no more than a couple of words reporting only the most minimal success with his Internet inquiries.

'You want me to go in there?' he asked then, with a careless nod towards the house. 'Give that — what did you say? — old battleaxe a taste of the way we really do things?'

Harriet sighed.

'No, I don't think so, DS. I'll make sure I get to visit Robert Roughouse just as soon as he's fit to talk. In the meanwhile I need to find out everything I can about him. Then we may begin to see why he was the victim of that disguised egg. Out there in Gralethorpe last night I exchanged a few words with a man kneeling beside him, a close friend I gathered, one Matthew Jessop. Here's the card he handed me. Give him a ring and fix a time for me to meet him in London, a.s.a.p.'

'Simple task for the lower ranks, as per usual.'

'Yes, DS. And I'd be obliged to have that interview this very afternoon.'

Immersed in thoughts about what could possibly lie behind the attempt at assassination — it was assassination, it could be nothing else — Harriet at last became aware that Bolshy was stuffing the mobile back into the bulging pocket of his horribly loud jacket.

She waited till the process was over.

'Well?'

'Gave you a warning.'

A warning?

Harriet almost allowed herself to be caught by what she immediately guessed was a piece of junior officer's cunning. The man she had talked with across Robert Roughouse's slumped body could have had no warning of any seriousness to give.

'Well, DS . . . ?' she said, keeping fury just under hatches.

'Said parking's bloody imposs where he lives in smart old Notting Hill. And in any case he can't do nothing till tomorrow. Eleven a.m., not earlier. He said if that won't —'

He broke off.

'Hey,' he banged out, 'that cab that just come in the gates. Y'know who's in it?'

CHAPTER FOUR

Now why should I please bloody Bolshy by asking who it is he's seen, Harriet asked herself. She looked over towards the cab just coming to a halt outside the ivy-clad house. At that moment the sun broke through the grey clouds overhead and a dazzlingly bright reflection from the clinic's glass doors made it impossible to see anything of the passenger darting up the steps. Not even whether they were man or woman.

But a visitor entering? A possible visitor for Robert Roughouse?

'All right,' Harriet said to Bolshy. 'Tell me then. Who was that?'

'Can't be sure,' Bolshy answered, mulishly. 'But I'd say, ask me, it's that marathon runner, Charlie Nyam-something.'

'And what's so interesting about him?' Harriet asked, not without sharpness.

'Not him. Her. It's Charity Something-or-other. Don't you ever read the papers?

Always called Charlie in the sports pages. She's the one going to bring us a cert Gold next Olympics, so they say. Comes from Kenya, but British now, some reason. Nyambura, yeah, that's what she's called.'

'That's all very interesting, DS,' she said, finding in fact her own interest rapidly fading. 'But the sooner I get back to Headquarters the better. I do have to report to the ACC, you know.'

'But what you don't know,' Bolshy replied, ignoring that, 'is Charlie Nyambura must be here for the purpose of visiting one Robert Roughouse. They're an item. Saw it in the paper, other day. Tasty bit of gossip. Black Charlie seen out, some smarty restaurant, with new party leader, giving his ex-Tory chums a bloody nose.'

Over at the Clinic, as the sun was swallowed again by the grey pall above, the big glass doors came firmly together.

'But you want to be off,' Bolshy said. 'Mustn't keep the big boss waiting.'

'No,' Harriet said, disregarding the jibe. 'No, we'll wait here until your Miss Nyambura comes out. If as a sort of celebrity she fares better inside there than I did, a chat with her may be well worth having.'

Judging by the time that passed, it seemed Charity Nyambura had at least got past on-

CHAPTER
ONE

Penny Leighton didn't feel right. She hadn't been feeling right for a long time now. She couldn't remember how long it had been since she *had* felt right.

She was lying in her big marital bed. The Cornish winter sun had not yet risen and she could see the dark sky through a crack in her exuberant poppy curtains. She'd thought them so cheerful when she'd bought them. She looked at them now and closed her eyes.

She had to get up. She had an important call to take at eleven o'clock. She opened her eyes and squinted at her phone. Ten to seven.

"Morning, my love." Simon stirred and reached under the duvet to put his hand around her waist. "How did you sleep?"

She closed her eyes. "Hm."

"Is that a hm of yes or a hm of no?"

"Hm."

"Did Jenna wake up?"

Her look said it all.

"Oh dear. Why won't you wake me? I'm more than happy to see to her."

"Then why don't you?"

"I don't hear her."

"There doesn't seem any point in us both being awake then."

Simon thought better than to reply. Penny had not been herself recently, quick to criticize, withdrawn and moody. He'd felt the sharp side of her tongue too often of late. He decided to make some coffee and bring it up to her but the act of shifting the duvet, even slightly, caused her grievance. "Why do you always pull the bedding off me?" She pulled the duvet tight around her chin. "It *is* winter, you know."

"I didn't mean to. Coffee?"

Penny knew she'd been unkind and rolled over to face him as he sat on the edge of the bed, back towards her, slipping on his T-shirt from the day before. She reached out and stroked the side of his hip. "I'm sorry. Just a bit tired. I'd love some coffee, thank you." He stood up and she let her arm fall back onto the sheets.

She said, "I do love you, you know."

He ran his hands over his bald head and picked his glasses up from the bedside table. "I know. I love you too." He smiled at her and, putting a knee onto the mattress, leant over to kiss her. She put her hands on either side of his face and returned the gentle kiss. "Coffee, tea or me?" she smiled. From across the landing came the grizzly morning cry of their daughter, "Mumma? Dadda?"

"Shit!" groaned Penny.

Simon eased himself back off the bed. "I'll get her. Stay there and I'll bring you your coffee."

★ ★ ★

Penny had her coffee in the luxurious silence of her peaceful bed. Winter in Cornwall held a quiet all of its own. No tractors would be out until the sun came up. No bird would be stirring in its nest and no parishioners would be beating their way up the vicarage path to give Simon another burden of responsibility. Finishing her coffee she stretched and wriggled back down into the warmth of her covers. She'd wait five minutes, just three hundred tiny seconds, she said to herself, and then she'd feel strong enough to get up and face the day.

Unable to put off the inevitable any longer, Penny tore herself out of bed and stared into the bathroom mirror. First she examined the two spots on her chin and then the circles under her eyes. She stood sideways and lifted her nightie to see her pale and wobbly tummy. She'd seen fewer pleats in the curtains of the local cinema. Whose stomach *was* this? She wanted her own returned. The firm and rounded one that she'd taken for granted for all those pre-baby years. Dropping her nightie and shrugging on her dressing gown, which still smelt of Marmite even after a wash and half a day hanging on the line in the sun, she slopped down to the kitchen.

Jenna was in her high chair and Simon was attempting to spoon porridge into her. "That's good, isn't it?" he said encouragingly.

Jenna opened her mouth and grinned. Pushing her tongue out, she allowed the cereal to ooze down her chin. Simon spooned it back in.

It came out again, and before Simon could catch it Jenna had put her hands into it and rubbed it into her face and hair.

"Would you like a banana, then?" he asked, reaching for a baby wipe.

Jenna shook her head. She had just turned one. "Mumma."

"Mummy's a bit tired," said Simon.

Penny sat at the table. "Too right Mummy's tired."

"Get this down you." Simon passed her a fresh cup of coffee. "A caffeine hit should make everything look better. By the way, I've emptied the dishwasher for you."

Penny gave him a cold stare, suddenly irritated again. "You've emptied the dishwasher for me? Why for me? Because it's my job, is it? The woman's job is to empty the dishwasher? Is that it?"

"Oh Penny, you know what I meant. It's a figure of speech. Like when you tell me you've done my ironing for me."

"Well, that *is* for you. It's yours. Do you ever do the ironing for me?"

Simon took his glasses off and began polishing them. "You know what I mean."

Penny picked up Jenna's breakfast bowl. "Come on then, monster, have your porridge."

Jenna obligingly opened her mouth and tucked in.

Simon, returning his glasses to his face, tried a cheerful smile. "Good girl, Jenna, you wouldn't do that for Daddy, would you?"

"Why do you refer to yourself in the third person?" asked Penny. "Don't say Daddy, say me."

"It's just a fig —"

"A figure of speech." Penny popped the last spoonful into Jenna's mouth. "Everything is a figure of speech to you, isn't it? Pass me the wet wipes."

She expertly mopped Jenna's face and hands, hoping that Simon felt inadequate watching just how deftly she did it, then lifted her from the high chair and handed her to her father.

"I'm just going for a shower," she said.

He looked anxious. "How long will you be?"

"As long as it takes."

He looked at the kitchen clock.

"Well, I can give you ten minutes then I have to go."

"You can *give* me ten minutes? How very generous." Penny went to leave the kitchen.

"Sarcasm does not become you," Simon blurted.

"That wasn't sarcasm," she threw over her shoulder. "Sarcasm takes energy and wit and I am too tired for either."

Walking up the stairs was an effort. Her body was not responding to the caffeine. Everything was an effort nowadays. She looked forward to nothing, she laughed at nothing, her brain felt nothing. Nothing but an emptiness that — and may God forgive her — even Jenna's dear face couldn't always fill.

She turned on the shower, stripped off her nightclothes, stood under the hot water and cried.

★ ★ ★

The morning crept on. By ten thirty Penny had Jenna washed and changed and back in her cot for her morning sleep.

Simon had gone off to his parish meeting about the upcoming Nativity service, complaining that he'd be late, and porridge bowls still sat in the sink under cold and lumpy water.

Penny was in her room dragging a comb through her newly washed hair. She badly needed a cut and a colour, but trying to find a couple of hours when someone could mind Jenna was hard. She stared for the second time that day at her reflection. God, she'd aged. Crow's feet, jowls, a liver spot by her eyebrow . . . She'd had Jenna when she was well into her forties and it had been the hardest thing she'd ever done. Harder even than leaving her life in London.

In London she had been somebody: a busy, single, career woman; an award-winning television producer with her own production company, Penny Leighton Productions.

Now she hardly knew who she was. Again she felt guilty at how horrible she'd been to Simon. Taking a deep breath she slapped on a little mascara and lip gloss and vowed to present him with steak and a bottle of wine for supper.

She got downstairs and into her study two minutes before the phone rang on the dot of eleven. Penny took a deep breath and plastered on a cheery persona.

"Good morning, Jack."

"Hello, Penny, how is life at the vicarage treating you?"

Jack Bradbury was playing his usual game of feigned bonhomie. He laughed. "I still can't believe you're a vicar's wife."

"And a mother," she played along.

"And a mother. Good God, who'd have thought it. How is the son and heir?"

"The *daughter* and heir is doing very well, thank you."

"Ah yes, Jenny, isn't it?"

"Jenna."

"Jenna . . . of course."

The niceties were achieved.

"So, Penny . . ." She imagined Jack leaning back in his ergonomic chair and admiring his manicured hands. "We want more Mr Tibbs on Channel 7."

"That's good news. So do I." Penny reached for a wet wipe and rubbed at something sticky on the screen of her computer. Jenna had been gumming it yesterday.

"So, you've got hold of old Mave, have you?" asked Jack.

"I emailed her yesterday," said Penny.

"And how did she reply?"

"She hasn't yet. The ship is somewhere in the Pacific heading to or from the Panama Canal, I can't remember which."

Jack sounded impatient. "Does she spend her entire bloody life on a cruise? Does she never get off?"

"She likes it."

"I'd like it more if she wrote some more Mr bloody Tibbs scripts in between ordering another gin and tonic."

"I'll try to get her again today." Penny wiped her forehead with a clammy palm. She wasn't used to being on the back foot.

"Tell her that Channel 7 wants another six eps, pronto, plus a Christmas special. I want to start shooting the series in the summer, ready to air in the New Year."

"I *have* told her that and I'm sure she wants the same."

"I'm not fannying around on this for ever, Penny. David Cunningham's agent has already been on the blower. Needs to know if David will be playing Mr Tibbs again or he'll sign him up to a new Danish drama. And he's asking for more money."

"I want to talk to you about budget —"

"You bring me old Mave and then we'll talk money."

"Deal. I'll let you know as soon as I get hold of her."

"Phone me asap." He hung up before she said goodbye.

Old Mave was Mavis Crewe, an eighty-something powerhouse who had created her most famous character, Mr Tibbs, back in the late 1950s. Penny had snapped up the screen rights to the books for peanuts and the stories of the crime-solving bank manager and his sidekick secretary, Nancy Trumpet, had become the most watched period drama serial of the past three years.

Penny's problem was that she had now filmed all the books and needed Mavis to write some more. But Mavis, a law unto herself, was enjoying spending her unexpected new income by constantly circumnavigating the globe.

Penny rubbed a hand over her chin and found two or three fresh spiky hairs. She'd had no time to get them waxed and, right now, had no energy to go upstairs and locate her long-missing tweezers.

She pushed her laptop away and laid her head on the leather-topped desk. "I'm so tired . . ." she said to no one, and jumped when her computer replied with a trill. An email.

TO: PennyLeighton@tlx.com
FROM: MavisCrewe@sga.com
SUBJECT: Mr Tibbs

Dear Penny,
How simply thrilling that Mr Tibbs is wanted so badly by Channel 7 and the charming Jack Bradbury. It really is such a joy to know that one's lifework has a fresh impact on the next generation of viewing public.

Another six stories, *and* a Christmas special? But my dear, that is simply not possible.

I wrote those stories years ago as a young widow in order to feed my family. Mr Tibbs has done his job, I'd say and I don't have the patience to think up more adventures for him.

Can you not simply repeat the old ones?

Yesterday we went through the Panama Canal. Absolutely extraordinary. Very wide in parts and very narrow in others. We are now sailing in the Pacific and stopping off at Costa Rica tomorrow. Why don't you drop everything and join me for a few weeks? Enjoy our spoils from dear Mr Tibbs.

    With great affection,
    Mavis Crewe CBE

Penny couldn't move. She read the email again and broke into a cold sweat. No more Mr Tibbs? Put out repeats? Go and join her on a cruise? Did the woman have no idea that so many people's careers were hanging in the balance because she couldn't be arsed to write a half-baked whimsy about a fictional bloke who solved the mystery of a missing back-door key? Anger and frustration coursed through her. She pressed reply and started to type.

TO: MavisCrewe@sga.com
FROM: PennyLeighton@tlx.com
SUBJECT: Mr Tibbs

Dear Mavis,
    If we have no more bloody scripts there is no more Mr Tibbs. Do you want to throw away all that you've achieved? I certainly am not going to let you. The end of Mr Tibbs would mean the end of your cruising and the end of me. PLEASE write SOMETHING! And if you won't do that, I shall have to find someone else to write Mr Tibbs for me, with or without your help.
    Penny

She hovered over the send icon. No, she needed time to think. She couldn't afford to fall out with Mavis. She must sweet-talk her round. She pressed delete and began again.

Dear Mavis,
How lovely to hear from you and what a fabulous time you must be having!

I respect your wishes to put Mr Tibbs "to bed" as it were. He has indeed served you well and given much pleasure to our viewers.

Which brings me to a difficult question. If you won't write the next six episodes and a Christmas special, someone else will have to. Before I find that special someone, do you have anyone you would prefer to pick up your nib? Someone whose writing you admire and that you feel could imitate your style?

No one could be as good as you, of course, but this could be an exciting new future for the Mr Tibbs' franchise as I'm certain you agree.

With all my very best wishes — and have a tequila for me!
Penny xxx

She read it through once and pressed send.

"Right," she said to the empty room. "The office is now shut for the day". She switched off the computer and threw her iPhone into the desk drawer. "I am going to eat cake."

Jenna always woke from her morning nap at about twelve thirty, so Penny had some fruit cake with a milky cup of coffee and flicked through a magazine, all the while feeling a creeping anxiety about how Mavis would react to the email. Mavis was no pushover and would recognize Penny's bluffing for what it was. She was beginning to regret sending it. But what was the worst that could happen? Mavis refusing point-blank to write anything? So what. Penny would do as she threatened, find a new writer, pay them a quarter of Mavis's fee, and stuff her.

She heard Jenna's little voice calling from her cot upstairs.

"Coming, darling!" responded Penny, and she put all thought of Mavis out of her head.

Penny loved Jenna with a fierceness that was almost as big as the fear she had that she was not good enough to be her mother. She would gladly die for her, but the endless hours of playing peekaboo and looking repetitively at the same old picture books, pointing out the spider or the mouse or the fairy, was killing her. There were days when she couldn't wait to put Jenna to bed and then, while she was sleeping, would be riven with the horror of not being good enough.

Repetitive.

Exhausting.

Mind-numbing.

Frightening.

Nerve-shredding.

She watched in envy as the young mums in Pendruggan appeared to revel in picnics on the village green, swimming lessons, tumble tots, musical games and the endless coffee mornings with other women trading their inane chatter.

Penny had been invited to one once. As vicar's wife she tried to do the right thing, but the amount of snot and sick and stinking nappies — not to mention stories of leaking breastpads and painful episiotomies — really wasn't her thing.

The truth was she missed work when she was with Jenna, and she missed Jenna when she was at work. Her love for Jenna was overwhelming, so big that it was impossible to connect with it, but . . .

She missed an organized diary, a clear office with regular coffee, and power lunches.

She missed flying to LA. She missed being in control of her life.

And she missed her London flat.

She had kept it on when she married Simon, telling him that it would always be useful, a bolthole for both of them, although neither of them had been there since Jenna was born.

But Jenna was here now. Here to stay. How could Penny be lonely with this beautiful, perfect, loving little girl who depended on her for everything? Penny looked at her daughter, sitting in her pram, ready for a trip to Queenie's village shop, just for something to do. She bent down and tucked the chubby little legs under the blanket. "It's cold outside." Jenna lay back and smiled. "I love you, Jenna," said Penny. Tears pricked her eyes. She angrily wiped one away as it escaped down her cheek.

"Mumma," said Jenna. She held her hands out to Penny. "Mumma?"

"I'm fine. I'm fine, darling," Penny said with a tight throat. She found a tissue in her coat pocket and wiped her face. "Now then!" She stretched her mouth into its trademark grin. "Let's go and see Queenie, shall we? She might have some Christmas cards for us to buy."

" 'Ello, me duck." The indomitable Queenie was sitting behind her ancient counter opening a box of springy, multicoloured tinsel. " 'Ere, 'ave you 'eard the latest?"

"Nope," said Penny. "It'd better be good because I'm starved of news. Jenna's not too good a raconteur yet."

"Ah, she's beautiful. Wait till she does start talkin' — then you'll want 'er to shut up. Give 'er 'ere. And pull up a chair. You look wiped out."

Penny sank gratefully into one of the three tatty armchairs that had appeared recently in the shop. Queenie liked a chat and most of her customers enjoyed a sit down.

"This chair's very comfortable," sighed Penny, sinking into the feather seat.

"Ain't it? Simple Tony got them for me over St Eval. Someone was chucking them out." Queenie sat down with Jenna on her lap and Jenna reached up to pull at the rope of pink tinsel Queenie had thrown round her shoulders. "Real pretty that is, darling, ain't it? When you're a big girl you can come in 'ere and 'elp me get all this stuff out."

Jenna crammed a thumb in her mouth and sucked it ruminatively.

Penny shut her eyes and enjoyed the peace. "Tell me the gossip then, Queenie."

"Well, you know Marguerite Cottage what's just behind the vicarage?"

"Oh God, yes. The builders have been making a racket for months."

"Well, I had the estate agent in here the other day. Come in for her fags. Silk Cut. Not proper fags at all but that's what she wanted. Anyway, I asks her, 'Oh, who's buyin' Marguerite, then?' and she says, 'It's been let for a year by two fellas from up country.' I says, 'Well, good luck to 'em if they're 'appy together.' And she says, 'One of them is a doctor and the other an artist.' So I says, 'Stands to reason. These gay boys are very arty and nice-natured.' And she says, 'They've got dogs, too.' And I turn round and say, 'Well, they always 'ave dogs.' And she turns round and says —"

Queenie stopped mid-flow and looked at Penny. "Oi, Penny, 'ave you fallen asleep?"

CHAPTER
TWO

The following morning Simon crept out of bed and left Penny snoring quietly. She hadn't been sleeping well at all since Jenna had arrived, but she always refused his offer to share the night-time feeds. He knew how tired *he* was with a baby in the house, so goodness knows how tired she was. Simon stood on the landing and looked through its curtainless window. From here, in the winter before the trees were in leaf, you could just see the sea at Shellsand Bay. The waning moon was low in the sky and spilling its silver stream onto the dark waves. It was so peaceful. He sent a prayer of gratitude for his wife, his daughter and his life.

Downstairs he put the kettle on and, while he waited for it to boil, he tidied up the previous day's newspapers. Tomorrow was recycling day.

He enjoyed the order of recycling and was fastidious about doing it correctly. He opened the paper box. Someone — Penny presumably — had put a wine bottle in it. Swallowing his annoyance he picked it out, replacing it with the newspapers, then opened the box for glass. It was almost full. He counted eight wine bottles, not including the one in his hand. All were Penny's favourite. He put the lid back on and stood up.

So this was why Penny had been so moody. She was drinking.

Too much.

She had always liked a drink. When they first met she had never been without a vodka in her hand. But she'd settled, and although enjoying the odd glass of wine, he had not seen her the worse for wear since she'd been pregnant with Jenna.

Upstairs, he woke her gently. "Coffee's here, darling."

Penny opened one eye. Her wavy hair was over her face and she pushed it out of the way as she sat up. "Thank you."

"How are you feeling?" he asked.

She looked at him with suspicion. "Fine. How are *you* feeling?"

"Good. Yes. Very good." How was he to broach this new and tricky subject? "Shall I buy some more wine today? I think we're low on your — our — favourite."

"Are we? We polished off a bottle with the steak last night, I suppose."

Simon thought back to last night. She had been halfway down a bottle of red wine by the time he got home. "Yes," he said carefully.

"Well, if you're passing the off-licence, get some." She took the coffee cup he was proffering.

He took a mouthful of his own coffee. "We seem to have got through the last lot of wine quite quickly. And you *are* still breast-feeding."

She gave a heavy sigh. "Oh, I see. Are you lecturing me?"

"Heavens, no."

"It sounds like it." She put her cup down and got out of bed. "I need a pee — and, as it happens, an aspirin. I have a headache."

He pushed his glasses a little further up his nose and looked at the carpet.

"Don't give me that attitude." She glared at him. "I have a headache, not a hangover."

The morning followed its usual routine. Penny treated Simon with the cool indifference that had recently become second nature to her. (When had that habit started, she wondered.) And he trod round her as if on eggshells. Eventually he left the house to do God knew what and Penny saw to Jenna.

Jenna was washed and dressed, breakfasted, entertained and put down for her nap. She was overtired and it was making her silly and difficult. Penny checked her forehead. "Is it those naughty teeth?" she asked. Jenna nodded her pink-cheeked face and a string of drool dribbled from her mouth. "Poor old Jen." Penny kissed her daughter's damp head. "I'll get the Calpol."

Cuddled on Penny's lap, Jenna suckled at Penny's breast while keeping a sleepy eye on the picture book being read to her. She fell asleep before the end giving her mother a chance to drink in the sight, sound, and smell of her. The overwhelming love Penny had for Jenna hurt. It also filled her with a kind of panic. She had never been the maternal type and had honestly thought that she would never marry. She had had endless unsuitable affairs with glamorous and handsome men, not all of whom were single, but she hadn't ever imagined falling in love with someone. Or someone falling in love with her. But both things had happened when she'd found Pendruggan, the ideal location for Mr Tibbs. She had been cruel to Simon when she'd first arrived, had thought him a parochial innocent, a drippy village vicar, wearing his vocation on his sleeve.

He had originally been keen on her best friend Helen, who had just moved into the village. Penny had teased him, but Cupid had shot his arrows capriciously. The oddest of odd couples fell in love and were married. That was a miracle in itself, but Simon's God had one more surprise for them. Jenna. Penny leant her head back on the Edwardian nursing chair and looked around the nursery: soft colours and peaceful, the Noah's Ark night-light that the parishioners had presented to them on Jenna's birth, the cot given to her by her godparents, Helen and Piran, the photograph of Penny's father. How he would love his granddaughter. And next to his picture, legs dangling over the shelf, was her love-worn Sniffy, the bear her father had given her when *she* was a baby.

Penny shut her eyes for a moment and felt the familiar stab of grief. She missed her father every day. In her unsettled childhood he had meant everything to her, until he died. She spoke to him, "Daddy, look how lucky I am. Jenna, Simon, success." She felt her throat tighten. "Why aren't I happy, Daddy? Can you help me to feel happy? Help me to be nicer to Simon? A good wife?"

Once Jenna was tucked into her cot, Penny felt drained; if the pile of laundry on the landing hadn't been winking at her she'd have gone back to bed. The aspirin was working on her hangover but not her spirits. She heard the sound of raking from the garden and closed Jenna's door. Looking out of the landing window she saw Simon, returned from wherever he'd been, raking leaves on the back lawn. His breath was steaming in the chill air. He looked happy creating neat piles. He stopped for a moment, aware of her gaze. He waved up at her. She waved back and debated whether to take him out a cup of tea as a peace offering.

She took the tea out to him and gave him a kiss.

"What have I done to deserve this?" he asked, pulling off his warm gloves.

"It's a thank you," she said. "And an apology. I am so sorry I'm being a cow to live with. I don't know what's wrong with me."

He put an arm around her waist and hugged her. "You're just a bit tired. We both are. Babies do that, apparently. You'll be fine."

"Will I?"

"Absolutely. By Christmas you'll be as right as rain."

Penny nuzzled into the comfort of Simon's old gardening jumper. "I don't want to hear the C word."

Simon kissed the top of her head. "Well, there's a few weeks to go yet and Jenna is old enough to sit up and

24

enjoy it this year. You'll bring her to the Nativity service, won't you?"

"Only if I can put her in the manger and leave her there." She looked at Simon to check his reaction. "Only joking. Of course I'll bring her. She'll enjoy seeing her daddy at work."

Penny had commandeered the vicarage's old dining room as her office. Her desk sat under the big Victorian sash window through which the December sun shone weakly. She swung on her new office chair, watching the dust motes that sallied in the air. An estate agent might call this a "handsome room with tall ceilings, wood panelling, and magnificent large fireplace". Which was true. But it was also very cold. She thought about lighting the fire but couldn't muster the energy to find newspaper and kindling.

She opened her laptop and plugged in the charger, then fished her phone from the drawer where she'd chucked it yesterday.

There was a text from her best friend, Helen.

Hiya. Piran and I wondered if you and Simon would like to go into Trevay one night this week for a bite to eat. We'll go early so that Jenna can come too. I need a cuddle with my goddaughter! H xx

Penny read the message twice. Helen had been Penny's friend for almost twenty-five years. They'd worked together as young secretaries at the BBC and Helen had married a handsome womanizer with whom she had two children. Finally, tired of the repeated humiliation of finding the lipstick and earrings of other women in his car, she divorced him, left Chiswick, and found her paradise in Pendruggan, in a little cottage called Gull's Cry, just across the green from the vicarage. She was now happy with the handsome but difficult Piran.

Penny's eyes filled with tears again at the thoughtfulness of her friend. "We'll go early so that Jenna can come too." Helen knew how hard Penny found it to leave Jenna with a baby-sitter, the anxiety she felt about being apart from her little girl.

Helen understood Penny's determination to be a better mother to Jenna than her own had been to her.

She replied. *"Darling, how lovely. I'll talk to S. xxxx"*

She put the phone back in the drawer — ringer off — and checked her emails. She scanned to see if there was one from Mavis. There wasn't. What did that mean? Had Mavis read the email or not? A cold sweat of anxiety swept over Penny again. Oh God! If she didn't get Mavis to write more scripts she'd have to find a writer who could do them in a similar style. And quickly. And if that didn't work there would be no more Mr Tibbs, no more work with Channel 7, and she'd be a laughing stock in the industry, all her old foes sniggering and toasting her downfall. She shivered as a ghost walked over her grave. She remembered something Helen had once said to her, "Just because you're paranoid doesn't mean to say people aren't out to get you."

She pulled herself together and replied to all the easy emails, deleted the rubbish ones, and left the others for later.

She heard the back door swing open and Simon's voice. "Darling?" he called. "Any chance of another cuppa?"

She dropped her head into her hands and took a deep breath. She forced a smile onto her face and called back, "Perfect timing. I'm just finished here."

As it was almost lunchtime, the cuppa turned into scrambled eggs on toast. Jenna was still sleeping and both husband and wife were greatly appreciating the unexpected peace.

"By the way," said Penny, "I had a text from Helen. She'd like us to go to dinner in Trevay with her and Piran. Early, so that Jenna can come too."

"That sounds good." Simon put his knife and fork together, wiping the last toast crumbs from the corner of his mouth.

Simon sensed that Penny was in a better mood and felt confident enough to bring up a tricky subject. "Penny, I really do think a nanny to help you with Jenna is a good idea."

Penny looked at him wearily. "No thank you."

"But it would be such a help for you. You could concentrate on your work, go for lunch with Helen, have your hair done. The other day you were saying how you dreamt of spending the day at a spa. Massages and all that stuff."

"I can do that when she's older but not while she needs me."

"She'll always need you. You are her mum and a very good mum. But I worry about you and —"

"And you worry about how much I drink?"

Simon pulled an expression of regret. "Well, yes, if I'm truthful."

Penny carefully put her knife and fork together and folded her hands in her lap and said as calmly as she could muster, "Maybe a little more help from you would be good. Once Jenna has gone to bed for the night, where are you?"

Simon bridled. "We've been through all this before. I have to work."

"I'll tell you, shall I? Monday, confirmation class. Tuesday, bible study. Wednesday, the parish council. Thursday, sermon-writing night. Friday, the bloody under 16s disco night . . . Shall I go on?"

"No."

"And now it's almost bloody Christmas with all that entails! So which night is Penny night? Hm? Tell me."

"Well, that's what I'm saying. We get countless offers from ladies in the parish to mind Jenna and I know you don't want that. But if we had a nanny, someone you can trust, you could get out more. See Helen. It makes sense."

Penny put her hands to her temples and squeezed hard. What Simon said made some kind of sense, but why couldn't he see that she loved Jenna so much that no one could look after her like she did?

There was a loud knock at the front door. "I'll get it," said Simon, relieved by the timely interruption, and left the kitchen to walk down the hall to answer.

The knock had woken Jenna and Penny went to get her.

Jenna's dear face was pink and puffy with sleep. She put her arms around Penny's neck and rubbed into her neck.

"Hello, baby girl. Do you feel better after your sleep?"

Jenna looked over her mother's shoulder and gazed out of the window. "Woof woof," she said.

"Woof woof to you too, my love. Now, shall we change your nappy? Then have some nice lunch? Hm?"

"Woof-woofs," said Jenna, pointing at the window. Penny glanced down and saw two languid Afghan hounds sniffing round the garden. One cocked its leg on the old apple tree and the other was squatting on top of a heap of Simon's raked leaves with a look of serious intent.

Penny banged on the window. "Shoo! Shoo!"

The dogs looked up and the one who'd finished peeing wagged its tail and barked a greeting.

Hurriedly changing Jenna's nappy and wrapping her in a warm shawl, Penny ran downstairs, calling for Simon.

She found him loafing by the gate, hands in pockets rattling his small change and chatting to three men in matching sweatshirts. They were laughing together, plumes of steam escaping their warm mouths and hitting the cold air. Behind them was an enormous removal van blocking the gate to the vicarage.

"Woof-woof," said Jenna and started to giggle. Simon, hearing her, turned and said, "Ah, this is my wife, Penny, and my daughter, Jenna. Darling, these chaps have come all the way from Surrey. I said you wouldn't mind putting the kettle on for them. It's damned cold out here."

Penny fought the urge to scream and said coldly, "There are two dogs fouling my garden. Are they yours?"

The oldest of the matching sweatshirts, the foreman Penny guessed, rubbed his cold hands together then pointed to a man who was trying to open the front door of Marguerite Cottage, and said, "They belong to him."

A man in his early-thirties, scruffily dressed in old jeans and a T-shirt with a stripey jumper over the top, was patiently trying one key at a time from the bunch in his hand.

"Excuse me!" shouted Penny.

"No need to shout, darling," said Simon, taking her arm. She shrugged him off. "How can he hear me otherwise?" she hissed.

The man had got the door open and had turned to give the three removal men the thumbs up.

"Excuse me!" Penny shouted again. "Are these dogs yours?"

The man smiled and lifted his hand in an apologetic greeting.

"I'm awfully sorry." He came towards them and held out his hand. "Hello. My name is Kit and I'm your new neighbour. I'm moving into Marguerite Cottage."

Penny didn't take his hand. "Would you please remove your dogs from my garden and clear up any mess you find? My daughter is learning to walk and I like to keep the garden clean and safe."

"Oh yes, of course." Kit kept up his warm smile. "I'm so sorry." He called to the dogs. "Terry, Celia — come here." The animals ambled towards him and allowed him to rub their ears.

"Welcome to Pendruggan, Kit. I'm Simon." Simon held out his hand. "Lovely dogs."

Kit shook Simon's proffered hand. "Celia thinks she owns the world. She definitely rules me. Terry is very easy-going but don't try to befriend him. If he likes you, you'll know."

"Please don't let them come in to my garden again," said Penny.

"Woof-woofs," said Jenna, straining sideways to get out of Penny's arms and down to the dogs.

"No, darling, don't touch them. They may bite," she ordered.

Kit smiled at her. "Well, they haven't bitten anyone yet, but let's not tempt it on our first meeting, shall we?"

Penny switched her attention to the removal men who were clearly waiting for their cup of tea. "How long will you be blocking our drive?"

"I've said they can take as long as they like." Simon smiled. "It's easier for everybody if they tuck in here, off the road. Marguerite doesn't have easy access. And we don't need to go out again today, do we?"

"I may want to go out," Penny said through clenched teeth.

"What for?" smiled Simon.

While Penny was thinking of an answer Queenie, dressed in a moth-eaten fur coat and with a scarf wrapped round her head, approached them from the shop. She was going as fast as her arthritic hips would let her, keen not to miss out on a bit of village news.

"I saw the lorry and I thought, 'Ooh there's me new neighbours.' I like to welcome anyone new to the village, don't I, vicar?"

"You certainly do. Gentlemen, this is Queenie who runs the village shop and is the fountain of all local knowledge."

Queenie smiled and pretended to be abashed. "Oh, he's a charmer is our vicar. Anyways, I bet you boys are 'ungry, so I've brought you some of me famous pasties. They're yesterday's, but I've heated them up so they'll be fine."

"Thank you very much," said the chief removal man gratefully. "They'll go down lovely with a cup of tea." He looked hopefully at Penny who refused to catch his eye.

Inside the vicarage, the phone began to ring. Penny passed Jenna to Simon. "I'll get it. And don't put Jenna anywhere near those dogs or their poo."

Queenie watched her go. "She's always busy, that one. I don't think you'll get a cup of tea out of her today. Eat them pasties before they go cold and I'll go and make the tea. Come up to the shop in a minute, 'cause I can't carry an 'eavy tray down 'ere."

She patted the pockets of her original 1950s fur coat. "I nearly forgot. This 'ere is the post what's come for the new tenants of Marguerite Cottage." She handed over several letters. "Most of them is the electric company and water and so on but one of them looks like a card. Probably welcoming them boys into their new 'ome." She screwed up her eyes and squinted through her rather greasy spectacles. "Doctor Adam Beauchamp and —" Simon stopped her from continuing. "Queenie, this is Kit, our new neighbour. I think that post is for him."

Queenie was unembarrassed. "Pleased to meet you, I'm sure. Our postman, Freddie, 'e's ever so good, he asked me to look after these for you." She handed the envelopes to their rightful owner.

"Thank you." He took them from her. "Those pasties smell awfully good."

"Oh they are," grinned Queenie. "Come with me up the shop and I'll get one for you if you help me with the tea tray."

"It would be my pleasure. Do you mind if the dogs come too?"

"Not at all. I 'eard you two had dogs. That's lovely. Like children to you, I 'spect. By the way I'm not just the village shop, I'm the postmistress too, you know."

Simon watched them go and felt it safe to let Jenna down from his arms.

Penny shouted at him from the front door, "Simon! Please come. Quickly. Something terrible has happened." She was pale with shock.

Simon picked up Jenna and ran to his wife.

CHAPTER
THREE

"What on earth is it?" Simon steered Penny with one hand, all the while gripping Jenna who was wriggling under his opposite arm, into the drawing room. "Sit down and tell me."

Penny sat shakily, her hands in her lap, her fingers weaving restlessly. She stared, unfocussed, at their wedding picture on the wall.

Simon waited.

"Mumma?" Jenna put her arms out and whined for reassurance. "Mumma?"

Penny spoke. "It's my mother. An old friend just rang. Thought I should know. She's dead."

Simon frowned and put his hand on Penny's. "Your mother is dead?"

Penny nodded, her face almost grey with shock.

"Is she sure, your friend? How does she know?"

"It was announced in the local paper."

"When?"

"Last week, but she's only just seen it."

"But why didn't Suzie tell you?"

Penny shrugged helplessly. "We haven't spoken since that terrible lunch. Maybe she thought I didn't want to know? Maybe she thought I wouldn't speak to her if she had called? Or maybe," she brushed a tear from her eye, "she's punishing me just a little bit more."

"But, darling." Simon stood before her his hands in his corduroy trousers, out of his depth. Penny had never told him what had happened over that lunch. He hadn't known her then and she had steadfastly refused to discuss either her mother or her sister since, other than that they were cut from her life. He said, "Maybe she just doesn't know how to approach you? Could you ring her?"

Penny shook her head. "No. You are my family now, Simon. And I'm so grateful to you for loving me."

"Oh that's the easy bit. You are very lovable." He put Jenna down. "You're in shock. Your mother has died and you need time to process it all. There's plenty of time to think about the future. How about a drink? Tea — coffee? Or would you prefer something stronger?"

Penny gave him a wry smile. "This morning I was drinking too much, wasn't I?"

"Yes, well. I think this calls for a drink."

Instead of the kitchen he walked towards the drinks cupboard. "Brandy? I've some lovage cordial too — shall I put some in?"

Penny said nothing. Jenna climbed onto her lap and, putting a thumb in her mouth, stroked Penny's hair.

"Get this down you." Simon placed the glass in front of her.

Penny was just seven when her father had his first heart attack. That day she had woken early, about six, she supposed. The sun was already up because it was summer. She had heard the back door open and click shut. Her father must be checking on his greenhouse. She crept out of bed and just missed the creaking floorboard outside her mother's bedroom. She stopped and listened for anyone stirring. All quiet.

In the garden the birds were busy chatting to each other and a fat thrush was pulling at an early worm. She threaded her way across the dew-soaked lawn, past the scented orange blossom bush and under the golden hop archway into the vegetable garden. There was her father, a cigarette in the corner of his mouth, his eyes screwed up against the smoke as he tied up a stray branch of cucumber.

He jumped when he saw her and closed his eyes, holding his chest. "Oh my goodness, Penny. You gave me a fright." Then he laughed and she giggled as he held his arms out to wedge her on his hip, the cigarette still dangling from his lips.

"Naughty, naughty," Penny admonished him.

"Don't tell Mum," he said conspiratorially, stubbing it out in a flowerpot.

She smiled. She liked sharing his secrets. "I won't," she said.

"Good girl." He looked up towards the house. "All quiet on the Western Front?"

She nodded.

"Want a cup of coffee?"

"With sugar?" she asked hopefully.

"Of course."

In the far corner of his greenhouse was hidden a little camping stove, a bottle of water, jars of coffee and sugar and a tin of Carnation milk. There was also, hidden in a large cardboard box, a bottle of Gordon's gin: another delicious secret that no one else shared.

The smell of the methylated spirits and the match as it caught the flame for the camping stove was intoxicating.

"Do take a seat, madam." Her father snapped open a rickety folding chair and placed an ancient chintz cushion on the seat. She sat, her bare feet, with sodden grass stalks sticking to them, barely touching the gravel floor.

"Are you warm enough?" he asked. "You must be cold in your nightie. Here, would you like my cardigan?"

She nodded and enjoyed the warmth of his body heat stored in the wool as he draped it over her shoulders. The kettle was boiling and he made them drinks. He had two spoons of coffee, no sugar and black. She had one teaspoon of coffee, two of sugar and a large dollop of the condensed milk. She didn't really like coffee but she didn't want to hurt him by saying so.

He sat on an old wooden crate and pulled a serious face.

"So, young lady, what have you got on at school today? Latin? Quantum Physics? Or a little light dissection?"

She giggled. "Daddy, I'm only seven. I've got reading. Sums, I think. Music and playing."

"A full and busy day then."

She nodded. "Yep. What about you?"

He lit another cigarette. Rothmans. Penny thought them terribly glamorous.

"Well, I've got to show a lady and a man around a very nice house that I think they should buy."

"Why do you think they should buy it?"

"Because it is pretty, has a sunny garden, and their little boy will be able to play cricket on the lawn."

Penny drank her coffee. The sugar and the Carnation milk made it just about bearable. "Can I come and see it?"

"No. Sorry, madam."

"Is it as nice as our house?"

"Gosh, no. Ours is much nicer. And do you know why it's nicer?"

Penny shook her head.

"Because you live in it."

"And Suzie. And Mummy," she said loyally.

Her father stubbed out his cigarette. "Of course. Them too. Now, are you going to help me open these roof lights? It's going to be hot today."

For twenty minutes or so she helped him with the windows and fed the little goldfish in the pond and put out some birdseed while he pottered in the veg patch checking on the peas and lettuces.

They heard the back door open. Her mother stood on the step. "Mike? Are you out there with Penny?"

"Yes, my love." He smiled and waved to his wife. "We've just been doing the early jobs."

"Well, come in or she'll be late for school."

Penny couldn't recall the next hour or so, although over the years she had tried. There must have been breakfast, getting ready for school, kissing her mother goodbye and hugging her baby sister. But try as she might there was a blank. Her memory jumped straight from her father holding her hand as they walked back across the lawn, to the interior of her father's car. It was big and dark green and the leather seats were warm under her bare legs. When it was just the two of them her father let her sit in the front next to him. Sometimes he let her change gear, instructing her when and how to do it. This morning was one of those days.

"And into third. Good girl. And up into fourth."

It was a happy morning. Even the man on the radio reading the news sounded happy. When the news ended and some music came on, her father lit another cigarette and opened his window, leaning his right elbow out into the warm air and tapping the steering wheel with his fingers. She was looking out of her window at a little dog walking smartly on a lead with a pretty lady in a pink coat when they stopped at the traffic lights. The noise and impact of the car running into the back of them was like an earthquake.

There was silence and then she started to cry. Her father asked in a rasping voice, "Are you OK?"

"Yes," she said through shocked tears.

"Thank God." Her father, ashen, and with a sheen of sweat on his forehead, was finding it hard to speak, gasping for every word. Penny was scared. "Daddy? What's the matter?"

Her father's lips were going blue and his eyes were starey.

A man watching from the pavement ran towards them and spoke through the open window.

"You OK, sir? I saw it happen. Wasn't your fault, it was the bloke behind."

Her father didn't answer him. He was still struggling for breath but was now clutching at his left arm.

"Daddy!" Penny was frightened. "Daddy, what's the matter?"

The man called the gathering crowd for help. "Quick, someone call an ambulance. This bloke's having a heart attack."

The police were very kind to Penny and a young police lady took her to school. Years later, when she was an adult, Penny wondered why she'd been taken to school at all. Let alone by a policewoman. Had they phoned her mother and she'd suggested it? That would make sense as it meant her mother could then go straight to the hospital. But who had looked after Suzie? Either way, Penny's next memory was of being called out of her reading class and being taken to the headmistress's study.

"Ah, Penny," she'd said, "do sit down. You've had quite an adventure this morning."

Penny didn't know how to answer this so she just nodded.

"Your daddy has been taken ill but the doctors are looking after him. Hopefully he'll be OK but you may have to prepare yourself to be a very brave girl." Mrs Tyler looked directly into Penny's eyes. "You understand?"

Penny didn't understand, but said, "Yes."

"Good girl. Now, off you pop and be good for Mummy when you get home tonight."

Penny spent the rest of the day in fear.

Somebody must have taken her home from school. It certainly wasn't her mother because she was already home when Penny returned.

Penny ran to her and hugged her with relief. "How's Daddy?"

Margot unwrapped herself from Penny. "He's been very silly. He's been smoking too many cigarettes and drinking too much gin. I'm very cross with him and so are the doctors."

"I told him off this morning," Penny said without thinking.

"Told him off? Why?"

Penny was afraid she'd got her father into trouble. "Because . . ."

"Was he smoking in the garden?"

Penny said nothing.

Her mother strode in to the kitchen and wrenched the back door open. Penny ran after her but couldn't stop her finding the two cigarette butts. "Was he smoking these?" Margot held them up.

Penny nodded and moved instinctively to protect the large cardboard box containing the contraband gin. Margot reached past her and opened the box.

She pulled out the bottle. "Did you know this was here?"

Penny remained mute. Margot shouted. *"Did you know this was here?"*

"Yes," Penny said, feeling like a traitor.

Her mother looked at Penny with poison. "So *you* are responsible. It's your fault he's in the hospital. If you had stopped him, we wouldn't be in this mess but if he dies now we won't have anything. No Daddy, no money. If we are thrown out of this house it will be *your* fault. I hope you remember that." Penny lived in fear for several days, expecting to hear that her father had died and that it was all her fault. But he came back to her. That time.

Penny's hand shook as she took a mouthful of the brandy and lovage. "She hated me."

"Hate is a very strong word. I'm sure she didn't hate you," said Simon, reasonably.

"You never met her though, did you?"

"I would have liked to."

"She'd have hated you too."

"Well, we'll never know." Simon had a fresh thought. "I still can't understand why Suzie hasn't phoned you."

Penny drained her glass. "Why would she?"

"She's your sister when all is said and done."

"We burnt our bridges the last time we saw each other."

"Please tell me what happened."

"No."

"It might help. After all, it must be five years ago now."

42

"It doesn't matter now my mother's dead." Penny swallowed the remains of her drink and hugged Jenna tightly. "I don't want to think about it. And it really, really doesn't matter now."

Simon sat down next to her. "Exactly, Penny, love, she can't hurt you any more."

When he and Penny had decided to get married, Penny had refused point-blank to invite them to the wedding.

"But this is a chance to rebuild the relationship," Simon had told her. "To forgive."

Penny had been adamant. "I don't want them infecting my life again. I don't want them to tell you things about me that will stop you loving me."

"You don't know that — and anyway, I could never stop loving you."

"Believe me, they would try."

Simon had attempted to bring the conversation up a handful of times since, but each time Penny had become tearful and finally he dropped the subject.

Penny took his hand and held it against her chest. "I'm so lucky to have you."

"And me you." He dropped a kiss on to the top of her head and she released him. "When is the funeral?"

She looked surprised. "Oh God! I forgot to ask."

"Will you go?"

"I don't want to."

"It may help. The ending resolved and all that stuff."

Penny gave a small bark of laughter. "I don't think so."

Penny's head dropped as she rubbed her face into Jenna's soft hair. Simon could tell she was crying. "Darling Penny — was it really that bad?"

Penny nodded her head, not trusting herself to speak.

Simon persisted gently. "But you have a sister. Jenna has an aunt. Wouldn't you like to have your family reunited again?"

Penny lifted her face to him. In that moment wishing she could tell him the truth but she was unable to confront the pain it caused her. "I *have* my family. You and Jenna and Helen — *you* are my family."

CHAPTER
FOUR

ELLA

It was a Sunday and it was raining in Clapham. The branches of the cherry trees in Mandalay Road were bare, their leaves long ago dropped damply onto the windscreens of the cars parked on either side of the street. Rain bounced off the slate roofs like heavy artillery fire and swilled down drainpipes, startling flat-eared cats who skittered off to their catflaps. At intervals, passing cars shooshed through the deep puddles ploughing up sheets of water to drench already bedraggled pedestrians. It was a road of good neighbours and occasional street parties. The Queen's Jubilee and the Royal Wedding were still fresh in the residents' memories. Now, Christmas trees were already appearing in bay windows, their lights flashing and twinkling brightly.

No 47, Mandalay Road was identical in design to all the others in the terrace: an early Edwardian, two-up two-down with a small front garden. Its front door and window frames were painted in a delicate lilac, complementing the pale blues, pinks and yellows of its neighbours.

Inside, Ella was lolling on a sofa that was strewn with shawls to hide the decades of wear and tear. There was little spring left in its base but it had been Ella's grandmother's and was therefore treasured. She looked contentedly at the Christmas tree she had put up that afternoon.

A pot of tea, now stewed, and a half-empty mug sat on a tray by her side. On the television Julie Andrews was yodelling. All was well with the world.

She heard the creak of the floorboards above and the tread on the stairs before the door to the sitting room opened. Her brother came in, rubbing his stubbly chin and yawning.

"What you watching?" he said. "Shift yourself."

She moved her legs and he sat in the space she'd created. She said, "What do you think of the tree?"

He looked at it. "Oh yeah. Nice."

"One of Granny's baubles had broken."

"Inevitable after all these years."

"I know, but it upsets me. Each year a little more of our history gone."

"What's made you so cheerful?" he asked, prodding her with his elbow.

"Christmas is a time for reflection," she said primly.

He grunted and watched as Julie Andrews and the von Trapp children worked the little puppets. "So, you hungry?" he asked.

She nodded. "I've got fish fingers and waffles in the freezer."

"I fancy an Indian."

"Have we got enough money?"

"Bollocks to that. I'll put it on my credit card."

"Are you going to eat that bhaji?" Henry reached with his fork to spear it but Ella got there first. "Mine! I'm starving." Henry mopped up the last of his tarka dahl with his peshwari naan and sat back, contentedly munching. "God, that was good."

"Don't speak with your mouth full; you're spitting desiccated coconut on the rug."

He grinned at her. "Don't care. Want a beer?"

"We've only got one can left."

"Share?"

She nodded and he got up to get it from the fridge.

They were sitting on the threadbare Aubusson rug — another of Granny's hand-me-downs — backs against the sofa, watching a rerun of *The Mr Tibbs Mysteries* on a satellite channel.

Henry reappeared with the last tin of beer and settled himself back down. "I rather fancy old Nancy," he said.

"She's very glam," agreed Ella. "But then Mr Tibbs is very handsome too."

"I read somewhere that in real life he's a bit of a goer," Henry said.

"Really? He looks like the perfect gentleman." They watched as Mr Tibbs climbed in through an open window at the suspect's house. He was closely followed by his secretary and sleuthing sidekick, Nancy Trumpet, who revealed a lacy stocking top as she slid over the casement.

"Phwoar!" murmured Henry.

Ella tutted.

"What?" her brother said.

"You know what."

"What do you expect me to do when I see a lacy stocking top and a glimpse of suspender? My generation are sold short on all that stuff. You girls and your tights and big pants and boring bras! I was born too late."

Ella laughed. "So Jools has blown you out, has she?"

"No."

"When did you last see her then?"

"The other day."

"Where?"

"Can't remember."

"So what happened?"

"She blew me out."

"Ha. Why?"

"She said she liked me and all that, but . . ." Henry pitched his voice higher and posher, "she couldn't see a future for us and anyway, she wanted to be free to see other people."

"Like who?"

"Justin."

"Justin no socks and loafers?"

"Yeah."

Ella was offended on her brother's behalf.

"Well, she's welcome to that total prick."

"He is a prick, isn't he?"

"Total."

They sat quietly thinking about Justin and Jools and watching the television screen as Mr Tibbs slipped his penknife into the lock of the desk drawer and revealed the stolen diary he'd been searching for. The camera cut to Nancy, a lock of hair falling alluringly over one eye and a button or two of her silk blouse undone more than was strictly necessary. Henry was rapt.

"Stop looking at her cleavage."

"I'm not."

"Yes, you are."

"If you must know, I was looking at the gorgeous scenery." The screen was now on a wide shot of a Cornish beach, the wind whipping white horses off the crests of the waves. Henry sighed. "I miss Cornwall."

Ella sighed too. "Yep. We haven't been back for a long time, have we?" She poked him with her foot. "If you ever get a girlfriend you can take her down. Give her the romantic tour of Trevay — Granny's old house, our old school — and she'd be putty in your hands."

That night, lying in her bed and listening to the rain still hurling itself at No 47, Ella thought about what her brother had said after they'd finished watching TV. She did need a job. She'd had plenty of them since getting her art degree from Swindon where she had trained to be an illustrator specializing in children's books, but none of them had been as an illustrator. She'd been a chalet maid in Val d'Isere, a nanny in Ibiza, Holland and Scotland and a barmaid in countless pubs and bars in South London. Henry had taken pity on her and offered her a room in No 47, a house he'd bought from his best friend when he'd left to get married. Henry was working his way up in a firm of commercial surveyors but he was making it very clear that he couldn't afford to have his sister as a non-rent paying guest for ever, even if she had brought her share of Granny's furniture with her.

She thumped her pillows into a more comfortable shape and sent a little prayer to her grandmother. "Granny, would you find me a nice job? Either someone who'd like me to illustrate a book or a publisher who wants to print *Hedgerow Adventures*? Please Granny. Night-night."

In the morning Ella felt refreshed and hopeful. The sun was shining and every rain cloud had vanished, leaving the sky periwinkle blue. She sang along to the radio as she washed up last night's curry plates and put some bacon under the grill. Henry appeared. "Bacon? Ella, you're a darling."

"It's the last few rashers but enough for sandwiches."

"What sort of day have you got planned?" he asked as she plonked a bottle of ketchup in front of him.

She had good news. "I'm going to look for a job." He raised his eyebrows at her as he bit into his sandwich. She raised hers back. "A *proper* job. And I'm going to send out *Hedgerow Adventures* to another literary agent."

He couldn't hide his frustration. "Not another one?"

"Yes," she said defiantly. "It's a good story and the pictures are some of my best. Every child I've ever nannied for has loved it."

He shrugged. "Ever thought they may have been being polite?"

"Charming! Thank you, you really know how to boost confidence, don't you? Ever thought of life coaching? Writing a best-selling personal help book, such as *Achieve The Ultimate You* by Henry Huntley, Fuckwit with Hons?"

"Ella, I'm trying to be helpful. *Hedgerow Adventures* is very charming, but it's not going to turn you into J.K. Rowling overnight, is it?"

She couldn't disagree.

"So . . ." He stood up and put his plate in the sink before doing up the top button of his shirt and straightening his tie. "By all means send it to a new agent — but promise me you'll check out the job agencies too?"

It was lunchtime and her feet were tired. Not having enough money to top up her Oyster card she'd walked for miles, checking every job agency before setting off on the long hike up to Bedford Square and the offices of the latest hotshot literary agent she'd read about in *The Bookseller*.

The brass plaque outside was freshly polished. She walked up the short flight of steps and pushed the doorbell on the intercom. A buzzer sounded and the blackly glossy front door opened to reveal a silent marble hall with a grand staircase curling up to the right. On her left was an open doorway and a smart young man behind the desk spoke without looking up. "Can I help you?"

"Thank you, yes. I was wondering if I could have a meeting with someone about my book."

His eyes scanned her from head to toe and back again. Expressionless, he asked, "Do you have an appointment?"

"No, but perhaps I could —"

"I'm sorry, but we don't accept unsolicited manuscripts."

"I see. It's a very short story, it would only take a few min —"

"You must have an appointment first."

"May I make one?"

"Has anyone asked to see your manuscript?"

"Well no, but —"

"Then I can't make an appointment."

"But how do I make an appointment if no one's read my book? And how do I get someone to read my book if I can't get an appointment?"

He smiled wanly. "It's a very difficult business."

The phone on his desk rang and he took the call, making it clear that he'd terminated his dealings with her.

Ella was angry and felt humiliated to boot. She pulled herself up tall and walked back into the hall to let herself out.

Running down the staircase was a young woman with her hair scraped messily back from her face and a smudge of red ink on her cheek. She was heading for the front door as Ella was struggling with the handle.

"Here, let me help you," said the woman.

The door opened with ease under her practised touch. She smiled at Ella. "Are you Gilda's temp?"

Ella wished she were. "No, but . . ."

The woman spotted Ella's manuscript.

"Oh, an author?"

"Well, not exactly, I —"

The woman smiled knowingly. "Supercilious Louis wouldn't let you hand it in? Give it to me and I'll read it. You've got your contact details on it, I assume?"

"Yes, on the front page."

"Great. Sorry, I must rush. Meeting someone for a coffee. I'll be in touch. You never know, this just might be our lucky day. Bye!"

Ella watched as the woman walked quickly across the square.

"Granny," she murmured, "what have you done?"

CHAPTER
FIVE

In the vicarage in Pendruggan the sun was still hiding behind the cliffs — and Penny wished she could hide under her covers. She felt lightheaded. She hadn't slept well because Jenna had had her up three times in the night. Teething was horrible for both of them. Night feeds were usually rather special. Jenna and she would sit in the silence, staring into each other's eyes, sharing comfort and love. But last night had been awful. Jenna had wanted to bite down on Penny's nipples to relieve the pain in her gums but she did it once too often and Penny tapped her leg in anger. In the split second before she opened her lungs and screamed, Penny saw her look of shock and disbelief.

"Jenna, darling! I'm so sorry. Shh, Daddy's sleeping. Shh. I'm so sorry. I'm so sorry." Penny was beside herself. How could she have hurt Jenna like that? She wrapped her up in a cot blanket and held her close as she carried her downstairs. She went to her study, the room furthest from their bedroom, so that Simon wouldn't be disturbed.

"Darling, shh, shh. I love you. I'm so so sorry." She rocked Jenna back and forwards until she calmed a little and reached out to touch Penny's face. Penny kissed the tiny palm and smiled. "Forgiven?"

She fumbled for her handbag, which was on the floor next to her desk, and found the travelling sachets of Calpol. "Here, darling, open wide." Then she found the teething ring she'd bought the day before and offered that to Jenna too. At last peace reigned again.

Penny got herself and Jenna comfy in her desk chair and she idly turned on her computer to see if there were any messages from Mavis. There were about fifty messages. She scrolled through them. The first dozen were spam or unimportant. Then she saw Jack Bradbury's name. Three emails, one after the other, all of them with the same subject. URGENT: MR TIBBS

She felt her pulse quickening and her breathing become shallow. Her fingers were shaking. She couldn't make herself open the emails. She scrolled down to see if Mavis had replied. Nothing. A black dread settled over her. She heard the roar of her own blood in her ears. Shit shit shit. What was she going to do? Where was the old Penny who would have known what to do and would have done it? Overwhelming grief at the loss of herself bore down on her shoulders and she wept silently, her tears falling on the sleeping Jenna. She deleted Jack's emails and shut her computer down again.

And now it was just after midday and she was exhausted, but this feeling was not simply tiredness. Since she'd heard about the death of her mother an extra layer of darkness, an invisible membrane, was separating her from the world. She had often felt like this as a child, particularly after her father had died. A feeling that she didn't really exist, that life rushed around her and she simply glided through it like a ghost. Occasionally she'd reach out a hand to touch a wall or her leg, just to make sure she was real, but it still didn't feel right.

As a child, she had tried explaining it to her mother. "You're liverish," Margot had sniffed.

"What does that mean?"

"That there's nothing wrong with you."

It was one of the many things she looked up in later life. Her computer dictionary gave the meaning as "slightly ill as in having a liver disorder" or "unhappy and bad-tempered".

Well, she'd certainly been unhappy.

And now her mother was dead and the feeling had come back. She wandered through the downstairs rooms and hovered at the closed door to her office. She told herself that she should go in and get on with some work. Work had always been her salvation; a raft to cling to when storms raged.

"Keep going, Penny, keep going," her father had told her when she started to learn to use her Hula Hoop. She had kept going every day of the summer holidays until she became really very good at it. It was the same mantra she had applied to her work and to every contraction that had squeezed Jenna into the world.

Keep going, Penny, keep going.

Now, standing outside her office door she said it to herself again. "Keep going, Penny. Just open the door. Keep going."

"Hellooo." A stranger's voice came from the back door and startled her.

She jumped in fright.

Her heart was in her mouth. "Hello? Who's there?"

Thank God Simon had taken Jenna out for the day. If she was to be murdered by a stranger at least they were safe.

The voice called out again. "Hello? It's your new neighbour. Kit?"

The bloody man with the uncontrollable dogs! She'd tell him where to go.

Penny stomped to the kitchen where she found Kit standing apologetically at the open back door with a large bunch of flowers. He smiled, not unattractively she was annoyed to notice, and proffered them to her. "Good morning. These are from Terry and Celia and me."

Penny's pursed lips were not the reaction he had expected but he continued valiantly, "As way of an apology for the way they behaved yesterday."

"I'm very busy, but thank you." She took the flowers. "I'd offer you tea or something but —"

He stepped over the threshold. "That's very kind of you. I'd love a coffee. I won't keep you long as I have a busy afternoon ahead."

Penny frowned. She had been about to tell *him* that she had a busy afternoon ahead. "I don't have much time myself," she said acidly.

He pulled a chair out from under the table and sat down. "What a lovely kitchen."

"Thank you." She filled the kettle whilst quietly hating him.

"Are all the cupboards original?" he asked, looking around.

"Yes. Do you take milk? Sugar?"

"Black, two sugars. They look Edwardian."

"They are." What was this, *Bargain Hunt*? "Here's your coffee."

"Thanks. How long have you been here?"

"A while." She looked pointedly at the wall clock above the Aga.

"I'm sorry — I'm being intrusive. I'm just interested in getting to know the village and my neighbours and all that stuff before Adam comes down."

In spite of herself she was interested. "Ah yes. Where is he at the moment?"

"Finishing off some odds and ends at his old practice — he'll be here before Christmas though. I've been sent ahead to get the cottage set up with all his little home comforts. I've got a builder coming later this morning. I have permission to put in a couple of skylights."

"Oh? I thought all the building work had been finished." She took a mouthful of coffee and thought of all the noise and dust she had just endured.

"I'm a painter. The spare bedroom will be my studio and the roof windows will give me the northern light that is so good."

"Who's your builder?"

"Bob. Bob the builder." Kit laughed at his own joke.

Penny smiled and said "Sinewy bloke? Very brown? Favours short shorts and always has a cigarette on?"

"That's him."

"He's known as Gasping Bob."

"Behind his back, I hope?"

"No, no. To his face. Almost all the locals have nicknames here: Dreadlock Dave, Flappy, Twitcher, Simple Tony —"

"Simple Tony? That's a bit un-PC, isn't it?"

"Not here, and anyway, it's what he likes to be called. He's a dear man and a very good gardener."

"I'm looking for a gardener. Perhaps you could give me his number?"

"He doesn't have a phone. He says they make him go all fizzy or something. But you'll find him in the back garden of Candle Cottage. Polly owns the house and she lets Tony have the Shepherd's Hut there. Best let Polly introduce you to Tony as he's a bit shy."

"Is he good? At gardening?"

"Well, put it this way, a couple of years ago Alan Titchmarsh came to open the village summer fayre and Tony gave him a few tips."

Kit drained the last of his coffee. "Great. I'll get in touch." He looked at his watch. "Well, I'd best be off. Gasping Bob said he'd be here by two thirty and I know you've got a lot to do."

Penny felt a sudden fear of being left on her own in the house. Simon had taken Jenna out in order to let her absorb the news of her mother and think more about contacting her sister. "Go for a walk on the beach," he'd said. "The fresh air will help clarify your thoughts." But now she found the company of Kit, a stranger, very important to her sanity.

"Don't go. Not yet. Bob's not known for his timekeeping. Let me make you another coffee?"

Kit looked surprised but he accepted and watched as Penny filled the kettle from the old brass tap over the butler's sink.

With her back still to him, she said, "I'm sorry if I've been rude. I had some bad news yesterday. My mother died."

Kit looked at her with concern. "I'm so sorry. And it's me who has been rude. I shouldn't be here. Would you like me to go?"

"No. Please stay. She and I didn't get on very well and I haven't seen her for quite a while. But, it's still been a shock."

"It must be."

Penny nodded. "I'm sorry. I don't know why I'm telling you this. It's made me feel rather numb and . . . I can't explain it." She brushed away the embarrassing tears that had sprung from nowhere. "It feels unreal."

"I'm a good listener and very discreet if you want to talk?"

She shook her head. "That's kind, but I'm fine. It has felt good just being able to say the words out loud to somebody. I am going to have to say it a lot more now, I suppose. I have to tell people that my mother is dead. It's convention, isn't it?"

"I don't know. We could practise it a few times if you like." She shook her head and wiped her nose on the back of her hand.

He continued, "Or we could talk about something else?"

"Oh, let's talk about something else." She tucked a strand of hair behind her ear and rubbed at her tired eyes. "Let's talk about you. What do you paint?"

"Ah well, I paint landscapes for myself, and portraits for money. That's why I've come down here with Adam, actually. I have a commission to paint Lady Carolyn Chafford of Chafford Hall, near Launceston."

"How very posh!"

"Not quite as she sounds. She and her husband bought the title — feudal, of course, so not in the peerage — with the manor, but they are very nice and very loaded, so she'll do for me."

"And tell me about your partner, Adam."

"Partner?" A frown wrinkled Kit's clear brow then he started to laugh. "He's not my *partner*. He's my cousin." He sat back in his chair and tipped his head to the ceiling, letting out a deeply infectious laugh. "Oh my God, that's why Queenie said the dogs were like children to me!" He reached for a handkerchief in his jeans and wiped his eyes. "She's very open-minded, I'll give her that. Wait till I tell Adam."

Penny was smiling too. "Typical Queenie. She loves a gossip. She was convinced you were going to be the only gays in the village."

Kit blew his nose and put his handkerchief back. "Oh, that's so funny. Sorry to disappoint her, but Adam and I have lived together, practically from birth. Adam lost his dad in the Falklands War and so his brother, my dad, took him and Auntie Aileen in and we grew up as brothers."

Penny's mobile phone interrupted him. Penny looked at the screen and saw it was Jack Bradbury from Channel 7. A familiar surge of panic made her clench her hands. She could feel her pulse quickening. She reached for the phone and cancelled the call.

Kit felt her mood change. "Are you OK?"

"Fine, yeah."

"I barely know you but I can see you are upset," he said gently.

Penny flashed a wide smile at him and pushed the phone under a pile of newspapers. "Just a work thing. It can wait. Want a biscuit?"

Penny and Kit spent the rest of the lunchtime swapping snippets about their lives, work and village characters.

"Just look out for Queenie," Penny warned, "she's not the sweet innocent old lady that she likes to pretend to be. She has a sharp business head with a love of gossip but a heart of gold. Pendruggan wouldn't be the same without her." Penny hesitated for a moment then added mischievously, "Let's not tell her just yet that you and Adam aren't a couple."

"You are very naughty for a vicar's wife, aren't you!" Kit nudged Penny's arm with his elbow

Penny sighed. "Well, I used to be naughty — before I married — but let's just say this last couple of hours have been the most entertaining I've had in a long time."

"Intriguing. What was your life before this one?" he asked.

Penny told him about what she did, about her production company and Mr Tibbs, her thrilling time in Hollywood with the film *Hats Off Trevay*.

"That was your film?" asked Kit in amazement.

"Yep. Well, me and quite a few other people too, but it was amazing."

"What a life you've had. How on earth have you managed to settle down in sleepy Pendruggan?"

She shrugged. "Oh. You know. I have a wonderful husband and Jenna my gorgeous daughter. Lots of blessings."

"You must miss the excitement of your old life, though?"

She picked up their coffee mugs and took them to the sink. "Maybe. A bit." She kept her back turned so that Kit wouldn't see the disloyalty she felt at having suggested her marriage wasn't happy. She and Simon were going through a difficult patch admittedly. Everything he did annoyed her. The way he ate, breathed, looked — She pulled herself up sharply at these terrifying thoughts. Keep going, Penny, keep going.

"Well, I'd better be off." Kit was standing and tying his stripey jumper round his neck.

Startled, Penny stood up straight. "Yes of course. Well, thanks again for the flowers and the company."

She opened the back door to let him out and found her best friend Helen rounding the corner.

"Oh Helen, you must meet Kit. Helen, this is Kit, our new neighbour at Marguerite Cottage."

Helen shook his hand. "Lovely to meet you. Queenie is all agog with the news of two young men arriving in Pendruggan."

"We'll try not to disappoint," smiled Kit, tapping his nose conspiratorially.

Penny turned to him. "If you want any fish or lobster, Helen is the woman to go to. Her partner, Piran, catches them all the time."

"Sounds amazing. Adam loves my curried lobster."

Helen beamed excitedly at him. "Oh, Piran and I love curry."

"Well, I must cook for you when we're settled." Kit bent to kiss Penny's cheek and shook Helen's hand. "Lovely to meet you, but I have a date with Puffing Bob."

"Gasping Bob!" Helen and Penny shouted in unison and they watched Kit stroll over to Marguerite Cottage just as Gasping Bob's rusty Rascal van rattled its way towards him.

"He seems nice," said Helen.

"He is. Very," said Penny, and immediately burst into tears.

Helen bundled Penny back into the kitchen. "What's happened, darling?"

"It's my mother," sobbed Penny. "She's dead."

"What?" Helen was shocked. "When?"

When Helen had heard the whole story, short though it was, she became very practical.

"You must phone your sister and ask her when the funeral is."

"I don't think I have her number." Penny's head was in her hands. "And the last time we spoke it was so awful. I can't ring her."

"For goodness' sake, Penny, she's your sister. She should have phoned you by now, anyway." Helen stood up and looked purposeful. "Right, where is your address book?"

Penny looked at her, pale-faced. "In my office somewhere."

"In your desk?"

"Probably."

"Right. I'll get it and we'll call her."

"I'm not sure I'm up to that." Penny struggled out of her chair and followed her friend to the office. "Please, Helen. I can't. I need to feel a bit stronger before I —"

It was too late. Helen was in the office and pulling at a drawer. As she did so the house phone rang.

"Don't answer it!" Penny almost screamed. "Leave it."

The two women stared at each other before the answerphone picked up. They listened to Penny's recorded voice telling the caller that she was unavailable and to please leave a message. She would get back as soon as possible.

It was Jack Bradbury.

He was shouting. "Penny! *Jesus.* Don't you ever answer your calls or look at your emails? Mavis Crewe is pulling out and if you don't get me six new scripts and a Christmas special *soon* I can promise you that you will never work for me or Channel 7 ever again!"

He hung up.

Helen looked at her friend properly.

Penny shoved her hands inside the saggy pockets of her ancient cashmere cardigan dropping her pale, swollen-nosed and red-eyed face to the floor.

It was the first time in twenty-five years that Helen had ever seen Penny Leighton look defeated. "Open your emails," she said.

Penny hovered for a moment; she'd got into an awful habit of hiding things and Helen would be cross with her if she knew the emails were deleted. She took a deep breath and then made her decision. She went to the kitchen and poured herself a glass of wine.

CHAPTER
SIX

Helen was back in Gull's Cry, her cosy cottage across the village green from the vicarage. She'd listened to Penny as she'd sunk a bottle of wine and then eventually been persuaded to go to bed. Helen nestled the phone between her shoulder and chin and put a pan of water onto the Aga for spaghetti. "I'm really worried about her, Simon."

Simon, sitting in his study, phone in one hand, his head in the other, was feeling helpless. "She's just a bit tired, that's all."

"I think it's more than that." Helen saw her boyfriend, Piran, walking up the path with a brace of mackerel in his hand. "I think she should go to the doctor." Piran pushed open the front door and Helen put her finger to her lips and mouthed "Simon" at him before pointing to a bottle of wine and a corkscrew.

She heard Simon attempt a half-hearted laugh before he said, "I'm not sure she needs the doctor, just a couple of good nights' sleep. Jenna's teething, work's a bit stressful, and her mother dying . . ."

Helen rolled her eyes at Piran and said, "Simon, seriously, for my sake, could you go to the doc's with her? Tell her you've made an appointment to check on

Jenna's teeth or something. Go together, the three of you. Then throw in that you're worried about Penny. Please?"

Simon fiddled with his propelling pencil, a wedding gift from his parishioners, and sighed. "OK."

Helen was relieved. "Good. Is she still asleep?"

"Yes. I checked on her a little while ago and she's fine. What actually happened earlier?"

"I think Mavis Crewe isn't going to write any more Mr Tibbs scripts and Jack Bradbury is taking it out on Penny. Also, I think she really should get in contact with her sister about when the funeral is. But when I suggested that she looked so . . . well, the only way I can describe it is that she seemed to have all her legendary courage drained from her. I ran her a bath and popped a hot water bottle in her bed and she didn't argue. Just did it and got into bed. That's not like her, is it?"

Simon pushed his glasses up onto his forehead and rubbed his eyes. "No. It isn't."

"Can you phone the sister?" asked Helen hopefully.

"I'm not sure. Pen won't want me interfering behind her back. She never talks about them, not even when Jenna was born. I don't want her more upset than she is."

"Understood. Let's see how she is tomorrow." Piran handed Helen a glass of chilled Sancerre and sauntered into the small drawing room where Helen heard him turn on the television news. The water on the Aga began to boil. "Simon, I must go . . ."

Simon drooped in his chair a little. "One last thing, Helen: do you think a nanny might be a good idea? A little help with Jenna might help Penny a lot."

"Yes I do. Just try persuading her of that."

★   ★   ★

Upstairs, Penny had woken from her sleep and was furtively searching for her tablet. She found it in her bedside drawer. She got back into bed and listened carefully in case Simon had heard her. Nothing. She turned the tablet on and the stream of ignored emails plus others popped up. She deleted a fair majority and managed to answer the simple ones. The three she'd deleted from Jack, she retrieved but there were two new ones, one of which sent a flood of panic through her abdomen. It was from Mavis. The other was from an old school friend, Marion Watson. A jolly hockey sticks sort of girl who married well and became an MP. The subject line said SUZIE. Penny didn't know which to go for first.

The one from Mavis could be good, could be bad.

The one from Marion spooked her, so that had to be last.

The ones from Jack? Well, at least they wouldn't hold any surprises.

She opened Jack's first email.

TO: Penny Leighton
FROM: Jack Bradbury
SUBJECT: URGENT: MR TIBBS

P,
    Mavis has flatly refused to write any more scripts.
    What are you going to do about it?
    Bloody call me.
    J.

Penny thought it could have been worse. It could have been the sack.

She hovered between opening the next two.

She opened the one from Mavis.

TO: Penny Leighton
FROM: Mavis Crewe
SUBJECT: Jack Bradbury

Dearest Penny,

I really cannot deal with Mr Bradbury any longer. What an arrogant bully. Even if I were able to write more Mr Tibbs tales, I would never again let them go to Channel 7.

I can see now why your last email was trying to butter me up. Oh yes, I can tell. I wasn't born yesterday. The odious Mr Bradbury has been leaning on you, hasn't he? No wonder you made the wild suggestion that another writer could take over. No no no, my dear. That is *never* going to happen. Mr Tibbs is *my* creation and I will never give permission for another writer to take on the franchise while I have the copyright.

I understand this may be inconvenient for you and Penny Leighton Productions, but all good things come to an end, don't they?

I have adored working with you and am still waiting to hear that you can come and join me on this marvellous cruise. How about hopping over for LA?

With affectionate regards,
Mavis

the-watch Tonelle, and presumably on up to see that icier proposition, Mrs Fishlock. But the wait in their tucked-away parking space proved to be longer than any encounter with Mrs Fishlock was likely to take.

Can this celebrity athlete, Harriet thought, have somehow got permission to see Robert Roughouse, however little conscious he is? Is she there beside him now? And — if he is perhaps able to talk a little — is she learning anything about what happened last night? Even why it happened? If Roughouse knows why, or has some inkling of it, isn't this girl the most likely person for him to confide in? Always providing they are, as the gossip pages told Bolshy, an item?

The minutes went on ticking by.

Harriet, still irritated by the remains of cheroot odour in the car, wondered idly if she could somehow get a replacement for Bolshy, secure a more energetic DS — and one less obnoxious. Her thoughts drifted into contemplating bright-smiling, irreverent Tonelle and the way she had hurriedly pushed out of sight her illicit copy of the *Guardian.*

Hadn't that copy in fact — Yes, this was what came into my mind as I walked past her — hadn't that *Guardian* looked very like, not yesterday's paper but last Saturday's issue, the one John takes for its book reviews and fiendish weekend crossword? But, hey, yes, if it's so much against clinic regulations openly to display a newspaper while on reception duty, then maybe I've got . . .

'Right,' she said, 'I'm going back in there. See if I can at least find out from that receptionist what's happening. I think, actually, I've got a way to put a little pressure on the young lady, if I have to. Not much, but something.'

Then, just as she set off, another thought occurred to her.

She turned back and told Bolshy to come to the house with her.

If my piece of pressure doesn't work with Tonelle, then perhaps Bolshy's cruder methods will.

At the foot of the steps up to the glass doors she tapped on the window of the waiting taxi. The driver looked up.

'Sorry, love, booked by the lady, take her back to Birchester station.'

'It's Charity Nyambura, the marathon runner, isn't it?' she asked.

'Yeah, that's her.'

'And did she say how long she thought she'd be in there?'

'She didn't. And I haven't got a clue. But I'm happy, clock's ticking away.'

Inside, Harriet, telling Bolshy to wait by the doors, went straight across to Tonelle and asked her point-blank how it had come about that Charity Nyambura was in the house when she herself had had such a hard time even getting as far as seeing Mrs Fishlock.

All she got by way of reply was a dazzling smile and 'Well, you saw old Fishlock eventually, didn't you?'

'But only to get my nose bitten off.'

'All right. But I did warn you, didn't I?'

And again a big, perfectly friendly smile. And nothing more.

So, time for a touch of the Hard Detective.

'Oh, yes, you warned me all right. But you shouldn't have sent me up to that dragon when you knew perfectly well I'd get no further. So why don't you tell me now what really made you let in Charity Nyambura just now and how it is she's still here?'

Bright red generous lips set in a sudden firm line.

' 'Fraid I can't do that. No way.'

'Oh, come on. You can tell me. Why ever not? And then I won't have to say anything to Mrs Fishlock about her receptionist sitting here reading a newspaper. Maybe lose you your job.'

But this simply provoked a coolly calculating look.

'Don't think you'd do that.'

No go, Harriet registered. She's right. I'd never tell that unpleasant dragon of a woman that her receptionist defied the no-newspapers-on-duty rule. And Tonelle's guessed I wouldn't.

But Tonelle evidently thought something of an excuse was still necessary.

'Look,' she said, 'it was the crossword. I'd got totally caught up by it. I'm not stupid, but some of those clues didn't make an atom of sense to me. Listen, this is what I was on when you came in. Something about — what was it? — yeah, just listen to this. *Up with a tent for* — can't remember. Oh, yes, I can *For not quite a blonde.* And then there was a little bit on the end, too. Yeah, *East not zero leads to dug-out.* How about that? Mean anything to you?'

'Not a thing. But then I won't ever even glance at a crossword. Fear of looking a fool, I suppose. Still, according to my husband, who always finishes the Saturday *Guardian* one, its clues do sometimes go beyond the rules of the game.'

Then an idea came to her. It might well be worth getting firmly on the right side of Tonelle. I'll almost certainly have to come back here.

'If I remember,' she said, 'I'll ask John if he made anything of that one. Let you know.'

'Well, thanks. Something like that nags and nags at me till sometimes I can't bloody get to sleep.'

All right, lines of sympathy established. But no answer to how Charity Nyambura got in, nor to where she is now.

She turned to go. But, as she passed Bolshy standing just inside, she murmured 'Have a word with the lady'.

But she had not been sitting in the car, windows wound well down to dissipate the cheroot smell, for much more than fifteen minutes when she saw Bolshy emerge from the house and come tramping towards her, face heavy with resentment.

So Tonelle's defeated even his by no means subtle tactics, she thought. All right, a tough young woman. Yet I can't help sympathising with her, however useful it would have been to get to see Roughouse in the way that Charity Nyambura seems possibly to have done.

Bolshy jerked open the door on his side.

'Stupid bitch,' he said. 'All alike them blacks. Sticking together. Just went on and on saying bloody Charity was one of her own, what she called a sporting icon. A fucking icon, how about that?'

'And she didn't give an inch, not however unpleasant you hinted you might be?'

'Didn't bloody hint. I was. And *icon, icon, icon* she kept yacking. *I bent the rules 'cos Charity's an icon for all us blacks.* I dunno.'

'Well, DS, you can console yourself with remembering that my somewhat subtler approach was equally a failure. So let's wait a little longer and see if Charity Nyambura, when she appears, will tell us rather more.'

They sat waiting again. And waiting.

After a while Harriet, feeling cold with the car windows still open, turned to Bolshy.

'Look,' she said, 'I ought to be at Headquarters, certainly in half an hour from now. I'll have to go. But I want you to stay here till Charity comes out, however long that is. And when she does I want you to ask whether she got to see Roughhouse. If it turns out he was fit to talk, don't press her to tell you what he said. Just get an address and phone number for her and say I'll be coming to see her. You'll have to call a taxi to get you back. But I dare say our black friend at reception will let you ring a local firm, however much of a hard time you gave her.'

'Your orders,' Bolshy said. 'Pity they did no good, as per —'

Then he decided better of it.

CHAPTER FIVE

At Waterloo Gardens, after a sticky half-hour fending off the ACC's questions and suggestions, Harriet found Bolshy already back. He was sitting at his ease in the newly set-up incident room — Happy Hapgood had already worked his miracle — another nasty little cheroot jutting from his mouth. She saw, too, that he was busily scribbling down his expenses on the left-hand pages of his notebook, doubtless adding a substantial extra to the taxi fare he had just paid.

'Right, DS,' she said to him. 'My office.'

There, telling him to extinguish the cheroot before he set foot inside, she asked at once whether he had seen Charity Nyambura.

'Came waltzing out just after you'd gone, made a dive for her cab. But yours truly was up to that.'

'You stopped her? Good work.'

'Not much came of it, as per usual.'

'Oh, and why was that?'

'She wasn't going to tell me nothing. No more than she bloody well had to. So, it was *Yes, I saw him, and, no, he wasn't able to talk*. And that was it, more or less.'

'But you got a phone number for her, as I asked?'

'I do know what I'm about.' Long pause. 'Ma'am.'

Then a quick look.

'Want the address? It's 26–27 Colville Road, London W11, Flat 9, if I remember right.'

'You noted it down, I trust.'

'Did, matter of fact. But if you want me to check . . .'

With a great deal of tugging and twisting he pulled out his notebook and then began slowly flipping through its scrawled-over pages.

Damn it, he's deliberately keeping me waiting, Harriet realised. Shall I get rid of the insolent bugger, come what may? Should have said something about him when I saw the ACC just now.

Then Bolshy saved himself. He showed her Charity Nyambura's scrawled phone number and her address which, it seemed, he had remembered perfectly correctly. And he did better.

'Oh, yeah, ma'am, something I forgot to tell you. That Roughouse, found he's got a nice old country mansion. Not far away, matter of fact.'

'You forgot to tell me?' Harriet snapped out. 'Don't you ever let me hear you saying that again, not while you're assigned to me. Yes?'

'All right.' But, once more, the long pause. 'Ma'am.'

'OK. So tell me about this place of Roughouse's, every last thing.'

'Ain't much. But this is what I got, for what it's worth. It's a bloody manor house, out a bit beyond the Masterton place. Gartham Manor, it's called. Plus he's got a London pad, what they call a service flat. I dug that out for you, too. It's somewhere in posh Chelsea.'

Harriet thought for a moment.

All right, tomorrow while I'm seeing Matthew Jessop in hard-to-park Notting Hill bloody Bolshy can go on to Chelsea and have a snoop round that service flat. Might be something to be learnt there before my search order comes through. Simple task like that should be right up his street. Then he can come and collect me from Charity Nyambura's. Her place in W11 shouldn't be far from Jessop's house.

She began then to go through the wearisome protocol of informing the Met that, next day, officers from another force would be entering their territory on duty.

'All right,' she said to Bolshy, as at last she put down the phone, 'we'll go right away now to — what did you say the place was called? — Gartham Manor.'

'No rest for the bloody wicked.'

'No, DS, there isn't.'

With Bolshy at the wheel — he was at least a good driver, with an excellent bump of locality — they had no difficulty in finding isolated Gartham Manor. Harriet made him halt just inside its gates, held wide open by the entwined tufts of autumn-dry grass climbing up them. Then she took a long assessing look at the house ahead.

Plainly it lacked altogether the discreet smartness of the Masterton's well-painted white woodwork contrasting with its swathes of lushly green ivy. Robert Roughouse, it seemed, can have taken few pains, however wealthy he is, to keep the place in good repair. The paint on its window frames was grey rather than white. The bare walls were streaked and stained by damp.

It all tells me more about Roughouse? Of course. That he's ever eager for something new. Think of his Innovation Party. Or of his insisting, when anti-hunting protests are flavour of the month, on putting himself on display, calculatedly challenging in his riding get-up. All right, a brave, appealing figure, but impulsive. So, little doubt that his 'ancestral pile' has been long neglected in favour of a ties-free Chelsea service flat and its opportunities to throw himself into whatever happens to catch his fancy.

In a sudden switch, she thought of her own home life. Rock-steady husband and two sons who had followed her into her own profession — until there had come the moment when that terrorist bomb had ended Graham's life and injured Malcolm, wrecking his career.

But how truly close had the boys actually felt to us, she asked herself. Would they have one day, like Robert Roughouse, abandoned their first careers and gone off, say, to America, in search of the new? Become distant, hardly known, figures? They might have done. But now I find it hard not to think of them both almost every day of my life. Look at the absurd way I even carry about with me everywhere that little bright-coloured mobile Malcolm once gave Graham.

But no time now for thoughts like those.

There's a trickle of smoke coming from one of the chimneys down there. Somebody, perhaps even several people, must be inside. So let's find out what's there to be learnt.

Leaving Bolshy in the car again, no doubt to fill it once more with vile-smelling cheroot smoke, she set off down the long slope of the weed-pocked gravel drive. But at the door of the big, decaying mansion it seemed as hard to gain entry as it had been to get into the Masterton. Or even harder. A tug at the long-unpolished bell-pull beside the time-seamed oak door resulted in nothing. Blank, still silence. Only, somewhere in the distance, a solitary cow could be heard bleakly mooing.

All right, try again.

A more vigorous triple pull appeared to do no more than produce a long discordant jangling from somewhere deep inside.

Then at last she thought she heard footsteps, though not very evident ones, hardly more than a distant weary shuffle, far removed from the ponderous steps of the butler or footman the house might have provided in its prime.

And, yes, it was an elderly apron-clad woman, even a very elderly woman, who eventually dragged open by a foot or so the heavy oak door.

'Good afternoon,' Harriet said briskly. 'I am Detective Superintendent Martens, Greater Birchester Police. I am making inquiries in connection with the bomb attack which, as you may know, severely injured Mr Robert Roughouse last night.'

'Mr Robert hurt?' the old woman cried out. 'No one's told me. Is he bad? He's not in hospital, is he?'

'I'm afraid he is. Or, rather, he's in the Masterton Clinic, if you know it. And I'm sorry to have to tell you that he has not yet recovered consciousness.'

'Oh, my gracious, my poor little Robbie. Did you say a bomb? What sort of a bomb? Was it one of those terrorists you hear about? Why did they want to go throwing one of their bombs at Mr Robert?'

'We don't know yet what exactly took place,' Harriet answered, as soothingly as she could. 'I'm here to see if you, or anybody else in the house, can help us in the police find out more about Mr Roughouse's life in recent months. Something that may give us an indication why the attack on him happened.'

'Oh. Oh, well, there's nobody here but me. Mr Robert comes only once in a blue moon nowadays. So his old Nanna is the only one left to look after the place. Yes. The only one.'

Harriet felt a small descent in her hopes. Not much to be learnt about Roughhouse's current activities from his 'old Nanna'. Hardly likely that tales of his childhood will yield anything worth having.

But perhaps a look indoors . . .

'Tell me,' she said, 'does Mr Roughhouse have a study or an office of any sort here? Could I perhaps have a look at it, if he does?'

'Oh, no. No, he did use to have his desk in the Book Room. But he emptied it of everything, every last thing, when he decided it'd be best to spend his time down in London. Though why he should want to live in a nasty place like that is more than I can understand, country-loving lad as he always was. No, he only comes up here these days when —'

She came to a full halt.

'Yes? When what?'

Harriet saw now that a faint blush had crept on Nanna's withered cheeks. A moment's thought, and she guessed why that might be.

'Is it when he comes with a young lady guest?' she asked, making the question sound as innocuous as she could.

'Well, yes. Yes, that's what it was just the

weekend before last, when he brought that
— when he came . . .'

She fell altogether silent.

What on earth's causing her all this awk-
wardness?

And at once she thought what it might be.
Didn't Bolshy tell me Charity Nyambura
and Robert are an item? If Kenyan Charity
was the young lady Roughouse brought to
Gartham Manor a fortnight ago, won't that
be something this old retainer doesn't want
to talk about? Even think about?

But how to overcome her reticence?

Mercifully, Old Nanna conquered it for
herself.

'They hardly spent any time at all here.
Just that one night, you know,' she said, as
if somehow one night could more easily be
blotted from her memory. 'And what a
gentleman like Mr Robert does is not for
me to think about. I know my place, even
though I had all the upbringing of him
when his poor mother and father died in
that same terrible car accident.'

'That must have been difficult for you,'
Harriet said, doing what she could to gain
Nanna's confidence.

'Well, it was, and it wasn't, so to speak.
You see, the trustees saw to it that I had
everything I needed, for myself as well as

the poor wee child. And then, as soon as he got to be seven, away he was taken to boarding school, the little mite. Not that he was so little. A good healthy youngster, big for his age and up to everything.'

'So after that you saw less of him?'

'I did. He'd come for a few days either side of term-time at school and in what they call the vacations when he went to Cambridge University. All I had to do was see to his washing and that, and then off he'd go to stay with one of the trustees. So all I really did was look after the house. And I still do. The bank sends me my money every month, on the first, except when that comes at a weekend. So I never want for anything, and I'm able to ask for whatever's needed for what they call the upkeep.'

'The trustees?' Harriet jumped in. 'Can you tell me who they are?'

'Well, I could. But — But, you see, they're both dead now. They died quite a time ago. Just after Mr Robert left Cambridge it was.'

'I see.'

Harriet thought for a moment. And ventured.

'I wonder,' she said, 'could I have a quick look at the bedroom Mr Roughouse used on that recent visit of his? You see, it's possible he left something there, a letter or

71

something, anything of any sort. Something that might give us a clue to why someone carried out that attack on him.'

But, instead of agreeing, the old woman blushed once more, a deeper shade than before.

'You know, it may be really important,' Harriet said quickly. 'And if I have to take anything away, I'll show you what it is, and, of course, give you a receipt.'

Nanna shook her head in perplexity. Then she straightened her back and gave Harriet a straight-in-the-eye look.

'Well, you see, miss,' she said, 'the fact of the matter is I've never got up there to make the bed and straighten things out.'

'I perfectly understand,' Harriet replied, beginning to suspect what might be making Nanna so reluctant. 'And I promise I won't take any notice of whatever — er — untidiness there may be. But I really must see if there's anything there that would help me.'

'Oh, if you think there might be something really useful, miss, I'll show you up.'

In the big bedroom, as Nanna baulking at entering hovered outside, Harriet's rapid search — drawers jerked open, quick digs down between chair cushions and glances underneath — revealed no carelessly left-behind letter, nor anything else at all helpful. All she saw, flicking a look as she ducked to see under at the wide unmade bed with its flung-aside pillows, was what she had guessed Nanna had not wanted her to find, the marks she herself rather liked to call by the charming French name, *traces d'amour.*

All right, she thought as they drove away, if Charity Nyambura's as intimate with Roughouse as those stains indicated, she's likely to know a good deal about him. I really must get to see her.

'Pull in a moment,' she said to Bolshy. 'I want you to phone Charity Nyambura and fix a definite time tomorrow for me to see her. Make it a little after midday, if she can manage that. Or any time in the afternoon.'

'Don't need to pull in, use the mobile,' Bolshy answered. 'I can drive, you know.'

'Nevertheless, DS, while I'm in a car with you we'll stick to the rules of the road as recently laid down. You don't drive and use a mobile at the same time, not unless you've got a fixed handset.'

'Ma'am.'

She sat, turned away while Bolshy, pulling over to the verge, took his time about reaching Charity.

Damn him, she thought, I should have made the call myself. No need for me, sitting in this seat, even to have had the car halted.

She pulled a face.

All right, the reason I didn't make the call was because I was ashamed, in front of this damn man, to take out the only mobile I've got with me, the bright-coloured toy that belonged to Graham. Bloody Bolshy would make plenty of it if he'd seen the famous Hard Detective using a kid's plaything.

Damn, I've not been listening to him. Isn't he being rather long. Is he making some sort of a mess of finding a time for Charity to see me? Didn't he label all black women as stupid bitches? He's going to alienate her. I know he will.

For an instant she contemplated reaching over and cutting his call.

I'll use my mobile. Hell with its toy-like look.

But she was saved from the humiliation. Bolshy was now stuffing his phone away.

'Yeah,' he said. 'Wasn't at home. But I remembered where she goes to train. Comes of always having a good read of the sports pages. Got hold of her there, just off the track an' puffing away like a sodding steam-engine. Said she'd be free tomorrow afternoon. I made it for three o'clock. Want me to drive you down to the Smoke then?'

Knowing there was nothing Bolshy liked better than getting out of any hard work by driving anywhere at all, usually at top speed, Harriet was tempted to say she intended to go down by train. But a lazy thought checked her. Being swept away to London by a first-class driver was altogether more tempting than making a weary train journey with at the end of it a battle with public transport.

'All right,' she said. 'You can do that. But . . . But, yes, you can go down to Chelsea when you've dropped me in Notting Hill and see what you can find out about that service flat Roughouse has. I'll buzz you when I've finished at Colville Road.'

Bolshy looked grudgingly pleased.

Worthwhile? We'll see.

CHAPTER SIX

What matters most at this point, Harriet thought as she reached for the bell-push at Mathew Jessop's pretty Notting Hill house, is not discovering what in Robert Roughouse's life caused him to become the victim of that purple egg but finding out just why Roughouse was taken away from a first-class hospital like St Ozzie's and swept out to the Masterton Clinic. Almost certainly Jessop, there after all when Roughouse was hit by the bomb, will at least have had a hand in arranging that high-speed transfer. If Matthew Jessop and Roughouse were friends *since school and all that* — think those were his exact words there in the dark — he may even have been one of the dawn raiding party, along with that surgeon, Edgesomething.

The door in front of her opened almost as soon as the bell inside had tinkled out a pretty little tune, and Matthew Jessop stood there, looking very different from the man in the portico of Gralethorpe's shabby town hall kneeling beside blood-covered Robert Roughouse. The all-over-the-place thatch of pale hair, his only physical feature that had made any impression, was now brushed neatly into place. It gave his whole face, straight little nose, pair of pink ears pinned close to the head and almost rosebud mouth, an air of compactness. They were set off, too, by a fresh laundry-white shirt with at its neck a carefully knotted club tie in white and earth-red stripes.

'Detective Superintendent Martens,' he said. 'So we meet again.'

'We do. But in rather different circumstances. I could hardly make out anything of you in the darkness there, with the jagged remains of that bomb all around. And now here you are looking as spruce, if I may say so, as if you'd just come from your barber's.'

Jessop laughed.

'So I'm spruce, am I? I hope that goes further than just having had my hair cut.'

'It does. That's a very nice tie there.'

Harriet had intended the compliment as being nothing more than a way to increase the friendly atmosphere and get her questions freely answered. But it had an altogether different effect.

For an instant Jessop's neatly featured face looked sharply disconcerted.

'It — It's an old-school tie, as a matter of fact,' he brought out at last. 'The Zeal School, you know. I — I dare say what caught your eye were the tiny black circles on each of the red stripes. They're just a little addition indicating membership of a sort of club some of us have. But come in, come in.'

With some haste he led the way — it left her without a moment to account for that sudden change of attitude — along a narrow hallway, past a slim polished table holding a folded copy of the pink *Financial Times,* completed crossword uppermost, and into the room immediately to the right.

But the glimpse of the crossword prevented her, momentarily, from conducting the swift clockwise inspection which customarily told her more about the owner of a house than any number of questions. Instead, she found buzzing in her head the absurd crossword clue that had baffled bright-eyed Tonelle. *Up with a tent for not quite a blonde* and, yes, *east not zero leads to* something. Right, to *dug-out.* Must remember to ask John what the answer was, or it'll bug me for ever.

But, now, start observing. Look all round,

and without in the least showing it.

OK, white-painted double doors leading into a back-room that — Yes, a work-station and a bookcase full of untidy-looking volumes. Office or study uncompromisingly devoted to business. Now, on the wall facing me, elegant fireplace with no sign of a fire. Along the mantelpiece a row of silver objects — christening mug, eighteenth-century card case, former tea-caddy — with three, no, four, invitation cards. All too tucked away to be read, damn it. Softly coloured Chinese carpet over parquet flooring, French windows looking on the street, white-painted shutters half-concealed by narrow-striped plum-coloured curtains. Pale grey sofa in inlaid wood and a button-back nursing chair in the same grey material. Finally, just beside me, rather out-of-place against that mock eighteenth-century wallpaper of nesting game-birds, two large photographs in stark black-and-white. One a village street in some dusty country, and the other — same location, I think — a man with his back to the camera holding, in a noticeably stagey manner, a pistol.

'I see you're looking at my photographs,' Matthew Jessop said.

Caught out, Harriet thought, and before I've quite completed my survey. He must be pretty alert. I like to think people never notice that I'm sussing out their way of life.

'They're yours? Your work?' she said. 'Excuse the way I was staring, but they're both rather unusual, besides being so striking. Where was this street scene? It doesn't look like anywhere in this country.'

Once again Jessop stood in silence, looking almost in a trance at the photograph in which a scatter of dirty-faced children were playing in the dust of a tumbledown sunlit street. His silence began to go on so long that Harriet wondered if she should break into it. But, just as she was scrabbling in her mind for something innocuous to say, he turned away.

'It's a still from a little film I made,' he said. 'Both those photographs are, in fact. Films are my business, actually. In a comparatively small way.'

He came to a momentary halt again. Then he gabbled out a burst of words, as if he felt he ought somehow to account for his silence. 'It — It's a street in a place called Transabistan, one of those almost unknown, little breakaway countries in the Caucasus. I was filming there to get some publicity for Rob's book, *Marching Through Georgia*. Did you ever read it?'

'No, I didn't. But, now you mention its

title, I think my husband —'

But Jessop ignored her.

'Funny place, Transabistan,' he torrented on. 'Ruled by a cross between a politician and a — well, a brigand, to be frank. Chap called Olengovili. Total dictator, of course.'

Harriet could make little of all the outpouring, except to ask herself why Jessop was so ill at ease.

'You said you are a comparatively small film-maker,' she put in, attempting to calm him a little. 'How small is that, if I may ask?'

The change of subject did bring back something of a smile to Jessop's neat features.

'Good question,' he said. 'And not altogether easy to answer. I began, of course, in the smallest of all possible ways, little more than as an amateur with a single cine-camera.'

'Another Satyajit Ray,' Harriet put in quickly, thinking of those first films of his that had so enchanted her, and counting on the comparison to calm the nervy fellow to a point where she could get coherent answers to her questions.

'Well, a little like Ray's early days, if you like. But I don't claim to be any sort of a film genius. No, I've risen to the point of having made — produced, that is — one full-length feature. It was directed, in fact, by someone I hope one day is going to become a name in British cinema. But, otherwise, I've just made a few documentaries, with some success I think I can say. At least I've learnt a lot working on them, even such simple things as the need for organisation on set. Rules about where things are to be put, and kept. Absolutely vital when everything around is bound to be chaotic.'

Does the extreme neatness about him account for that insistence on order, Harriet wondered. Bit of a fusspot about his personal appearance, too? Golly, how it must have upset him to be in such a mess crouching there with the remains of that grenade all round and his friend of old covered in blood almost from head to foot.

'But, look, can I give you some sherry? Not much too early, I think.'

Harriet accepted. She was still far away from asking her questions about the dawn raid on St Ozzie's. But go roundabout towards that.

'So are you making a film at the moment?' she asked, taking a sip of the sherry, something she recognised as being distinctly out-of-the-common.

'Indeed, I am. It's why I couldn't find a time to meet you till now. I was up all hours yesterday on a night shoot. I'm using that same young, well, youngish director. But this time, I'm happy to say, I've got a really bankable star, and I like to think an interesting story.'

'Oh, yes?'

Jessop gave a bark of a laugh, half-deprecating, half-proud.

'It's the basic tale of that long Tennyson poem *Maud,*' he said. 'Of course, most people, if they know it at all, know only those verses made into that drawing-room song, *Come into the garden, Maud.* Much mocked. But the actual story is a cut above that, a considerable cut. It's in fact an account of the circumstances leading to a duel to the death, at a time when duelling had just been made strictly illegal in this country but when fighting one was still seen, in some reaches of society, as an obligation of honour. So, you see, there's a lot of tension there. Statute law versus an older code of expected behaviour. And, of course, it reflects on aspects of society today, clashes between the laws and what people think they've a right to be able to do. Much really what lies behind all the agitation over making hunting illegal.'

'Yes,' Harriet said, hardly finding this a way-in to asking about the dawn raid on St

83

Ozzie's. 'Though I must admit I haven't been following all that very closely. Too busy devising ways of stopping drunken hooligans disturbing the Queen's Peace.'

'Something that needs to be done,' Jessop chimed in. 'At least that's what I think. My upbringing, I suppose. You know, the Zeal School, where Rob and I were, may have been a little unorthodox, but, morally speaking, it was absolutely conventional, what even nowadays might seem distinctly old-fashioned. As you'd probably expect from a place where the fees are rather higher than Eton's.'

She remembered Jessop saying there in the dark at Gralethorpe that anyone who, like Roughouse, aspired to run a pack of foxhounds had to be rich, and that *rich* was a word it was not quite the done thing to use unless *filthy,* deprecatingly, was put in front of it.

Am I at last getting somewhere, she wondered. Isn't he talking now about a stratum of society where there's a huge amount of money about. And money, real money, has its own ways of doing things. So can there have been some reason for taking Roughouse off in that private ambulance altogether more weighty than a simple wish to avoid publicity? Was Roughouse shot at, not by some Animal Rights maniac, for heaven's sake, but for some quite other reason? One not easy for your average citizen to conceive of? Something even that's altogether beyond the law? Or even above it? His Innovation Party, could it somehow have been seen as a threat to some secret organisation with a great deal at stake?

All right, let's go on a bit. But circuitously.

'The Zeal School?' she said. 'I'm afraid I haven't actually heard of it.'

'No, not everybody has, by any means. The founder, Dr Jakob Kettner, made a point of avoiding any sort of publicity. Not because there was anything secret about his regime, but because he believed outside interference would affect his theories.'

'But the regime there was — you said — unorthodox?'

'Yes. Yes, it was. Dr Kettner put much more emphasis on rigorous character-building, as it used to be called, than on the academic or even on religion. We were held to a totally strict timetable from five a.m. till an early, exhausted bedtime. Physical testing to near breaking-point, cold baths, long runs, hard-played games.'

'Yow,' Harriet felt obliged to put in.

'Oh, yes. We even had something you'll no

doubt think totally bizarre, called the Clamber, a fierce competitive trial under, I quote, *the unarguable rules of gladiatorial combat.* Boys, paired one against another, had to climb an appallingly jagged rockface and be first to touch what was supposed to be the scroll of the Ten Commandments held out by bearded old Moses.'

'So the Zeal School,' Harriet asked, 'is named from the huge amount of zeal that's expected of its pupils?'

'You're not entirely wrong there, though actually it's called the Zeal School simply because it's near a place called Zeal on the northern edge of Dartmoor. But, oh yes, zeal was expected. It still is. Long after one's left the place. We're called Zealots, us old boys, and things are always being demanded of us.'

Harriet, when Jessop smiled disarmingly as he brought his account to an end, found she had a new idea in her head about how to find out why really that raid on St Ozzie's had been launched. Since Jessop wasn't on any night shoot when he had been accompanying his school friend of old to Gralethorpe, he would have had ample opportunity at dawn the day after to accompany that surgeon — Yeah, Jackson Edgeworth — in the private ambulance.

Can I just ask him outright? Act the Hard Detective? I'll have to ask, sooner or later. So, here goes.

'Tell me, were you one of the people who went to St Oswald's Hospital in Birchester and had Robert Roughouse transferred to a place called the Masterton Clinic?'

Matthew Jessop hesitated, but for only an instant.

'Yes. Yes, I was. It's true. We took Rob to the Masterton because we thought he'd do better there. Have a quieter time, that sort of thing.'

'I see,' Harriet said, though she hardly saw this as any sort of a reason for moving a patient in as fragile a state as Roughouse had been.

All right, another question.

'But wasn't that move made with somewhat excessive haste? I mean, it must have been a risk for someone that badly injured.'

Another tiny hesitation.

'One of us there was, in fact, a surgeon, one with a considerable reputation, comparatively young though he is. A chap called Jackson Edgeworth. So his opinion —'

But Harriet interrupted.

'I've been told Dr Edgeworth was —'

A counter interruption now from Matthew Jessop.

'Not *Doctor*. I told you: he's a surgeon. He's Mr Edgeworth.'

Harriet felt a jounce of fury.

How could I have fallen into such a solecism? However ridiculous it is to call surgeons, by custom, Mister, something I was even told about when I was at school.

'As I was saying,' Matthew Jessop began smoothly to go on.

But Harriet cut in.

'Mr Jessop, tell me. Is your *Mr* Edgeworth — What did you say you called your fellow ex-pupils? — a Zealot?'

Something like a blush now on Jessop's cat-neat features.

'Yes. Yes, he was actually at the Zeal with myself and Rob. But that's got nothing to do with it. Nothing. I was simply pointing out that his medical opinion would have been convincing to the authorities at St Oswald's Hospital.'

'I see. But I understand there were three of you there.'

'Yes, you're right. There were three of us, though only myself and Jackson actually took Rob on to the clinic.'

'But was the third person also a Zealot?'

Jessop gave her a quick cold glance, almost a glare.

'As a matter of fact he was. But that's

hardly strange. As I've indicated to you, people who were at the Zeal tend to stick together afterwards. We've all shared what you might call a unique experience.'

'Very well. But who, actually, was this third Zealot?'

A hesitation. Not the first.

'He's a chap called Drummond.'

'That's his proper name? Does he have a forename to go with it?'

A visible change of mood in reaction to that, marked by another of those markedly genuine smiles.

'You could say he has two forenames, if you like. He was actually christened Valentine, but he's known to his friends, and sometimes to the gossip pages come to that, as Tigger. Name he got at school when, one term, he brought down with him a little mechanical tiger he'd put together. In fact he now runs a very successful firm making that thing called Tiger Man.'

'Oh, I know about Tiger Man. Even years ago my sons each had an early model. The all-conquering mini-hero. So, it was Tiger Man who freed Robert Roughhouse from his captors at St Ozzie's?'

Another smile from Jessop.

'If you like to put it that way. Old Tigger may be just a toy manufacturer, but he's a dab hand as an organiser. Always was, even at school. So it wasn't surprising that he came along.'

'Ah, yes. Your rapid action. But, tell me, why actually was it needed?'

One more hesitation. This time even more prolonged.

'Well, put it this way. It was obvious, even out there in Gralethorpe, that the missile that almost killed Rob was meant for him and nobody else. So, if that was the case, it might well be, we thought, that someone — whoever it had been in Gralethorpe — would make another attempt. Isn't that reason enough for his friends to take what precautions they could?'

Someone. That vague, Harriet thought. So it looks unlikely I'm going to find out from Jessop here anything about what was behind that attempt.

'It didn't occur to you,' she said, 'that Greater Birchester Police would have taken appropriate precautions in view of the possibility of a second attempt? I instigated them myself, as a matter of fact.'

'Well, I suppose I wasn't thinking very clearly after I left Gralethorpe. I simply rang a few friends to tell them what had happened, and the idea of taking Rob into safety just came up.'

'All right. I suppose, if you all have the money you seem to have, you might decide between you on a private initiative. Though, I must say, it seems to me a bit over the top.'

One more smile from Jessop, if not quite as warm as before.

'Well, may I suggest it might seem over the top to you because you, even as a senior police officer, are not used to having the sort of money most of us Zealots happen to have. What are by ordinary standards large sums, even very large, don't mean a great deal to most of us.'

Harriet fought down her innate prejudices, perhaps as deep-seated as those of Bolshy Woodcock.

Nevertheless, she thought, I do smell something a bit . . . a bit unpalatable here. Though I certainly can't lay a finger on it. And, if what I've learnt about the money floating around in that circle means anything, there could be something there that made those three Zealots act. Would it be a reason of even more weight than providing safer protection to anything Greater Birchester Police offered?

But none of all this can be other, just now, than pure speculation.

So is there anything else to be eased out

of Matthew Jessop, minor film producer?

Yes, there's this.

'Mr Jessop, have you any idea, when all's said and done, why anyone should have wanted to kill Robert Roughouse? Or perhaps to have him killed?'

Matthew Jessop gave her, for a long moment, no answer. But then he shook his head.

'No,' he said. 'No, I can't find any answer to that. Of course, I've been asking myself why ever since they took poor Rob off to Birchester.' A choked sort of laugh. 'But rack my brains as I may, I cannot conceive of any answer.'

Harriet looked at him.

More to come? Why do I think that?

Her mind stayed blank, and Jessop stayed silent.

Time perhaps to go?

All right, Jessop hasn't always answered me with quite as much frankness as he might have done. Something surely a bit fishy there. Yet I very much doubt if he'll give me the least bit more just now. But I'll be back. If Matthew Jessop is my way forward, then he's soon going to find himself face-to-face with me once more.

CHAPTER SEVEN

Harriet found Charity Nyambura's flat was in a building just off the Portobello Road. A plaque over its door announced that it was owned by a housing trust and called Daley Thompson House, in honour of the record-breaking black athlete.

OK, she said to herself, I see why Charity lives here. Coming from Kenya, probably with not a great deal of money, certainly not by London standards, what better place could she have found than this sort of shrine to a fellow black athlete?

As she prepared to mount the steps up to the doors and buzz the entry-phone, something flicked at the edge of her vision. A man walking towards the Portobello market had come to a sudden standstill. The abrupt cessation of movement must have just caught her eye.

Looking back for an instant, she saw the stock-still man was not at all the sort of person one might have expected to be going to the cheap and cheerful market ahead. Further along, where antiques were on sale, yes. But here, no. He had been, she realised even as he abruptly swung away into the side-street next door, altogether too well-dressed. An immaculate summer suit in a shade of butter-yellow, a pale blue shirt — glimpse of a smart striped tie? — and well-polished tan shoes, sun glinting off their toe-caps.

For a moment she contemplated turning round and going to get a better look. But at once she decided it would be ridiculous. However out-of-place the man had looked, he must be no more than a chance passer-by who had suddenly remembered something.

What's he to me? Or I to him? What's Hecuba to him, or he to Hecuba?

No, enough Shakespeare.

She trotted quickly up the steps of Daley Thompson House and thumbed the entry-phone for Flat 9.

'Who is it?' came a distinctly African voice.

Harriet identified herself and was told to come up to the top floor.

There, she found the flat's door wide open and a young black woman in a white top and jeans, the latter plainly tight-stretched by muscular legs.

94

Yet, despite a wide, welcoming smile, Charity Nyambura, she thought, seems clearly to be fighting back some deep underlying anxiety.

'Come in. Just go through, straight ahead. You want a coffee?'

'That would be nice.'

Charity popped into the kitchenette next to the door and flipped down the switch on a green kettle.

'Sweetener suit you? I don't have nothing else. Have to watch the weight. But there's plenty of milk.'

'Milk'll be fine,' Harriet, who detested pills in her coffee, answered quickly. In the room she had stepped into she made, once again, her customary survey.

Less to take in here than over at Matthew Jessop's elegant little house, a good deal less. The room was not large, though with its plain walls colour-washed in pale orange and big radiator painted in the same shade, it was airy and pleasant. Not a great deal of furniture, a small sofa in plain grey-green leatherette and two rather narrow armchairs in the same material — Harriet thought she had seen such three-piece suites in many a shop-window — and wall-to-wall carpeting worn enough to have been laid when Daley Thompson House was first built. Otherwise

95

almost nothing to take note of except, hanging on the wall opposite the two large uncurtained windows, a wood carving of a male African face, broad-nosed, deep-eyed, a little threatening.

Charity came in, once more smiling, mug of coffee in each hand. Something then decided Harriet to go straight in.

'I saw you on Wednesday at the Masterton Clinic outside Birchester,' she said.

And got a reaction. The smile on Charity's boot-polish brown face slowly fading away.

'OK, I was there.'

'May I ask why?'

Charity's guarded look became yet more wary.

'You ought to know why I was there,' she said. 'That detective who questioned me must have been with you. So, let me tell you, I didn't at all like the way he spoke to me. All right, I'm black, and maybe I have to expect hassle from the police sometimes. But he just went too far.'

Bloody bloody Bolshy, Harriet thought. Didn't I tell him he wasn't to press her? So what did he do? Gave her a hard time. Still, I suppose I should have been more explicit in tasking him, seeing the way he's so prejudiced.

'Look,' she said to Charity, 'I must

apologise.' She checked herself: no name, no official complaint. 'That officer should certainly never have spoken to you otherwise than strictly politely. I never gave him any instructions that might have authorised anything else.'

The smile returned, if not as broadly as before.

'All right,' Harriet went on. 'You were at the Masterton to see Robert Roughouse, if you could. And you did see him. But did you tell my sergeant everything that occurred when you were inside there? Was Robert in fact able to say something, anything at all?'

'No. No, he wasn't. What I told your bullyboy was the simple truth. When I came into Rob's room I saw straightaway he was totally unconscious, and he never opened his eyes and hardly even stirred the whole time I was there.'

'But all the same you did get to see him,' she went on. 'So, tell me, how was it you were allowed right in there, when earlier I had the devil of a time even getting to see the Administrator? And on police business?'

Charity suddenly grinned.

'Simple,' she said. 'Tonelle on Reception's an old friend.'

And then came a sudden close-down.

Harriet pretended not to notice. But something here, she thought, not quite as might be expected?

'So that accounts for it,' she said easily. 'And I suppose you never even saw that dragon, Mrs Fishlock?'

Another grin, if a little more slow to come.

'No. No, I didn't. Tonelle told me where to find Rob, and I just went along there, slipped into the room and told the nurse on duty I'd got permission. But, hey, sit down, sit down. Can't have you standing there, about to tip coffee all over the carpet. Not that it'd matter. Grubby old thing, here in the flat when I got it.'

Harriet lowered herself into one of the narrow armchairs, while Charity slid gracefully into the other.

'Look,' Harriet said to her, 'the reason I'm here is that we in the police have really no idea why Robert was attacked. Nothing's come to light. So, you know him well, can you give me any idea about any enemies he might have? Or whether he's done something — anything — that might make somebody want . . . want him not to be here any more?'

'No. No, no. There's nothing, — er — Superintendent.'

'Oh, drop the rank and all that. It's

Harriet.'

'OK, Harriet. Well, we met, Rob and I — it was quite a long time ago, actually — at one of those big parties they held to whip up interest in London's bid for the Olympics. And . . . and we just took to each other straightaway, in spite of being so different. And not only in our ages, nearly twenty years between us, you know. I mean there's me, a Kenyan girl from nowhere at all, and there's Rob, kind of ruling class, like in the old days when they all dressed up specially to eat their dinner. Always said they had to do that, you know, though God knows who'd told them to.'

'But did Rob ever say anything to you, even the least hint, that, looking back, might give you an idea of why anyone should want him dead?'

'No, hardly a word,' Charity said. 'That's the trouble, really. If I knew anything, if I had the least idea, I'd not feel so awful. Had a terrible day training yesterday.'

'I can imagine. You've got an event coming up?'

'Yeah, a ten-thousand metres at Manchester in a couple of weeks. If I can get fit enough. You have to keep at top level all the time, you know. And . . .'

'Yes, I understand.'

99

Again a silence. Something she's trying to recollect? Something half-buried in her mind?

'No, he never said anything. Not a word.'

'But tell me about yourself and Rob,' Harriet said, groping for more. 'You said you've known him quite a long time.'

Charity's nose abruptly wrinkled up in a what-the-hell grimace.

'Suppose there's no harm in telling you really,' she said. 'Rob and I are lovers, though I hope you won't go blabbing to the papers about it.'

'To the papers? I promise you the thought would never enter my mind. I'm not too keen on those people. So that means you and Rob see a good deal of each other?'

'Oh, we do. We do. Most nights, matter of fact.'

'Good. And does he tell you then about what he's been doing during the day?'

'Well, it's funny, but he doesn't really. Or not all that much. We've got other things to talk about, you know. And in some ways Rob's a bit cagey. I mean, I know a lot about when he was a boy, the family house and that, and about his travels, like the ones he wrote that book about, *Marching Through Georgia*.'

'Ah, yes. I've heard of that. In fact . . . I

suppose I couldn't borrow your copy? I'd give you a receipt, of course, and see you got it back as soon as I'd finished it.'

A look of what might be a pang of misery came on Charity's bright brown face.

'Rob never gave me one,' she said. 'Though I've asked him often enough.'

Alertness sprang up in Harriet's mind.

'That's a bit odd, isn't it?' she asked.

'Well, Rob is odd about some things. I mean, there's stuff I hardly know anything at all about. That Innovation Party he's started up — Rob hardly mentions it — and, even more, there's a little bunch of his school friends he almost never talks about, a sort of secret-ish club. They call it something. Rob said it, just once. Yeah, the Cobbles, I think that's what he said. But he never says the least thing about it. Only, he told me once, they invented a whole set of rules for themselves. Ones they're sworn to keep to. Bit silly, it seemed to me. Little boys' game. But, of course, I didn't say that to Rob.'

'So there's really nothing he ever said that makes you think he could have acquired an enemy who, that night in Gralethorpe, launched that attack on him?'

'No. No, really I can't think of anything. I know it's strange, when we're so close really.

But Rob has got some funny ways. I think it's that crazy school he went to. What a place. I mean, almost all Rob's friends from there are a bit odd. And the man who's president or something of the whole outfit — the Zealots they call themselves — he's a real nutter. A judge, I think, he is. Somebody Cotmore. Certainly rules the roost like he's a judge. Rob even *Yes, sirs* when he's talking to him.'

'I find that a little hard to picture. Not much like the Robert Roughouse I saw berating that crowd of anti-hunt protesters.'

'Oh, Rob's only like that when he puts on his Zealot hat — well, Zealot tie actually, big red and white stripes. That's when he gets all stiff and silly.'

'That's men all over,' Harriet said.

In the companionable silence that followed she wondered if perhaps she had learnt all she could from Charity. But then that moment of shut-down when Charity had said she and Tonelle were old friends came back to her mind. It was more than a little curious. How could a Kenyan athlete living in London and a girl working at a clinic in distant Birrshire be *old friends?* It isn't as if Tonelle, ebony black, looks in any way like this boot-polish brown Kenyan. And Tonelle, from her speech and fly knowledge of the scene, is clearly British-born, perhaps even second generation.

'Tell me,' she cautiously asked Charity, 'how does it happen that you know the Masterton as well as you seem to?'

Charity bit her lower lip.

'Oh, well,' she said, after a silence that seemed to have lasted almost a whole minute, 'I was there as a patient once. It — It's got quite a reputation for — for treating sports injuries, you know.'

A quick look, as if to see how that had gone down.

Harriet, who had no idea what sort of medicine the Masterton practised, let Charity assume that what she had said raised no doubts.

'Reputation for that, has it?' she said. 'I don't know much about the place, except that it's there.'

The relief on Charity's face was too evident to miss. But Harriet made a point of seeming not to notice.

'Oh, yes, there is one other thing I meant to ask,' she said. 'How did you come to know that Robert had been taken to the Masterton in the first place?'

'I heard from a man called Matthew Jessop,' Charity answered. 'He's Rob's best friend, and he rang me. He actually said he thought I shouldn't go up there and see him, though he never said why. But, of course, I started out as soon as he'd rung off.'

'Good for you,' Harriet said.

'Glad you think so. But is there anything else you want to know?'

Harriet rose to her feet.

'No. No, I don't think there is.'

She thought for a moment. Got all I could have hoped for? I suppose so.

'Right. Well, thanks for your help. And, if anything you've forgotten comes back to you, here's my card with a phone number.'

Descending the stairs, Harriet felt she had been left with a good deal to think about. Curious little mysteries. Why had Charity, who had seemed to be a nice, open creature, hesitated before saying how it had come about that she knew Tonelle? All right, she had accounted for it by saying the Masterton specialised in sports injuries. But then she had left it at that. Not a word about what particular injury she had suffered, or how it had come about that the Masterton rather than a clinic in London had treated her. Nothing criminal in that, of course. But odd. Odd.

And then, too, what she told me about Roughouse was somehow not quite right.

She had implied she was fully in his confidence, an ear for his pillow talk. But she had also said he was cagey about much of his day-to-day activities. Was that really true? Were there things she didn't want, or didn't for some reason dare, to tell me about? Does she know more than she let me believe? Can it be, in fact, that someone . . . that someone's already threatened her into silence?

All right, I did learn from her that there's a small inner group of old boys from the Zeal School who call themselves — was that really right? — the Cobbles. And does Charity actually know more about them than that curious name? Did her Rob confide something to her, but swear her to secrecy by the same sort of schoolboy rules she told me the group goes by? And does she feel, with Robert after all alive, she owes him her silence?

Something worth pursuing there? Though I implied to Charity that I'd learnt everything I wanted to, that's by no means in fact the case.

CHAPTER EIGHT

Outside, Harriet used her toy-mobile to summon Bolshy from Roughouse's Chelsea service flat. She had been in two minds about whether it had been sensible to give Bolshy his task. Will he, she asked herself now, have carried it out as sloppily as when he was asked to do nothing more difficult than find some details of Roughouse's everyday existence?

But, she shrugged, I have to make use of such help as, thanks to the ACC, I've been given. And in fact, even if I get a search warrant, there's not likely to be much to learn at somewhere as impersonal as a service flat. Roughouse's bank, his solicitor's office, even the headquarters of the Innovation Party will probably be better sources of information. But they will be sources for me to tackle, or perhaps, by phone, reliable old Happy Hapgood. Still, Bolshy had to be found something to do.

As she waited for him to come, she thought for a moment of exploring the street next to Daley Thompson House where the man who had come to that sudden halt had vanished. Did he stop like that because it was me he saw there looking up at this building? But why should he have? Yet what is it that makes me feel there is something. Something about him which makes me curious?

But, no. No will-of-the wisps. This is as good a time as any to go over in my mind once again everything Charity Nyambura said. Was there something I missed when she was talking about the Masterton? I feel there was. But no, damn it, can't even think at this minute. I'll get back to it in the end, but not by puzzling away now.

She crossed the road and looked through the high railings of the big playground gardens opposite.

Take a stroll there? No, might miss Bolshy, and God knows whether he'd wait here if I did. So, just have a peek down that little street after all?

Looking across, she saw it was called Colville Houses. *Colville Houses.* The mere curiousness of that as a street name — somehow not one conventionally right for any city street — finally decided her. She crossed back and looked along its short length. A row of small newish houses on one side, probably built after wartime bomb damage, and, opposite, tall and narrow much older ones, to judge from the uniform appearance of their brightly painted fronts let out as cheap flats. So not at all the kind of street an expensively dressed man was likely to have business in. Unless there was a prostitute somewhere there.

She walked up to the top — it was a cul-de-sac — looked all round, and, since there was nothing at all to see, made her way back.

But this definitely was another puzzle, the butter-yellow linen suit, the just glimpsed silky-looking tie, the polished tan shoes. In this unlikely setting?

It may mean nothing, of course. London full of unexplained oddities. But . . . but all the oddities that I've noticed here have at least been connected — if this last of them only remotely — with the unexplained attack on Robert Roughouse.

And there's yet another puzzle, she thought now. Matthew Jessop, that friendly man, when he'd rung to tell Charity that her Rob was injured and in the Masterton Clinic, had said she ought not to visit him. And no explanation. Why? Knowing, as he must do that they are a couple, he can't but have realised she would want to go to him straightaway. It's not as if he had said there was no point in visiting when a phone inquiry would tell her all there was to be learnt. No, he had just said she shouldn't go. That, and no more.

Worthwhile, as soon as Bolshy's picked me up, nipping back to that pretty little house and having another word with Matthew Jessop? I think so. A few carefully put questions, face-to-face, may lead me somewhere. A stone not to be left unturned.

She used her toy-like memento of Graham to make sure Jessop was still at home. But no go. A recorded voice. *Matthew Jessop is not in at present. If you want to leave a message, speak after the tone.*

All right, already off filming somewhere, I imagine. He seems to do that almost every day. But if he's not there in — what's it? — Rutland Place, he's not. Another little oddity to keep in mind.

A car came to a brakes-squealing halt just in front of her. Bolshy, the cock-a-hoop fast driver.

She opened the door, got in. For once not much of a smell of cheroots. He must have had a window open, nice afternoon as it is.

At once she embarked on some sharp questioning about Roughouse's Chelsea flat. To her surprise, Bolshy emerged with a degree of credit.

'Doorman at the block didn't know next to nothing. Seems old Roughers don't even eat in the flat. Goes to what that doorman called *his sodding club.*'

'And is that all you found out, DS?'

'Matter o' fact, it ain't.'

He gave her a quick look, blue-grey eyes at once flicking away.

'I do know my way around,' he said. 'Guessed a doorman like that feller was bound to be a bit dodgy, so told him pretty quick I'd sussed out his little ways and he'd better turn the old blind eye to what it'd do him no harm not to know. Next thing I was inside the flat. Quick look at a fancy-looking address book on the desk. Just a lot of names, though I did spot a solicitor and a bank manager. In my notebook for you.'

'Good work, DS, though I'd have preferred not to hear that you entered illegally.'

'Suit yourself, ma'am. But that's not all I found in there.'

Harriet sighed.

'So, what else?'

'Lot o' locked file cases labelled *Innovation Party.* Went through 'em all.'

'Locked files, DS?'

'Yeah, not bad locks either. But I done better.'

'All right. What did you find in them then?'

'Not a bleeding thing. Lot o' bollocks every page, ask me.'

Ask him or not, Harriet said to herself, can I trust him? All right, he's no doubt got a nose for anything dodgy. But he's also perfectly capable of polishing up evidence for his own ends. If I accept what he's telling me, he'll hope to be let off making more inquiries, hope I'll assume the Innovation Party is eliminated from the inquiry. Look at the way he told me only what he thought would satisfy me about Charity Nyambura. It was barely a tenth of what I learnt myself.

No, he's done something of a good job at the Chelsea flat, even if he went further beyond the rules and regs than I like to think about. But as to trusting him, I can't. I won't.

Back at Waterloo Gardens in the business-like surroundings of the Incident Room, she found its full, if meagre, team of DCs active under Happy Hapgood's directions. The results of the inquiries at Gralethorpe which might still produce a description of someone seen running from the scene had all been filed and cross-filed. And more, Happy had waiting for her the early forensic report on the mortar-like machine that had sent the purple egg flying to within a foot of Robert Roughouse's head. In her office, devouring the close-typed pages she learnt that the contraption had probably been constructed, to judge by its workmanship, by a skilled craftsman. It was, too, clearly a one-off, designed for that one occasion it had been used. And no identifiable traces of the person who had fired it had been found.

A hired killer then who had looked ahead even against the eventuality of his having to abandon his machine. A real professional. The implications began to slot themselves into place in her mind. For some reason somebody, or some people, with plenty of money must have thought it necessary to get rid of Robert Roughouse. Not, for heaven's sake, as a potential Master of Foxhounds, and not, surely, even as head of the Innovation Party. But, after somehow learning he was to speak in out-of-the-way Gralethorpe — information more or less freely available — they must have seized that opportunity to have him killed and make it look like the work of some Animal Rights extremists. It was a scheme which, but for that single-minded, armigerous old fool Percival Pidgeon, could well have left not the least trace.

No, it's plain now, if it wasn't totally so before, that this is an affair of real importance. Think of the large sum involved in having the hitman make the device and its cunning little explosive egg. All right, that may look now as if it's beyond the resources of any Animal Rights activists, but had the person who fired that shot been able to take the device away with them, no one would ever have known how elaborately it had been constructed. But, thanks again to Percival Flappant Ears, they had been forced to leave it behind for us to find and the forensics people to analyse.

But should I go to the ACC and say I think the case is now a matter for Special Branch, however much the handling of it might restore my reputation? Show him I'm not the woman I was when I learnt about — about Graham's death, and Malcolm, so terribly —

A sharp tap on the door.

'Come in.'

An oddly anonymous-looking man stepped inside, grey sports jacket and dark trousers, plain blue tie on plain blue shirt.

Clearly, from his merely being here on his own, in the heart of Birchester's main police station, he must be a police officer. Yet I'm certain he's nobody I've ever seen. Unless that oddly blank face of his has made me forget.

'Detective Superintendent Martens?'

'My office. My name.'

'Good evening, ma'am. DI Peters, Special Branch. From London.'

What's this? I'm just thinking Roughouse's death may after all be a matter for the secret ways of Special Branch and in steps none other than an SB officer.

'I'm up here seeing your ACC (Crime). He's been in touch with us about the attack on Robert Roughouse. He was concerned that political matters, possibly to do with the Innovation Party, were at the back of it.'

So who's been trying to show cocky Detective Superintendent Martens that, though she may have been right about the Animal Rights people, she's way behind in seeing that the case does have political implications? And, yes, galling that I've only just worked that out myself.

'And he's sent you to tell me that the SB is taking over? Well, I suppose that's probably for the best. You've got the knowledge, and the resources.'

DI Peters unexpectedly grinned. A sudden gleam on the poface.

'That's true, ma'am, we have got the

knowledge. Knowledge about the Innovation Party. And it's this. They're a nice lot of old buffers — some young, of course, and some female — who are going to be about as effective in politics as any other here-today, gone-tomorrow outfit. Haven't got the funds, haven't got any real backing.'

Well, well. So Bolshy's forage through those locked files in Roughouse's flat got it right. *Lot o' bollocks, every page.*

'You mean, the party's not likely to have been involved in any way in the attack on Roughouse?'

'We don't think so, ma'am, not for a moment. You know, we always take an interest in any new outfit like the Innovation Party. Put someone inside, see what they're really up to. And it turns out that nine times out of ten — probably ninety-nine out of a hundred — they're just pretending they're for real. They're having a nice little time, all on their own.'

'I see. Well, I don't mind telling you I'd just arrived at the same conclusion as my ACC, though he didn't actually say to me he was getting in touch with you. Right, it turns out we were both wrong. I'm in good company, it seems.'

DI Peters offered no comment.

'There is one other thing,' Harriet said in

115

face of that discreet silence. 'How shall I put it? Yes. Do you know whether any other body, besides the Innovation Party, may have an interest in Roughhouse?'

'There's a fairly simple answer to that. As far as I know, no group with any serious activity in mind is likely to be interested in him. He's a nice well-meaning chap, from all I hear, and a brave one. But in any political context he's a lightweight. Blown this way and that at any puff of anything.'

'Thank you for telling me, DI.'

'So, ma'am,' he said with a tiny hint of a smile still on his firmly blank face, 'looks like I'm leaving you with a mystery motive.'

Sitting staring at the door that DI Peters had closed behind him on his way back to London, Harriet felt she had more than a little new to think about. A mystery motive. DI Peters couldn't have got it more right. If it wasn't an Animal Rights maniac who had all but killed Robert Roughhouse, and if there's no faction inside the Innovation Party with plans that go beyond the unwritten rules of British political life, then why on earth did an assassination attempt take place at all? But it did. It happened. And from that moment onwards it's been all mystery and murk.

But something still to do, and at once.

Lips set in an inflexible line, she rang the Masterton's guardian dragon.

'No, Superintendent,' Mrs Fishlock said in answer to a carefully worded inquiry, 'Mr Roughouse has, of course, undergone the operation on his head. But he has still to recover consciousness. However, I can tell you that our medical staff are well pleased with their work and have informed me that the patient's condition remains stable. And now let me add this: I am, as you scarcely seem to have recognised, a very busy woman. I have innumerable important duties. I cannot spend the whole of my time answering all these inquiries about Mr Roughouse, wherever they come from.'

'It's no concern of mine however many inquiries you have,' Harriet snapped, returning blow for blow. 'But, when Mr Roughouse is at all able to talk, will you see that I am informed immediately? It is essential that I interview him, however briefly, at whatever hour of the day or night, as soon as he's fit to be spoken to.'

A silence at the far end. Broken eventually.

'Very well, Superintendent. But I must warn you that any interview you have must depend on the medical staff advising me that it will not adversely affect the patient. Is that understood?'

'Of course.'

Harriet put down the phone before another fiery puff of dragon's breath could reach her. She turned with a sigh to writing up her mandatory Policy File, the hour-to-hour record of her own thoughts and ideas. Always a mistake to leave it till later. Scribbling away with a snatched-up ballpoint, she set down her certainty that the attack on Roughouse had been the work of a professional hitman and not of any Animal Rights militant nor of any rogue group within the harmless Innovation Party.

Her reasoning was promptly confirmed when a message came in from New Scotland Yard. There was, it said, no reason at present to believe that any of the Animal Rights activists kept under regular surveillance were involved in *the Gralethorpe incident,* nor had their undercover officers had any hint of extreme action being planned.

At last she locked the Policy File safely away and set off for home.

It was only as she stood at her front door, fishing in her bag for her key, that the question she had last been reminded of by the pink copy of the *Financial Times* on Matthew Jessop's hall-table came back, full-blown, into her mind. The question John, very likely wondering at this moment if this was going to be another get-your-own supper evening, would in all probability have an instant answer to.

She found the key, opened the door.

As soon as she caught the look of mild relief on John's face she dived into the kitchen and snatched up her blue-and-red heavy-duty apron. Then she went back and, before anything intervened, blurted out her question.

'Up with a tent for not quite a blonde, east not zero leads to dug-out?'

John blinked only once.

'Eleven across, I think it was. Last Saturday. But why do you want to know? You're the one who makes a point of never so much as looking at a crossword.'

She grinned.

'It's police business, something to please a possibly useful contact. Nice girl called Tonelle, the receptionist at the Masterton Clinic.'

'Must be bright as well as nice, if she has a go at the *Guardian* crossword on a Saturday.'

'Yes, she is bright. Certainly bright enough to foist off a nosy detective superintendent wanting to talk to a patient at the Masterton.'

John's eyebrows rose.

'The Masterton Clinic, all those pop singers and drink-problem footballers? What were you doing there? If it isn't a secret.'

'No, not secret at all. I was there to talk, if I could, to Robert Roughouse. At dawn yesterday he was taken away from St Ozzie's, where he was being perfectly well looked after, by some of his rich friends. Besides needing to talk to him, I want to know exactly why they did that.'

'I'm not surprised you do. Moved to the Masterton at dawn? I'd certainly want some sort of explanation for that.'

'And, when I asked for one there, I was simply not given it. But I've a notion that, through Tonelle, I could perhaps find out more. If I'm useful to her, she may be useful to me. So, *Up with a tent . . .*'

'All right, tell her that eleven across was *pitchblende.*'

'Pitchblende? That's the answer? How on earth did you make that out?'

'Simple enough.'

'OK, Mr Clever, unless you explain I'll hand over my apron and you'll cook supper.'

'Answer coming straightaway then. What do you do when you put up a tent?'

'Ah, I see it. Pretty easy really. You pitch it. Half of *pitchblende* accounted for.'

'Right. Then, if you've pitched a tent for *not quite a blonde,* what comes into your mind next?'

'Nothing. So what came into your mind, if it wasn't a lascivious thought?'

'Heaven forbid. No, this is crossword business, we're playing by the unwritten rules. Crosswords are games. And if you're playing a game you need rules as to how it's to be played, even if they're not all actually formulated. They make the game possible, and, if they're broken, what you get is chaos. And chaos is something to be avoided in this world whenever it can be. Yes?'

'Yes.'

'So never knock unwritten rules, however much breaching them is, *by all the laws known to the world* as old Trollope says, something you can do if you want to.'

'OK, OK. But that still leaves me wanting to know how *Pitchblende* comes to be that answer.'

'Right. According to the rules of crossword solving —'

'Unwritten.'

'Yes, unwritten but convenient. OK, an expression like *not quite* in a clue may mean you have to alter in some way the word or words following.'

'Ah, wait. Yes, I sort of get it. Not *blonde* but *blende.* Perhaps I will take up cross-words after all.'

'Oh, no, you won't. Not unless you can explain how that particular change had to be made. After all, you already knew the final answer.'

Harriet put her tongue out at him.

'No, damn it, tell me. I'm not going to waste half the evening fiddling about with a crossword. I've got to go and cook.'

'Your choice. No one ever says you have to do a crossword.'

A little too deliberately, John took up the book he had been reading.

'All right,' Harriet said. 'That clue kept young Tonelle awake half the night. So, for her sake, tell me please.'

John smiled. Rather too tolerantly, she thought.

'*East not zero,*' he said. 'Not too difficult. In place of *zero,* i.e. an *O,* put *East,* i.e. —'

'No, I've got it. *E* for east, and it goes from *blonde* to *blende.*'

'All right. But, remember, the setter is bound by the infrangible rules to indicate as well what the final answer is, though sometimes of course that rule is *franged.*'

'Right, the bit tagged on at the end.

Something about a *dug-out.* Not that I can see how that can possibly mean *pitchblende.* And what is pitchblende anyhow?'

'One answer to both questions. Pitch-blende, so-called because from its curious lustre it resembles pitch, is a mineral, a source of uranium among other things. And it has to be dug out of the earth, though I'm not altogether sure that making *dug-out* one word was strictly according to the rules, but —'

'Hey, you knew that about pitchblende? Does someone have to know an obscure fact like that before they can complete a wretched crossword? No wonder it foxed little Tonelle — not so little actually, rather on the buxom side.'

'Well, I didn't know exactly what the stuff was myself till I looked it up.'

'Cheat.'

'No, I looked it up only after I'd finished the puzzle. Just to satisfy my curiosity.'

'OK. You win: I'm cooking. But, when I see my friend Tonelle again, I'll have a present for her.'

'And, when you give it to her, you think you'll start to get somewhere? I've the impression you're fully engaged in this investigation.'

'I am. By God, I am.'

'So thoughts of resignation no longer with you?'

'They may not be, or they may be. Depends whether the case gets me a result, or not. The whole business seems to be wrapped in layer on layer of things that I suspect are relevant but can't at all see why or how. It's infuriating. At last, after months of piddling jobs, I manage to get myself one worth having, and —'

'Has it ever struck you,' John broke in, 'that the powers-that-be might feel reluctant to task you with anything really onerous after . . .'

'After me having one of my sons killed by a terrorist bomb. Say it.'

'Well, I do say it. We've had an agreement between ourselves — another unwritten one — not to bring up Graham's death unless it's inescapable. I manage to stick to it, though often enough I want to break down and have a good weep. But I thought now this was a moment to —'

'Yes. Yes, I know. I must bring myself to be able to talk about it. And so far I just haven't been able to, not in any meaningful sense.'

'I know. If only from the way you still carry about, somewhere deep in the mysteries of a woman's handbag, that toy mobile of Graham's.'

'You know about that?'

'Well, yes. I do keep an eye on you.'

'All right, and I suppose I know that's what you've been doing. But, however ridiculous that thing looks, it does work, you know. All the same, do you really think I should put it away, go back to my old one?'

'Only if you want to.'

For a long moment she thought.

'No,' she said at last. 'I don't want to, silly though I am about it. But I don't. And, what's more, I don't think cherishing it the way I do makes me in any way unfit to conduct a major investigation. As some people, not you of course, think that I am.'

'Well, if *some people* has been thinking that, he seems to have given up the idea now. You could hardly have been tasked with a more important investigation than the attempted murder of Robert Roughouse, ex-MP, party leader.'

'I had to insist on having it, though. And I got it. But what if that was only in the belief that I'd fail, and the stiff-necked idiot could get rid of me?'

John gave her a carefully judged smile.

'Don't fail then,' he said.

CHAPTER NINE

The moment Harriet entered her office next morning she decided — no trusting Mrs Fishlock's word — it was time to ring the Masterton again in case she had not been told that Robert Roughouse was now fit enough to talk.

Or . . . or, she thought, can it be he's no longer alive?

She picked up her phone.

One minute later she knew she was not going to find out for some time to come whether Roughouse himself had any idea why that purple egg had been shot at him. 'Mr Roughouse is showing some more hopeful signs. But he is still far from being fit to hold conversations. In fact, he is not able to talk at all.'

Cold dragon's breath.

Glum in the face of the blank negative, she had to remind herself that there was still Matthew Jessop to pursue. What reason could he have had to say to Charity that she should not come up here to Birchester?

Was he just, in fact, somewhat disapproving of the affair between his well-padded and well-educated friend — the Zeal School, extraordinary place — and an athlete from heaven knows what background in Kenya? Perhaps he hoped Robert's stay in the clinic, which might be a long one even if he soon regained consciousness, would gradually make the love affair fade away. All right, that could be it. But it's not somehow altogether likely.

She picked up her phone, and this time succeeded in reaching Jessop in person. He had, he explained without fuss, left for a country location as soon as he had seen her go yesterday. No point, she thought, in questioning him by phone, unable to see his face let alone any tics in his hands or minute shiftings of his feet. But, when she asked if she could come to talk to him today there was a distinctly long silence.

'Well, that's impossible,' he said at last, sounding an edge more hostile than when they had been talking face-to-face. 'No. No, you see, I shall be down in the country again. We're doing the most important exterior sequence in the film. And — this is it — according to the forecast the weather's going to hold over all the weekend. We've got to seize the chance.'

'I could make it in the early evening,' Harriet tried.

'No. No, you see, I shan't be back till late. The pack-up's always a long business after a day in the mud.' A cough of a laugh and a burst of rapid chatter. 'Still, better mud than the jagged rocks and unutterably steep hillsides when I filmed Rob's Georgia trek. Georgia and beyond, wilder and wilder.'

What's wrong with the man, Harriet asked herself. Why is he blathering out all these excuses? And the weather's fine. He won't have had a day in the mud. Has he got something to hide then? Even if it's only something, perhaps embarrassing, he hopes a little evasiveness will save him from having to mention?

Well, he's not going to get away with that.

'I have other inquiries I have to make in London,' she said flatly. 'I'll call you again.'

She sat and considered, swinging to and fro in her deep-padded desk chair. Wasn't there, when you came down to it, something a bit curious, more than a bit curious, about all that flurry of excuses? Yes, I think —

The phone at her elbow rang into life.

It was Charity. And from the moment she identified herself, it was plain she was in distress.

'Calm down, love. Calm down. Take a deep breath. Then tell me what's the matter.'

Down the line, a choked sob, a silence. Then at last words that could be made out.

'I'm sorry. I'm sorry. Yes, got to pull myself together. It's not very terrible, really. It's just . . .'

'Just what, Charity? Tell me.'

'I — I — I've had someone on my entry-phone. A man. Didn't recognise who. But classy voice. Yeah, classy.'

'And he said what?'

'He — Soon as I answered, he just said *Do not go and see Robert Roughhouse. Understand. You are not to go. If you do, it's likely to be the last thing you ever do.* That was it. I've told you it exactly. It was only a minute or two ago. Harriet, who was he? Why did he say that? Does he mean it? Will — Will he really kill me, have me killed, if I go near the Masterton? Harriet, what's happening? What is it?'

What is it indeed? First Jessop simply saying Charity should not come up here to see her Rob, and now a plain threat — could it be from the man in that smart yellow summer suit? — aimed at keeping her well away.

'Look,' she said. 'I absolutely see why you're upset. But, listen. First of all, it may be just some silly practical joke. You said it was a classy voice. Do any of Rob's friends go in for that sort of thing, thoughtless practical jokes? It wasn't Matthew Jessop, was it? He's said once already you shouldn't go to see Rob. And he never really explained why. Isn't that right?'

'No, it wasn't Matthew's voice at all. I'd recognise that. All right, same sort of classiness. But, no, this was quite different. I don't know, sort of harsh, heavier than Matthew.'

'But it could be one of Rob's other friends? It's something people like that, those Zealots, might think was somehow funny.'

'I hadn't thought of that. The voice sounded so . . . But, yes. Yes, I suppose it could have been. Just.'

'OK. Can we leave it at that? But, all the same, if I were you, I wouldn't go out without taking very good care. Look about you all the time, if you have to go anywhere, anywhere at all, especially after dark. Or always go with someone, someone you know. And, Charity, I think for the time being you actually shouldn't attempt to come up here. Robert's still unconscious, I called the Masterton barely twenty minutes ago. So you don't absolutely need to come. OK?'

'Yes. Yes, suppose so. But I just want to see Rob again, even if he can't speak or anything.'

'I know. I understand. But take my advice. Stay where you are, be careful if you have to go out. I doubt if there's any real danger, after all a threat on your entry-phone doesn't sound too serious. And, listen, the moment I hear that Robert's regained consciousness I shall have to go to see him, and I'll pass on the news straightaway. OK?'

'Yeah. Yeah, thanks.'

She put the phone down, wondering whether she had said enough to reassure Charity and whether it might be a good thing to call her nearest PS — probably the big one at Paddington Green — and suggest Daley Thompson House merits special attention.

But almost at once the phone rang again.

'Superintendent Martens? This is Mrs Fishlock.'

She ringing me again? Now? What is this? What — My God, is Roughhouse dead? It can't be. But it might be. Yes. Oh, God.

'Mrs Fishlock, you've got news for me?'

'I have. Mr Roughhouse has fully recovered consciousness.'

Thank God, thank God. So now I may be . . . ?

'That's wonderful, Mrs Fishlock. Can I see him?'

'The medical staff have informed me that, now he's awake from the anaesthetic, they can say he has come very well through the minor operation on his neck.'

On his neck? It was an operation on his head earlier on. How obstructive can you get, Mrs Fishlock?

But she was still talking.

'The medical staff consider Mr Roughouse is able now to answer questions, provided they are not in any way aggressive.'

Aggressive? For heaven's sake, is the wretched she-dragon determined to find fault with Greater Birchester Police?

'I don't see there should be any need to be aggressive, Mrs Fishlock. No need at all. I simply need to learn if Mr Roughouse has any idea what might be behind the attempt on his life.'

'Very well. Would tomorrow morning at, say, ten o'clock suit you?'

Still being difficult, are we? Want to make it clear no one outranks the Masterton?

'No, Mrs Fishlock, it would not suit me.' Then she decided to soften that, if with a plain lie. 'Unfortunately I have an important interview to conduct in London tomorrow.'

'Oh. In that case shall we say in an hour's time?'

'That would suit me very well.'

She called Charity again straightaway.

'Oh, oh, that's marvellous. Marvellous. Oh, I'm so glad. So happy. Look, I know you said *Stay away,* but can't I come up now? Isn't it all right?'

'No. No, I'm sorry but it's still *Play safe.* Whoever it was on your entry-phone may quite likely still be somewhere nearby, perhaps sitting in those gardens opposite, waiting to see what your reaction to their message is. No, stay at the end of the phone, and when I've seen Rob myself — I should be finished easily within the next two hours — then I'll give you a bell and tell you how he is. After that we can discuss you coming up here. OK?'

'OK. I suppose.'

Mrs Fishlock herself led Harriet to Rough-ouse's room. A discreet tap on its door, just above a brass holder with a neatly written card giving his name, and, as soon as a solidly competent nurse appeared, the somewhat subdued dragon retreated to her lair.

Harriet took a quick stride inside.

There in the middle of a large hospital

133

bed, all protective metal bars and metallic lifting apparatus, lay the man she had knelt beside in the dark outside Gralethorpe's town hall, the odour of his blood sharp in her nostrils. The man she had watched, a picture of forcefulness and courage, defying the hostility of the crowd below.

But now all that she could see of him beneath a swathe of bandages was the upper part of his face, grey as a sheet of long-discarded paper. Drained, washed-out.

She went over — the bed seemed so hygienically clean that it had an odour of its own — and sat down on the mesh steel chair beside it.

Now she saw that two eyes were staring upwards, glinting, for all their surrounding turgid bloodshot streaks, with lapis lazuli points of life.

A glance at the watchful nurse standing at the bed's foot.

'It's all right to talk?'

'Yes, it is, Doctor said. But five minutes and no more.'

Harriet bent towards the drained face and spoke quietly but clearly as she could.

'Mr Roughouse, I am Detective Superintendent Martens, Greater Birchester Police. I've come to ask just a few questions about what happened to you in Gralethorpe. Have you been told that someone, someone unknown, projected a small grenade at you from the chapel opposite? You know that happened?'

'Yeh.'

The word hardly more than an articulated sigh. The bloodshot eyes unmoving, mired in fatigue.

'So, what I have to ask you now is: do you know why anyone, anyone at all, should have done that?'

The head on the starched-white pillow stirred from side to side. As if the man within was in the throes of some impossible decision.

But from the almost colourless lips there came not even the smallest murmur.

'Mr Roughhouse?'

Still no answer.

'Mr Roughhouse, can you tell me why someone wanted to kill you?'

'No.'

'No? You have no idea?'

'Can't . . .'

Then, slowly seeping in, a deeper torpor.

Harriet leant even nearer.

'What can't you, Mr Roughhouse? Try to tell me. We must stop this individual, or whoever may be behind him. You could be in danger again. Please.'

'Don't . . . think . . . can.'

'Why not, Mr Roughouse?' Harriet was unable to keep anxiety out of her voice. 'Is it that you simply don't know? Or . . . ? Is there some reason why you feel you can't tell me, can't tell anyone?'

Out of the corner of her eye she saw the nurse at the foot of the big bed peer forward as, once more, the head on the starched pillow began to twist and turn, almost feverishly now.

'Please, Mr Roughouse. Please, it's vitally important.'

A muttered word — or was it? — from the exhausted lips below her.

Something. Something almost impossible to make out.

'Mr Roughouse, what is it you're trying to say?'

'Loyal . . .'

The blood-webbed blue eyes closed. Shutters now all but down. And, in a moment, staying down.

Harriet looked across to the nurse.

'I think you should leave now.'

Object to that? Object to a too easily imposed edict?

No. Right's on her side.

She pushed herself up off the little chair.

One last look at the paper-dull face half-concealed by the heavy bandages.

No, plainly if he's to speak again, it'll have to be later. Perhaps hours and hours, even more than a day, later. Plainly, the doctors, if not dragon Fishlock, were too optimistic in allowing me in here.

But what was that word, that half-word, that he murmured? *Loyal?* But loyal to what? And it might have been something else, anything else. Loyal, royal, spoil, boil. Boil? But it could have been anything.

Poor bugger, she thought as the nurse softly closed the door behind her.

CHAPTER TEN

Back in her office, Harriet called Charity Nyambura and gave her as reassuring a report as she could. Then, swinging this way and that in her desk chair, she went over and over every last syllable Roughouse had uttered, had barely uttered, every least movement of his bandaged head. But pound away as she would, nothing came to light. Nothing that clearly said anything at all. *Loyal, royal, spoil?*

She took her Policy File from its drawer and simply recorded the facts. She drew no conclusions, suggested to herself no new way forward. Impasse.

File snapped shut, drawer pushed home and locked, she found her mind was scratching away at the little group of Zealots that Robert Roughouse had told Charity he belonged to, together presumably with Matthew Jessop. Was that dab hand as an organiser, Tigger Drummond, a member? And, yes, up-and-coming surgeon, Jackson Edge-worth? What was that name Charity had given the group? Yup, the Cobbles. Could the Cobbles — did she really have that name right? — be behind Roughouse being targeted by that purple egg bomb?

For what it is, this is perhaps the best lead I have.

Then she remembered someone else Charity had mentioned. A judge who was — yes — president of all the Zealots. Cotmore. That had been the name. Now could I learn something from him? If he's president of the whole society of the Zealots, with any luck he'll know at least something about the secretive Cobbles. If that's really the name? Charity, after all Kenyan by birth, could have misheard.

She turned to her computer, which produced quite quickly a magic answer. A London phone number for Mr Justice Phillip Cotmore.

But when Harriet kept her appointment with Mr Justice Cotmore, at precisely eleven next morning, she found him in a state of excessive confusion. He had given her the appointment over the phone himself, and she had expected from the plummy, pondering voice she had listened to that she would be received with some ceremony. Instead when she was shown into the study at his Knightsbridge house she found him looming bulkily over a papers-strewn desk. His big, flabby face, glistening with perspiration, had on it a look of something like despair.

'Oh, Superintendent, it's you,' he said, almost moaning as with a wide, hectic gesture he indicated the chair in front of the desk. 'I am afraid you have caught me at a very bad moment. You — You see — well, this is the point. Just this morning when the post came, disgracefully late as usual nowadays . . . really, I cannot think why the Post Office, which is after all charged with delivering the Royal Mail, Her Majesty's mail, cannot carry out its duty as, in my young days and in my father's before me, it invariably did. One got one's post at breakfast. That was how — oh, but, dear me, I have now been led somewhat astray. You must forgive me.'

Tremendous emphasis on the *must.*

Harriet was driven to think why actually *must* I forgive him? Shouldn't he have simply asked for my forgiveness, if he felt it was needed? But, no, out comes the formula, from high to low. *You must:* it's a law.

'You seem to be in some complicated

trouble,' she said to him. 'Would you like me to come back in, say, an hour?'

The judge puffed out a billowing sigh, somewhere between exasperation and politeness, if veering strongly towards the former.

'No, no,' he said. 'I gave you an appointment for this time, and I note that you have kept it to the minute. The least I can do is to give you my fullest attention.'

Then, with another barely suppressed groan, he proceeded to do the complete opposite.

'It's this letter. As you can see, a formal document. Yes, you could say that. A formal document. It requests me to provide the name by which, when I attend the ceremony of the conferring of my knighthood, I wish to be called by. You will know, of course, that I have recently been elevated to the High Court. And it is the rule that one is given a knighthood on that occasion. But this is the trouble. You see, I am never known other than by the second name I was given at my christening, Phillip. I am known as that to everybody. Everybody, except my late parents, I suppose. You see, I was in point of fact christened Cecil, and as a boy at home I was called by that name. Yes, Cecil.'

Will this ever end, Harriet asked herself. But it was clear that an ending, if it was to come at all, would not be reached for some time.

Can I crudely butt in, point out that I am here on police business? No. There are things one can do, and things one can't. Or not at least to someone just made a High Court Judge.

'But, and this is my difficulty, you understand,' the judge went relentlessly on, 'when I went up to Cambridge I thought — well, I thought that Cecil was not perhaps the sort of name to ensure one a certain amount of friendship. Naturally, at school I was known simply as Cotmore. Cotmore. But at Cambridge . . . Of course, I was very young then. Comparatively young, and even a little unsure of myself. So . . . Very well, I elected to be called there by one of my other names, and I chose Phillip. I even put it about that I should be known as Phil. Phil. But now, you see, I have had this request for my name, the name that is to appear on the official record, that will be pronounced by Her Majesty herself when she pleases to dub me. And I cannot decide what name I ought to set down. I believe, if I wished, I could be known as Sir Phillip Cotmore. But, after all, my formal name is Cecil. Cecil. So

142

should I be Sir Cecil Cotmore? You know, I really feel that is my duty. But then there are all the people who have known me as Phillip . . . I indicated, you know, when I had reached a certain eminence in society, when I became a judge in fact, that Phil was perhaps not altogether suitable, but —'

And now Harriet's patience did come to an end.

'Sir Cecil,' she said firmly. 'Might I say that name seems altogether right for you? Speaking, of course, as a mere observer.'

The judge subsided into the wide, padded chair behind his desk.

'It seems extraordinary,' he said slowly, 'that two or three words from — how shall I put it? — a chance visitor should decide me in what is, after all, a matter of some importance. But — But it seems that they have. Thank you.'

'I'm glad to have been of help,' Harriet replied, conscious she was adopting much the same weighty tone, if underneath she was wickedly pleased to be able at last to get the man to talk about what she wanted to discover. Did he, possibly, know anything of that close-knit group going by the un-likely name of the Cobbles?

But jump in at once, or the old boy will be off again.

'It's good of you to give me a few minutes of your time,' she said hastily. 'As I told you on the telephone, I am investigating the attack that took place in Gralethorpe last Tuesday on Mr Robert Roughouse.'

'Yes, yes. A disgraceful business. Roughouse is a prominent member of the Zealots, that is former pupils of the Zeal School, which doubtless you know of, and —'

'Yes, I do know about the Zealots,' Harriet darted in before the judicial windbag could get fully airborne. 'You are their president, I believe.'

'I have that honour. Indeed, I am wearing a Zealots tie at this moment, as I usually do. As I usually do.'

Harriet, scarcely giving the judge's earth-red and white tie a glance, bounced in again.

'It's in connection with the Zealots that I have come to see you, sir,' she said. 'It appears that a small number of Mr Roughouse's fellow Zealots may be at least tangentially involved, and —'

'Impossible. Impossible, my dear lady. You must have acquired a very wrong impression of the Zealots to have thought such a thing. I assure you that any boy who has had the unique experience of having been educated at the Zeal School has been imbued with the highest standards of probity and, more, of mutual loyalty. We pride ourselves on that. Pride ourselves.'

OK, Harriet said to herself, it was a bit of a stretch to say that some Zealots were somehow linked to the attack on Roughouse. But I can't help suspecting that the three of them who spirited him away to the Masterton in all that hurry were not acting purely in the interests of his recovery. Matthew Jessop, after all, never really provided a pertinent reason for the way he was taken away in such an excessive hurry.

'I am sure you are right, sir, to take pride in that education, that sense of loyalty,' she quickly slipped in. 'I have been talking to Mr Matthew Jessop, who was with Robert Roughouse when he was so nearly killed on Tuesday, and he told me a good deal about the Zealots. In fact — I don't know if you are aware of this — it was Mr Jessop who, with admirable loyalty, immediately arranged for Mr Roughouse to be transferred from St Oswald's, the Birchester hospital, to a private clinic.'

She watched the flabby red face intently.

'No, no, I am not, as a matter of fact, aware that Robert has been placed in a private clinic. But I have no doubt that his fellow Zealots would have been acting altogether in his best interests. Loyalty, that is

145

our keynote and mainstay.'

Abruptly he placed a large red forefinger on a dark grey paper-covered book among the chaotic strew of documents on his desk.

'The Register of every Zealot who has ever passed through the school,' he said. 'And I think I can safely assure you that not one —'

The booming voice abruptly faded away.

'I can assure you, Superintendent,' he resumed in a moment, 'I can assure you there is scarcely a person named here with whom I would not trust my life.'

He favoured Harriet with a look of deep-hued sincerity. Only to allow it once more to waver.

'No, I must tell you the absolute truth. There have never been within the Zealots any of those congeries and cabals one reads of in other societies, even in the most respectable of organisations, the unpleasant consequence of jealousies and distrust. No. But, it is true, there may be one or two names in this register in whose impeccable loyalty one could not put the fullest trust. But those names are from the earliest days of the Zeal, men now long in their graves. No, there is no one — well, yes . . . perhaps there is one — er — renegade in the list, still active in the world. Indeed, active in the legal profession, I am sorry to say.'

Harriet knew she ought not perhaps to pursue this. The judge had brought himself to make an admission which it must have pained him to utter. It would be kindest to pass over it. But she thought she would very much like to have that name in her head, if only learning it was yielding to an imp of malice. Seldom was she able to resist poking a pin into any passing balloon.

'And who would that be, Sir Cecil?' she asked sharply.

'Ah, no, no, dear lady. Not *Sir Cecil.* You must remember I am not Sir Cecil until Her Majesty has deigned to dub me such. One must adhere to protocol, you know.'

Harriet decided to give that no further acknowledgement, but to put her more sneaky question once more.

'You were about to tell me who the *renegade* gentleman is?'

'Yes. Well, I suppose it is hardly a matter of slander, under its legal definition, to tell you that. Doing so will, in fact, simply reinforce the claim I have made, nothing more. He is a Bengali gentleman. A Mr Kailash Gokhale.'

Harriet did her best not to let manifest itself the sudden dazzling view she had had of a way to bypass the convoluted, loyalty-obfuscated path through the inflated ego in front of her.

'Thank you, sir, for that extremely honest answer,' she said as impressively as she could. 'With what you have told me altogether about the Zealots, I think I can assure you now that any doubts I had about Mr Roughhouse's friends from his schooldays have firmly been put to rest. Thank you.'

As she made this little speech, she reached forward and slid her neat, black handbag down to the floor under her chair. Then she got to her feet.

'Allow me to show you out,' her host said. 'And may I thank you again for helping me to resolve the little difficulty brought to me by my post today. Sir Cecil, it shall be. Yes, Sir Cecil.'

So, when they had almost reached the heavy front door, Harriet produced her prepared gasp of dismay.

'Oh, good gracious. I must have left my handbag behind. Yes, I remember I put it underneath my chair. How silly of me.'

And, a skittish schoolgirl, she ran rapidly back into the judicial study.

One second to snatch up from the desk the slim grey paper-covered Zeal School Register. Two or three seconds to flip expertly through the pages to the big letter for Section G, mercifully not a long one. And there it was. *Gokhale, Kailash Q.C., 62 New Square, Lincoln's Inn.* Followed by two telephone numbers, *Home* and *Office* and two e-mail addresses.

CHAPTER ELEVEN

Harriet knew at once who, at her ring on the bell, had opened the outer door of Kailash Gokhale's Lincoln's Inn chambers. Despite the informality of jeans and a fine-knit roll-neck green pullover, she had no doubt the plumply dapper man there was the Bengali QC himself.

'Detective Superintendent Martens?' he asked, brown eyes brightly glowing.

'Mr Gokhale, it's very good of you to see me at such short notice.'

'Oh, not good at all. I am interested, curious. But come in, come in. You find me alone in these gloomily impressive quarters, the only person in the whole establishment, from the head of chambers to the tea lady, who delights in working on a Saturday. All of them, except perhaps Mrs Harris who presides over the tea trolley, hidebound by that never promulgated rule which says Saturdays and Sundays are what my Catholic friends might call Holidays of Obligation. I am the sole heretic, I fear.'

Harriet during all this had spotted to her left a solid oak door and she now turned towards it.

'Ah, no, no,' Kailash Gokhale said. 'No, that leads to the Clerk's Room and the waiting room. My room is on the second floor, something of a climb I'm afraid. We have yet to acknowledge the lift as a means of access. But let me lead the way.'

Harriet saw now that in the darkness beyond there was a flight of bare stone stairs.

'And you're happy for me to interrupt the labours you undertake on this sacred day?' she asked as she followed the plump QC.

'Oh, as I said on the phone — this way, this way — I am most . . . Ah, now right, go in, please, straight ahead. Yes. Now take a chair, take a chair.'

Harriet obediently sat in front of the large desk, which she saw had on it just a single sheet of thick, words-weighty paper.

Hopping round to the other side, the little barrister rubbed his hands briskly together.

'Yes, yes,' he went happily chattering on. 'My dear lady, you come as a breath of fresh air into this lawyers' world that I, and countless others, have allowed ourselves to be sucked into. A swamp. Yes, a veritable swamp. The law, you know, becomes so impregnated in every corner of one's mind from the earliest years of one's studies that one finds it eventually impossible to think in any other terms. One comes to believe the only way the world's problems can be dealt with, and indeed one's own too, is by following the law's laid-down precepts. Many of them necessary if society is to be carried on, though not perhaps all. Who was it who said — it must have been in the early years of the twentieth century — *All history is an effort to find clear rules?* I don't recall. But, alas, yes, I do regularly recall those somewhat grandiose, and only half-accurate, words.'

Harriet smiled. She couldn't help it.

'No, no, it's perfectly true about all us lawyers being held fast in that swamp,' the chubby QC raced on. 'No, wait, let me illustrate with a little anecdote, something that happened to me only last week.'

'Please do.'

'Very well. Walking along to my club on my way to lunch, I encountered an old college contemporary, a well-established solicitor, and since we were just outside the club I invited him to join me. But, just at that moment, a van came driving by quite close to the curb. And, as there happened to be a deepish puddle right beside us — we had been having a lot of rain, remember — it sent up a great swish of dirty water. All over the trousers of my friend, whom for the purposes of this account we shall call Freddy, which happens to be his real name. Very good, what would you have done in those circumstances? Emitted a most unladylike expression, I venture to say, and glared at the retreating vehicle.'

'I would. A very unladylike expression.'

'Naturally. But what did my friend Freddy do? At once he began considering whether the offence was actionable, what damages he might claim, such as the cost of a new pair of trousers on the flimsy grounds that they might no longer be wearable, together with a claim for distress caused by having to lunch at a reputable club in a state of disarray. The case he elaborated lasted us through the whole course of our meal. You see what I mean?'

'I do. And I rather think that, as a police officer, I am often mired in a similar swamp myself. We, too, are inclined to work under the belief that every crime can be resolved only by the means we have at our command.'

'Now, you are trying to offer me reassurance. And you are doing it. Only not in the way you think. You are doing it, I trust and hope, by bringing to me the case you spoke of when you telephoned. And, more, you indicated to me it marginally involves that appalling organisation, the Zealots.'

Harriet seized internally on *appalling*.

Is this bubbling Bengali, possibly the sole dissident in that loyalty-linked society puffy Sir Cecil spoke of so sonorously, going to give me at least some insight into Robert Roughouse's world?

'Yes, the Zealots,' she jumped in. 'I've learnt that some members of that society took Robert Roughouse by ambulance at dawn the day after he was so badly injured to a private clinic in Birrshire. My attempts to find out exactly why they acted with such urgency have so far met with no success.'

Kailash Gokhale's brown eyes shone more brightly.

'Yes, yes,' he said. 'Just the sort of thing I thought you might have to tell me. In my day at that extraordinary educational establishment, the Zeal School, I was only the third so-called black who had ever been there, and schoolboys, you know, are apt to be decidedly uninhibited. I might add that after their time at school they are still inclined to set aside the restraint necessary in civilised society.'

But Harriet had hardly taken in all that. Kailash Gokhale's reference to being the sole brown-skinned boy at the school had flicked her mind across to Sir Cecil earlier stating the *absolute truth* that his ever-loyal Zealots were never prey to *congeries and cabals*. And, in a sudden flash of insight, she had linked that expression to Charity Nyambura talking about 'the Cobbles'. Surely she must have meant — an unusual, dated word she's unlikely to know — the Cabal?

'Mr Gokhale,' she broke in. 'I'm sorry. But could you please tell me if, among the Zealots, there's a group that calls itself the Cabal?'

Kailash Gokhale blinked. Just once.

'Yes,' he said. 'Yes, there is. I'm surprised you know of it. They pride themselves on keeping their existence pretty much secret. But, yes, the Cabal has been going for some years. It was, incidentally, founded as a discussion and dining club with the very highest, if vague, aims, by none other than Rob Roughouse. A great one for founding things, Rob. A true optimist, poor fellow.'

'Poor fellow indeed.'

'Oh, yes. Though I had perhaps more in mind in using the word *poor,* Rob's invariable tendency to optimism, something always the better for a sharp dose of the truth. You know about his Innovation Party?'

'I do.'

'Very well, now the Cabal was originally no more than that simple dining club, although one that indulged itself with a whole train of mandatory rituals. I suspect, in fact, that Rob, who's always treated me in the friendliest way, would have liked me to join. Not that nowadays he might have regretted it if I'd agreed.'

'He would have thought you — what was it? — too held fast in your legal swamp to be acceptable?'

'A hit. And a palpable one. Because, yes, there has developed in the Cabal, as I have gathered from occasional hints and indiscretions, a tendency to favour ignoring the rule of law.'

'Has there indeed?'

'Well,' Kailash Gokhale said, 'don't be too quick to come to judgment on those people. On occasion I am capable of ignoring a law myself. Not, I hasten to say, any of those on the statute books, though I suppose when I'm retained for the Defence some of my arguments may be said to tend that way. But I have, quite frequently I regret to say, broken laws such organisations as the

Zealots delight in laying down.'

'Yes, I learnt as much earlier today from its president, Mr Justice Phillip Cotmore, who now, by the way, with his elevation to the High Court wishes to be called Sir Cecil.'

'Sir Cecil. I hasten to obey.'

'I don't doubt you will. But, now, can you be a little more specific about the Cabal? Do you know who its other members are? Or is that an impenetrable secret?'

'Oh, it's impenetrable indeed. So shall I tell you the names I do know?'

'Please.'

'All right, besides Robert there's his particular friend, Matthew Jessop.'

'With him when that grenade was launched.'

'I'd expect that. And who else is there? Let me see. Yes. There's that up-and-coming surgeon, Jackson Edgeworth, always top in science at school, the insolent swine. And a newish, rather older member than any of Rob's contemporaries, Sir Marcus Fledge, chairman of Pettifer's. If that means any-thing to you.'

'Pettifer's, the worldwide machinery-making firm? Yes, it could hardly not mean something to me, if it's only money, money, money.'

'As it is. Fledge, who was a little senior to myself at the Zeal School, I've always thought rather a dull chap. It's quite odd that, only recently I think, they've voted him in. Say what you like about the Cabal, they're a pretty lively lot, if misguided. But vote him in they did, as I have somehow learnt.'

'Right. That's four names. Can you produce more?'

'Oh, yes. There's that wretched fellow Tigger Drummond, inventor of the little Tiger Man toy, and a thoroughly bouncy pest at school. Then, yes, someone from a year above Rob and myself, Martin Cookbury, who now runs a very successful advertising firm. And another dullish chap, to my mind anyhow, Reginald Brown, senior partner in a firm of stockbrokers. Very useful to them, as you may come to realise. That's probably the core membership, though there will be a few more. But they're the ones I'm certain of.'

'I don't suppose you can give me their addresses?'

'No difficulty about that. I have, of course, tucked away somewhere in a cupboard here that invaluable work, the Zeal School Register.'

A little rummaging, and a copy of the

grey-covered booklet from which Harriet had contrived to secure Gokhale's phone number, lay on the open surface of the desk. Out came her notebook, down went the information.

'All right,' she said as she finished scribbling. 'So does the Cabal do anything beyond having high-flown thoughts like Robert Roughouse's?'

'Well, yes. I suspect, though with no actual evidence, that these days they — what shall I say? — do something. But what that something is I have no idea, no idea at all. What I can tell you, though, is that Rob has seemed in these past weeks to have a new attitude towards myself. Vaguely friendly as always, which is his nature, he's been doing more, recently, than ask after my health, comment on the news or whatever. He's actually been telling me things about himself, and, to a very small extent — a matter of hints and drawings-back — about some of his friends in the Cabal.'

'Oh, yes?'

'All right, I think I can tell you a little more. But you're not to make too much of it.'

'Yes?'

'When Rob and I meet in circumstances where there are other Zealots present, there's often about him a certain furtiveness. Yes, I think that's the word. A furtiveness altogether different from his normal attitude.'

'You're talking,' Harriet intervened, as much as anything to give him time cautiously to advance a little further, 'to someone who for a good quarter of an hour watched Robert Roughouse haranguing a mob of very angry anti-hunt supporters. Nothing furtive about him there.'

'You watched him? This was just before the attack?'

'It was. My husband and I happened to be going home after a midweek lunch party and had to pass through Gralethorpe. We found our way absolutely blocked by that demo, and stayed to watch for a little, largely because of Roughouse and the almost ridiculous courage he was showing. And then came that grenade, and I found myself what we in the police call the Investigating Officer, the first at the scene of a crime.'

'I see now why the case is one you feel more obliged than in the ordinary way to resolve. So let me help you as much as I reasonably can.'

'Thank you.'

'Very well, I rather think, from what I've

noticed about Rob, that he's on the point of getting the old heave-ho from that nice little dining club he himself instituted. Or perhaps he's been easing himself out of it because he didn't much like the company he had come to find himself in.'

Harriet thought for a moment.

'And . . . and do you think,' she asked, out on a limb, 'it's possible, at all possible, the rift in the Cabal, if that's what has happened, could go as far as them getting someone to attempt to kill Roughhouse?'

'My dear lady, I cannot possibly answer that.'

'No, I suppose not. But can't you manage a guess, however malicious?'

Kailash Gokhale laughed.

'All right, the malice is there, I admit. But, alas, so far without any basis.'

He paused for a moment, looked down at his almost clear desk.

'So what you're saying,' Harriet advanced cautiously, 'is that Robert Roughhouse has been having doubts about what the Cabal's up to?'

'Yes, *up to*. Not a term one would introduce in a court of law, but one that does indeed convey what I think, guess, wonder, might be happening.'

'But you've no idea what precisely that

might be?'

'I am the very last person who would be allowed even to hear a whisper of it.'

'Yes, I suppose so. But how then am I to get to know? Because I think I ought to.'

A second or two of silence.

'Really I've no idea. No, wait, there is one thing you might do.'

'Yes?'

'Have you chanced to see Rob's book, *Marching Through Georgia*?'

'Oh, God, no, I haven't. I've been meaning to look at it. But I haven't managed to get hold of a copy, though at the back of my mind . . .'

'Well, it's been some time since I read it myself, and I can't say I remember a great deal about the contents. Rob isn't one of the world's great writers, I have to say. But get hold of it, read it. That's the best by way of advice that I have to offer. All the advice, indeed.'

'I couldn't possibly borrow your copy, could I?'

Kailash Gokhale smiled.

'I'm afraid the lawyer says no. You see, I annotated it as I read, and some of my comments are undoubtedly libellous. You reading it would constitute publication.'

Is he joking, Harriet thought. Can I make

sheep's eyes at him and change his mind? Complex rules almost always create ways round them.

She glanced at her watch.

'Oh lord, I'd no idea it had got so late. Where's your nearest bookshop?'

'You won't find *Marching Through Georgia* in a bookshop. It's been out three years or more, and I even had some difficulty in getting hold of it then.'

The plump little barrister must have seen Harriet's face falling because he gave her a yet more impish grin, abruptly leant back in his chair and placed his fingers together in a pointedly storytelling mode.

'When I was a mere boy down in Bristol, where my father's job as a partner in a jute importing firm had brought us to live,' he began, 'I used to haunt the big public library. One evening in the reading room, deep into — I'm afraid — a detective story, though one of course with a legal hero, I looked up and saw I had failed, despite the hush all over the building — in those days, you know, the unspoken rule of silence still prevailed — even to hear the last warning bell. The whole room was deserted. I was locked in.'

He produced a dramatic pause. Harriet dutifully responded.

'And you got out? How? Was it by some legal device?'

'No, no. In those days I wasn't yet wholly a law-devouring machine. I simply sat there, quite pleased with my romantic circumstances. But then, some twenty minutes later, or even less, the cleaning lady came in as she pursued her laid-down round. With one bound I was free.'

'Nice story, I'll remember it. And, OK, I'll take your kind hint. The public library in Birchester should be still open, if I catch the next train. They're bound to have a copy, even several, of a book by a locally prominent man.'

Chapter Twelve

The train from London was delayed. Not once but twice. As it left the last station before Birchester, Harriet realised she was by no means certain of the library's opening hours. It might on a Saturday close early. Picturing the familiar building, it occurred to her that Kailash Gokhale had told his story of being locked in the library at Bristol, not just as a charming anecdote but so as to put a definite extra emphasis on reading *Marching Through Georgia*. He must — why have I only just thought of it? — remember the book as having in it a hint of why that egg bomb was manufactured.

Does he then know more than he's willing to say to me? Or is he making such a wild guess at whatever it is he suspects — God, how cautious law-impregnated people can be — that he dared not give me more than a clue, if I'm sharp enough to spot it, pointing towards . . . towards what, for heaven's sake?

She began looking at her watch at increasingly short intervals, its little hands hard to make out in the dim light of the carriage.

Stupid, stupid. It's still not a quarter to five. Must be. Plenty of time to go that short distance from the station to the library, even if it closes as early as five. And, in any case, what does it really matter if I do find it closed? All it'll mean is I'll have to wait a little longer till I read a book that I ought to have got hold of already. Unless it has some vital . . .

A jolting thud seemed to run all along the train.

She looked up, startled.

We've arrived. Probably just bumped the buffers.

She jerked open the heavy door beside her, jumped down to the platform, turned and pelted off, handbag on its narrow strap banging at her hip.

Which way? Yes, to the left. Turn left coming out.

Then run. Keep running.

The crossroads. Go all round via the zebras, or straight over? Yes, no traffic about. So, go straight, and trust no speeding car's just coming.

OK, over.

Quick look at watch. Can't quite see. Was it three minutes to? Or past?

Run again.

God, not used to pelting along like this. Must get back into . . . My duty.

But, yes. There it is, other side of this road. Can see the sign *Public Library.* Can't see if the doors are open, though. What time is — Hell with that. Just get across.

Wait. Look both ways. Early days in the Met, round of the primary schools . . . Road Drill.

No, come on. Looks safe.

Across.

Then at the foot of the steps leading up to the big, stone-built, Edwardianly pompous building she saw its sombre wooden doors — oak? — were firmly closed.

Shit.

But if . . .

She ran up the steps at a trot. Put a hand flat on the doors' right-hand leaf. Yet even before she leant any weight on it she knew it would not yield. The window above the transom was showing no light of any sort. As she slumped forward to draw breath, she saw the notice board just beside her. Painted on it with full municipal authority *Opening*

Hours 10 a.m. to 8 p.m. Sats 5 p.m. Closed Sunday.

She did not need to peer once more at her watch to know it would say at least five minutes past, if not almost ten.

Damn it, she thought as her mind slipped back into calmer waters. Caught by the inexorable progress of clock hands, fixed for all the nation by some early nineteenth-century Act of Parliament, and later for the whole world under the law of Greenwich Mean Time.

She looked once more at the locked oaken doors and the blackly forbidding window above. Last librarian on duty gone, heading for home on their bicycle. Week's work over.

No. That picture Gokhale painted for me. His young self, all alone in the locked Bristol library, having an adventure. Till, all too soon the cleaning lady arrives on her prescribed round, and with one bound . . .

A cleaning lady in here now? Very likely. So, I've done it. After all, I've . . .

But then Common sense Harriet came pouring back. A coolly rational flood. Hammer on these doors till I've attracted attention? More likely to attract the attention of some patrolling PC and then awkward explanations indeed. And, even if there is anyone in there, how easy am I going to find

168

it to persuade them that it's necessary for a senior police officer to go hunting among the shelves for one particular book?

No, come on, there's tomorrow. Tomorrow to find perhaps one of the only two or three copies of Local Author's *Marching Through Georgia*. But, damn it, no, it still won't be to hand then. Tomorrow's Sunday.

Ah, well.

Home James. Taxi, if I can spot one. Back at the station probably.

At the house, exhausted and hungry, when she spilled her tale of woe into sympathetic husbandly ears, there came a moment of unexpected irony. One of the copies of almost forgotten *Marching Through Georgia* borrowed from the library had been taken out by none other than Nose-in-a-book John.

'It's been in the house ever since, you know. Passing the library when I was doing a bit of shopping weeks ago, I suddenly thought — I'd decided originally not to buy something only marginally worth cramming into the shelves — that a book by a local man might after all be worth a quick browse.'

'And, natch, you had that.'

'I did, soon as I'd brought it home. Which

is why it's been there on the window-sill in the hall ever since, waiting to be taken back. Surprised the Hard Detective never noticed it.'

She decided to let that pass, especially as she now realised John had actually mentioned once that he had put it where he had.

'But was it worth it, your browse?' she asked.

'No. Not in the least. How can a man who's been an MP, and thinks he's fit to lead a new political party, write as unimaginatively as if he was compiling directions for using a video?'

'Nice to know what you think, since I'm going to settle down here and now to read my way through it, from first page to last.'

'Deep insights into the mind of attack victim, Robert Roughouse?'

'That's one thing I hope for. But I may also have had a hint, just perhaps, that I could get some sort of a clue from it to whoever projected that deadly egg. You saw it happen.'

'I did. But I have to say I doubt very much, however late you stay up, you'll find what you want.'

It was almost 4 a.m., sitting tensely reading as rain pattered steadily down on the roof above, before Harriet finished *Marching Through Georgia,* quite soon re-named *Trudging Through Georgia.*

And have I, she thought, however much I made myself concentrate over every line in it, found any hint of what Kailash Gokhale might have drawn to my attention? I have not. Towards the end, just after the third or fourth time I'd dipped the whole of my face in cold water, I'd begun to ask if the tricksy Bengali had been doing no more with his tale of the boy locked in the library than play a joke on me. *With one bound . . .*

But, no, I don't believe it was a joke. There must be something he remembered as being there that he thought would nudge me in the right direction.

And I haven't found it. So that's that. Perhaps, in a day or two if nothing more hopeful has turned up, I'll give the whole wretched book another go-over. But it is a wretched book. A wretched job of work. Even the title, I thought when I slapped it closed, is absurdly misleading. Roughouse marched through Georgia itself for not much more than thirty or forty pages. Three or four other countries in that much split-up area of the Caucasus had resounded to his trudging feet. He actually spent longer in tiny Transabistan, where Jessop took those photographs, than he did in Georgia itself.

Yes, she thought sliding muzzy-headed into bed beside faintly snoring John, Roughouse actually referred to the scene in one of those photographs in Matthew Jessop's elegant Notting Hill drawing-room.

What was it he wrote in his slap-happy way? Can't think.

Yes, I can. *A village full of little boys blackfaced and shiny as niggers because of the pitchblende pebbles they kept throwing at one another.*

Stop.

Can it . . . can it actually have been just that village, that street, that Gokhale wanted me to react to? Had Matthew Jessop, too, selected that scene out of all the dozens, even hundreds, of photographs he must have taken out there because it was somehow significant?

The pitchblende? But why should pitchblende be significant? Or seem so to my Bengali friend. Don't know. Can't think. God, I'm exhausted.

Then, with the slipping-away thought that she must remember when next at the Masterton to give Tonelle her crossword answer, she was deep in sleep.

She stayed sleeping longer than she had

meant to, and found when she got down-stairs that early-bird John was already at work in the garden, although since Graham's death he had never liked to be on his own for long, prey to the dim grey thoughts of what once had been. For a little she watched his bent back, dressed this Sunday morning in the colourful, student days shirt he liked to wear by way of cocking a snook at his fellow suit-clad Majestic executives. Another of his quotes came into her mind. One he sometimes produced when he had bedtime play in mind. Raymond Chandler, citing that once famous anthropology tome *The Golden Bough,* "our sexual habits are pure convention like wearing a black tie with a dinner jacket".

Clothes rules, she thought. How absurd they are.

Then, in a single grim flashback, the thought of herself at Graham's funeral, dressed head-to-foot in mandatory black. The memory sharp as a thorn pressed into flesh.

She fought her way, as nowadays she, like John, nearly always did, back to the every-day. Yes, look, John's already made his Sunday morning trip to the Aslough Parade bakery for oven-fresh croissants, my quota meticulously counted out on the shelf in front of the dishes cupboard.

She hurried over. Alas, all now limp.

She ate them nevertheless and took her share, again calculated to an exact half, of the coffee still steaming in its glass jug on the machine's hot-plate.

She thought then of ringing the Masterton, but decided it was too early to get a response she could rely upon.

Might be better in fact to arrive there, unannounced. On this day of the week perhaps Mrs Fishlock will be at church, or at least supervising Mr Fishlock — could the dragon have a mate? — in weeding their garden while the rain-soaked earth made it easy. If so, I might be able simply to make my way to Roughouse's room, as Charity did, and tell any nurse there that I have permission to enter. And if her patient is able to say more than that one *loyal* . . .

Last gulp of coffee, open the window, call out to John and jump into the car. Waterloo Gardens first, I think, pick up any messages at the incident room, get Bolshy, if he's come in, to drive me to the Masterton.

Bolshy was there in the incident room, early though it still was, sitting beside a waste-bin with cheroot smoke reeking out of it, defying equally a not-too-happy Happy Hapgood and the authority of the red-lettered *No Smoking* notice directly above him. Does he do it deliberately and defiantly, she asked herself as, with a jerk of her head, she directed him to follow her to her office? And should I, as a responsible senior officer do what Happy has decided to do and turn a blind eye?

She put off any decision.

'Right,' she said as soon as her door was shut, 'I'm off to have another go at seeing Roughhouse. He may be more fit to answer questions than he was before. No use ringing the Masterton to ask, I've a strong feeling I'd just be told he's no more able to talk at length than when I saw him before.'

Loyal, royal, spoil, she thought. If he really did try to pronounce that *loyal,* doesn't it mean, or at least indicate, there's some sort of conspiracy to which he both wants to remain loyal and simultaneously thinks he should not keep secret? And is that why really he's being kept virtually incommunicado?

'You going to get that Tony-whatsit to let you past?' Bolshy asked. 'You know she lives on the premises, there already?'

'Thank you for telling me. So, yes. I may see if she'll take me to Roughhouse. And her name's Tonelle. Not a very difficult one, DS.'

'OK, Tonelle, if that's what you want to call her. Want me to pave the way for you there? Put the fear of God into her again?'

'I don't think that will be necessary.'

'You going to bribe her with a promise or two then? She won't do nothing for you unless she gets something out of it, not a girl like that.'

Harriet took in a breath.

'As a matter of fact,' she said, 'I do have something to offer her.' She left a little pause. 'It's the answer to a tricky crossword clue.'

The expression on Bolshy's face then was satisfaction enough.

'And you think that'll please her?' he got out at last. 'A crossword clue? Straight from the jungle way she is?'

'Yes, I do think she'll be pleased. And I'd have thought you'd have realised that someone with a name like Tonelle is bound to be a second-generation Brit, if not a third.'

That did finally shut him up.

But they did not even get as far as the door before the phone rang.

What's this? On Sunday morning? This early?

She picked up.

'Detective Superintendent Martens?'

It's Mrs Fishlock. I'd recognise that voice

anywhere. Only . . . Only isn't there something a bit odd about it?

'Harriet Martens here.'

'Miss Martens, I'm ringing from my house. There — There's something — something terrible I have to tell you.'

Oh, no. Not that Robert Roughouse has died. Surely not? They said his condition was *stable.*

'Yes, Mrs Fishlock, what is it?'

'At some time during the night — I've only just this moment been told — someone entered the clinic. I don't know how. Our security . . .'

'Mrs Fishlock, someone entered the clinic and did what?'

'They murdered Robert Roughouse. Murdered him.'

CHAPTER THIRTEEN

Harriet's first reaction, one that followed so closely on that word *murdered* it might have been the same single thought, was that she had never arranged for a police watch at the Masterton. All right, she was still arguing to herself as Bolshy drove her at demon-speed, Matthew Jessop and his friends did spirit Roughouse away to the well-protected Masterton. It could be said doing so was precaution enough. Hadn't the Masterton always prided itself on the security it provided for de-toxing pop stars? Or, yes, for a celebrity athlete like Charity. Hadn't that been enough?

But, say what you like, is Roughouse's death really and truly down to me? Oughtn't I to have been aware that, even in the Masterton, he must be in danger? Shouldn't I have had a 24-hour guard put on the place? Or, at the very least, have warned . . . Warned who? Mrs Fishlock, I suppose. And, if what stopped me doing that was the damn dragon's I-know-best attitude, oughtn't I to have overcome my dislike of it? But, no. No, I simply believed Roughhouse's safety had been provided for. And really I was not altogether wrong.

Yet am I still to blame, she asked herself again and again as Bolshy spun the car down the narrow country lanes. But . . . But . . .

The question was still unresolved in her mind when they arrived, just minutes before the full panoply of necessary attendants at a murder, the Scene of Crime team, the police photographer, the video-taper and the civilian Scene Manager, temporary boss of them all, guardian of evidence in danger of contamination. Before leaving Waterloo Gardens she had, as Senior Investigating Officer, also requested the attendance of Dr Edwards, the Greater Birchester Police forensic pathologist, who would eventually carry out the autopsy. Bolshy meanwhile had been tasked with notifying the duty forensic physician — Harriet still thought of them as police surgeons — although it was likely to be some time before the moment came for them to declare, following laid-down protocol, that the dead victim was dead.

Dressed eventually in clumsy-looking white paper cover-all, hair inside clumsy white disposable hood, yet clumsier plastic galoshes on her feet, Harriet waited outside Roughouse's room, where only the Friday before she had heard him mutter that word *loyal,* possibly significant. As the minutes went infuriatingly slowly by, all she could do was watch through the partly open door as the Scene Manager, a first-class fusspot insisting always on his full surname, Montague-James, established access routes across the pale grey wall-to-wall carpet inside. She could just make out Roughouse's body, a mere covered-up shape on the hospital-style bed, in almost exactly the position he had been lying when she had last seen him. Except over the bandaged head she well remembered there was a white-starched pillow, marked by the deep impressions of two heavy fists.

But whose fists? Whose?

And how had the person who had held them there got into the room? By climbing up that thickly matted ivy all over the walls of the house? No, both sash windows were shut. By moving a little from side to side

180

she could see the bright brass catches on them were locked. Whoever it was who had got into the room must have made their entry into the house somewhere else.

'DS,' she called quietly to Bolshy, waiting further along the corridor, 'here a minute.'

She told him then to slip away and go, unobtrusively, round the whole building to see, if he could, where during the night hours someone might have broken in. The hours, she thought with a jet of frustration, when at home I was doing no more than plough through the interminable pages of *Marching Through Georgia* listening to the rain on the roof.

Bolshy stumped off, for once not looking displeased.

Inside the room it appeared that every conceivable surface had at last been pointed out for fingerprinting by ultra-pedantic Mr Montague-James. The flashes from the photographer's camera had come to an end. The video-taper, his awkward-looking machine dangling from his hand, was making his exit, tip-toeing along the taped-out route between the body and the door.

'You can come in now, Superintendent,' Montague-James called. 'You'll see the route tapes clearly laid out. But take particular care just inside. As we first went in, I observed the drying-out remains of a wet footmark there. It should provide a measure of identification, now that it's been satisfactorily photographed. But I still don't want it trampled on.'

Damn man, Harriet thought with a bite of the ill-temper which she had stored up while forbidden entry, praising himself for doing no more than work to the rules laid down for him. Why do all the scene managers I have ever watched make such a palaver over doing what they're meant to do? Glorying in every last twiddle of every last piece of procedure.

Ah well, I suppose that's the attraction of the job for a certain sort of ex-police officer, one of the go-by-the-book lot who shelter inside the great web of Police Regulations comforting themselves with the feeling that, even if they've got no useful result, they haven't put a foot wrong.

Dutifully keeping her hands deep in the pockets of her stiff paper cover-all, she walked the path laid down till she reached the body. The body, it came to her, of the man who thumping energetically at his keyboard, alive and pleased with himself, had written *Marching Through Georgia,* dully adding in all those other places in the Caucasus he tramped over.

For a long while she stood beside the hygienic hospital bed, methodically searching for the least thing that might indicate something about whoever had crept into the room in the hours when there had been no nurse present. Questions to be asked about that absence, too. Though most probably, the medical staff must have decided a constant watch was no longer necessary. *Condition: stable.* How often did I hear that repeated?

With a nod she agreed to Dr Edwards' request for the pillow over the head to be removed. Forensics would do what had to be done with it.

Blood-drained, the bandaged face looked little different from that of the semi-conscious man who, in answer to her gently insistent questions, had managed to utter only some half-dozen syllables, among them that single grunted-out word *loyal.* If it had actually been that.

'I think for once cause of death's pretty straightforward,' Dr Edwards said, 'even without taking into account other physical signs that may emerge, petechiae in the eyes and so forth. You saw the depth of the hand impressions on that pillow. They speak for themselves, subject to any unexpected forensic evidence, and I doubt if anything significant will emerge there, certainly no nice DNA. You can see from the marks that your man was wearing heavy gloves.'

'Or your woman,' Harriet more or less automatically put in.

'Oh, yes. Or woman, if you must. But I think the amount of continuous force used really does indicate masculine strength. But I'll allow you a healthy woman if you want.'

'Thank you.'

The almost statutory mild banter over any horribly murdered corpse brought to an end, Harriet gave her agreement to the body being taken away for the autopsy. Two of the waiting SOCO team at once advanced carrying their heavy plastic sheet.

She stayed on only until the rolled-up sheet had been safely sticky-taped together. Then, gratefully discarding her cover-all, she set off to see Mrs Fishlock. She had questions to ask.

Within minutes in the icy dragon's office she came to wish that the moment she had learnt the news on the phone she had put the questions which had at once sprung to her mind. How was it that the murder had not been discovered till that comparatively late hour of the morning? Why was there no nurse in the room? If a high degree of intensive care had no longer been thought necessary, what regular visits had been paid to the sick man? Who was it who had, in fact, found the body? And how exactly had the clinic's much-vaunted security come to have been breached?

But, on the phone, out of a feeling she owed someone in such a state of turmoil as icy Mrs Fishlock some consideration, she had failed to ask.

And now her witness was in full defensive mode.

'Of course,' she said, prickly with stiffness, 'it is our rule here that a patient who is sleeping should be left as long as is reasonable. Sleep, you may not realise, Superintendent, is the great healer.'

Oddly enough, Harriet thought with a jet of rage, I do know that. As does every woman in the world.

But the spate of excuses went tumbling on. It was of course altogether impossible that a patient in need of 24-hour supervision should not be given it. 'Our very well-regarded medical staff made their decision, and it was not the duty of anyone less qualified to question it.' Whatever way in which the person who entered Mr Roughouse's room had reached it, there could not possibly have been any fault in the clinic's security. Of course, it had been the nurse on morning duty, Nurse Smithson, who, entering at precisely her laid-down hour, had found the patient dead.

'Then I shall need to see Nurse Smithson.'

Harriet could no longer endure the endless parade of half-truth information.

'As soon as Smithson's urgent duties permit I shall arrange for that,' Mrs Fishlock immediately countered. 'Every patient at a clinic like ours requires personal nursing attention, you know.'

'Thank you. But could you perhaps, since it seems I must wait to see Nurse Smithson, explain to me now how it is that you were able to assure me that there cannot have been any fault in the clinic's security last night?'

'Superintendent, there is no possible method of entry to the house. When the building was purchased the most thorough investigations were made solely with security in mind. If anything was found to be less than satisfactory, improvements were at once put in place.'

'However, an intruder did enter.'

'That is as may be. But I can assure you it was not through any default in our system. The Masterton advertises its high degree of security all over the country. We have had in our care on many, many occasions actors and actresses of the highest standing.'

'Yes, I have heard that was so. But nevertheless someone got into the house, entered Mr Roughouse's room and suffocated him.'

'Well, it is your business to deal with that. We pay enough towards the upkeep of the Greater Birchester Police. We are entitled to see some activity from you.'

Harriet suppressed a new flare of rage. Wearily she put a few more questions, each of which was answered with much the same bureaucratic rigmarole, none of it hiding the fact that security at the Masterton, whatever it once might have been, had been penetrated.

At last she stood up to go.

'Very well,' she said, stamping down the least trace of irony, 'I think I have learnt all I wanted to know. If anything else arises, I will not hesitate to come to you again.'

Outside she found Bolshy looking, surprisingly, very unlike his usual gloomily resentful self.

'Got it,' he said the moment he saw her, his ever-darting pale eyes positively shining. 'Needed a bit of looking for, but there to be found.'

'Good work, DS. And your *it*, what exactly is that?'

Bolshy produced a rare grin.

'Just a little splinter of wood.'

Harriet reined back her impatience.

'And just where did you find this splinter?'

Bolshy's air of satisfaction visibly grew.

'Thought I'd first of all take a bit of a prowl round the whole outside. Best way. And what d'you think I came across?'

This time Harriet declined to provide any idiot question.

'A little old tucked-away window, that's what,' Bolshy said, after a long moment. 'Down at the end of a narrow sort-of passageway, left when that wing-building was tacked on some time. Dirty great bush, all over bloody thorns, growing all the way along it.'

'I think I know where you mean. I noticed the bush when we were sitting in the car looking at the house. So there's a window hidden behind it?'

'Yup. But what you don't know is just at the edge of that little square of a window — ain't been painted since the end of World War Two, ask me — there was my tiny splinter of fresh wood. Oh ho, I said soon as I spotted it, someone been digging a good strong knife-blade in here, or maybe a biggish screwdriver. So I followed suit, gave the frame a gentle hoick. Always carry a useful knife, you know.'

'Good practice,' Harriet put in by way of urging the story on.

'Certainly is. 'Cos I got that window open without making so much as a mark on it. Put my head inside, careful of dabs of course. And what did I see? Old storeroom or something, looked as if no one been in it for years. Nothing but a few empty crates on the floor. 'Cept a nice line of footprints. Wet shoes on the dust. Man's, of course, an' a nice pattern of ribbed stitching round the edge of the soles. Just like, I'll be bound, the shoe pattern old Monty-tonty was so chuffed at seeing. The prick.'

'You didn't go into that store-room?'

'No, ma'am. I am a detective. Went back in the house, worked my way round to where that store had to be, and, plain enough, its door — hadn't been opened for years, ask me — showed every sign of having just once been pushed wide and then shoved back into place. Rubbish swept right to one side.'

So the not unusual answer to any sort of a locked-room mystery: someone years earlier had not done what they ought to have done.

'Right then, DS. Go back up to your friend Monty-tonty and get him to send the photographer down there fast as he can. Then we'll have some useful evidence.'

'Be a pleasure,' Bolshy said.

'And one thing more, DS.'

Something that had been tapping obscurely at the back of her mind abruptly found its answer. Mrs Fishlock, in one of her not-so-subtle digs at the Greater Birchester Police, had complained about the number of times I had inquired about Roughouse's condition. But she had also implied there had been other persistent inquiries. Now it was clear they had been made by whoever it was who wanted to find out if unconscious Roughouse would ever be able to talk again.

But who that was —

'OK, ma'am, if I nip out for a smoke?'

She brought herself back to the immediate reality. Bloody Bolshy taking advantage.

'No, it's not OK. There's something I want you to do. As soon as the nurse who found the body is available I've got to hear exactly what she saw when she went into that room. But I'd also need to have a word with young Tonelle. I'd like to find out if, by any chance, someone came to the house last evening saying they wanted to know something or other about the clinic's routines, making out they were looking for somewhere for a rest cure, anything like that. Because, if there was, that'll have been the person who hoped to get to Roughhouse without having to break in.'

'Could be, I suppose. Worth asking that Tonelle anyhow.'

Hearing Tonelle called something other than a black bitch, Harriet abruptly remembered the present she had intended to give her.

'No. Wait a moment.'

She scrabbled in her bag, found an old shopping-list — one of several — put a line firmly through it, and on the back wrote *What's putting up a tent called? What happens to a blonde if in place of O for Zero you put E for East? And what has to be dug out of the earth? Pitchblende, that's what.* She added her two initials, and folded the flimsy list firmly in half.

'Give this to Tonelle from me before you ask her anything,' she told Bolshy. 'Let her have a moment to look at it, and then I think you'll find her as helpful as can be.'

Bolshy, of course, flipped the little piece of paper open.

'All gobbledygook to me,' he said.

'Never mind. See if it works.'

'Ma'am.'

'And congratulations, DS. I think you've solved the mystery of the house that couldn't be broken into, even if it was no

more than a mystery created by that bloody
woman in the office behind us.'

CHAPTER FOURTEEN

Nurse Smithson told Harriet that her night-duty colleague when they exchanged shifts had said that when she had last looked in on Robert Roughouse at midnight she had noticed nothing amiss. Consequently it had not been until 8.30 a.m. that, in accordance with standing instructions, she had gone to wake the patient, take his temperature and check his pulse. As soon as she had opened his door, she had seen the pillow over his face, one she even recognised as left ready not far from the bed. It had needed then no more investigation than touching the hand protruding from the bedclothes and finding it lifelessly cold. She had at once raised the alarm.

Very well, Harriet said to herself, after making sure Nurse Smithson had told her everything she could, what happened here during the night is surely clear now. Some-one came into the building via Bolshy's little storeroom, probably well after midnight. They then cautiously made their way to where they saw that brass card-holder *Mr Robert Roughhouse.* In the room, snatching up the convenient spare pillow, they had held it over the sleeping victim's face until they were sure life was extinct. No struggle, no chance of a shouted cry. Robert Roughouse's enfeebled state would have seen to that. And afterwards his murderer had simply opened the nearest convenient window and escaped down the ancient ivy.

But who was it? I've nothing to go on. Nothing at all.

Unless my guess turns out to be right and someone did come here in the afternoon or early evening and ask Tonelle a few careful questions.

Bolshy. Has he learnt anything from her?

Where is he anyhow? He ought to have got the answer by now, certainly if my shopping-list note made her as cooperative as I'd hoped. Is the damn fellow, puffed up by his moment of glory, idling away somewhere with one of his damn cheroots?

Right, I'm going to find out.

She discovered Bolshy, as she had more than half-expected to, sitting comfortably in the car, and, yes, enveloped in drifts of nose-wrinkling smoke.

'Oh, hello, guv,' he said. 'We off back to the nick now? Don't seem to be much more to do here. Or nothing Monty-tonty and his merry men can't take care of.'

'That's as may be, DS. But why haven't I heard from you whether anybody came to the door here yesterday asking questions?'

'Weren't nothing much to tell you.'

'Nevertheless I asked you to make an inquiry, and I expected to be told the result.'

'Oh, well then, if that's what you want. Yeah, there was a bloke come just after they'd locked the doors.'

'And what time was that, DS?'

'I dunno. Oh, yes. Yeah, I do. That Tonelle said. Doors locked every day at six sharp. Dunno why early as that. But what she said.'

You may not know why the doors are locked precisely at six, Harriet thought. But I do. It will be because Dragon Fishlock has laid it down. For no particular reason. Except that she likes issuing regulations of any sort, whether they serve a purpose or have just come into her head. I know the type. There's more than one or two of them in the Service.

'And did Tonelle by any chance,' she demanded, 'tell you what this man who came to the door looked like?'

'Yeah. Did get some sort of descrip out of her. White bloke, tall, six foot maybe, had a hat well down over his face, sort of brown felt like you see people wearing at the races on telly, she said.'

'Anything more than that to identify our man? If he was our man.'

'Could have been him,' Bolshy said. 'Like I told you when I went off to see that Tonelle.'

Oh, how I'd love to point out to this bloody insolent fellow that I was the one who thought the killer might have made an earlier recce. But, no, if I do, he'll just try and clam up on me, and I need to hear every scrap he learnt from Tonelle.

'So what did he actually say, this man?'

'Well, she weren't that interested in him. Far as she was concerned someone had just come making some sort of inquiries for some friend of his. Wanted to know if the beds were comfortable, bloody pooftah.'

'Did she say that? Tonelle? That this man appeared to be gay?'

'Nah. That's just what most of what they call *patients* here are, ask me.'

Damn it, damn it, damn it. I'm going to get rid of this wretched fellow, one way or another. Never mind how clever he was finding that means of access. And, no, she added to herself, I'm not even going to ask him now what reception my note to Tonelle got. Quite possible he never even remembered to give it to her.

'All right, DS,' she said. 'There's nothing more for us here at present. What I need now is for you to drive me down to London, fast as you like. There are people whose whereabouts last night I'd very much like to know, before they hear the news and have time to make up tales. Zip up and tell Mr Montague-James we're going. Then it's look in at the incident room to put in hand a house-to-house round the whole area here. Got to be done, even though there are hardly any houses to check. Somebody may have seen a stranger hanging about between six and whenever he got in through your little window. Then off to London.'

'Monty-fucking-tonty,' Bolshy muttered as he plodded off.

In London, despite her urgent need to check where at the time of the murder those Cabal members she knew of were, Harriet had no difficulty in deciding to see Charity Nyambura first. Somebody has to break the appalling news to her before it reaches the media, she thought. And she deserves to have it told her as thoughtfully as possible.

Yet, as they drew up outside Daley Thompson House, she found poking up in her mind the question she had asked herself after her last visit, *Isn't there something unexplained about Charity saying that she knew Tonelle?*

She tried to thrust the question to the back of her mind. Charity had terrible news to hear. Not the time now for catching her out over the fact that when, quite casually, I asked how it had come about that she had been a patient at the Masterton, far away from London, she had stayed silent for almost a full minute before saying the Masterton specialised in sports injuries. Something I didn't know it did, or does. A dark fly-spot on the immaculate surface I thought I was seeing? But this not the time now, in any way, to go probing into it.

She gave a firm buzz to the entry-phone. Faintly purring semi-silence from the grille of the little loudspeaker. Charity out? She may, somehow, have already learnt the news and is she wandering the streets stupefied with misery.

But no . . .

'Who's there?' Charity's unmistakable African voice, in it even just a touch of apprehension.

Harriet quickly identified herself, asked if

she could come in.

'Yeah, come up, come up. Good to hear you.'

So plainly she hasn't learnt yet.

Straightening her shoulders she began climbing the stairs.

Up, she thought, to a by no means *Good to hear you* encounter. Still, I've had to break terrible news like this before. Dozens, perhaps hundreds, of times. A policeman's lot, not at all a happy one. Or, more often, a policewoman's lot, some cowardly male having passed over the burden.

Yet, somehow, I feel it'll be a lot harder here. Charity, such a figure of hope. Her long journey from — what? — a comparatively impoverished life in distant Kenya to . . . to, in a way, the centre of the world. Or at least the centre of the sports world that plays such a part in so many people's lives now. Now very much in her grasp, come the year 2012 and the Olympics, a Gold. Her name enshrined in the records for ever. And she's about to hear that her lover, top-flight Robert Roughouse, ex-MP, Party leader, is dead. Has been murdered.

Inside the flat there was no immediate chance to say the words that had to be said. Charity, looking little different in jeans and T-shirt than she had done at their previous encounter, reached at once for her green kettle and busied herself, with a muttered *OK?*, in spooning coffee grains into mugs.

Harriet stood watching, somehow feeling herself cast back in time. Almost as if in a dream, she was thinking of Robert Roughouse as still alive, lying there in the big hygienic bed at the Masterton slowly recovering from his injuries. And soon able to answer every question fully and clearly.

But then, as Charity put a hot mug into her hand, the wishful daydream vanished.

'Charity,' she said, still standing there. 'Charity, I'm sorry, but I've got some bad news. Sit down. Sit down straightaway.'

Charity, her face suddenly a picture of dread, almost collapsed into the nearest little furniture-store armchair, and Harriet saw that telling her the news would be now a mere formality.

'Yes,' she said. 'I'm afraid it's what you think. But it's worse. Even worse. You see, in the middle of last night someone broke in at the Masterton and got into Robert's room. They put a pillow over his face as he slept and — and smothered him. He must have been dead for some time before Nurse Smithson — you must know her from when you were there — went in to wake him at eight-thirty this morning.'

Charity sat there in the too-small armchair saying nothing. Slowly she lowered her coffee mug to the floor, only at the last moment tilting it and spilling a spoonful or two of milky liquid on the battered old grey carpet.

Harriet wondered whether this was the time to put an arm round her shoulders. But after a moment there came a few leaden words.

'Rob dead? You're telling me Rob's been murdered?'

'Yes. Yes, I was. I am. Someone deliberately killed him. You have to face that. And, of course, I'm here not only to tell you he's gone, but because it's my duty to find out who it was who killed him.'

'Yeah. Yeah, you've got to find out who. Poor, poor Rob.' A long moment of reverie. 'The one who did that broke the worst law of all, the law everybody in the world knows. *Thou shalt not kill.* Yeah, Harriet, it's your duty to . . . bring them to justice. Put things right again.'

'I promise you, Charity, whatever I can do to see that duty is done, I will. And I'll make sure everyone in the investigation, too, does their very best from start to finish.'

Then, into her mind, came Bolshy's pallid, freckled face, dampened cheroot between his lips.

Have I promised too much? And it's not only Bolshy. Detectives are human beings. However determined they are the moment they're informed of a murder, they cannot all go on day after day working at the same demanding rate. And some of them will hardly try. Look at Bolshy. Did he even bother himself this morning to give Tonelle the shopping-list note I sent her? The friendly message that, shocked by the murder as she must be, would have induced her to tell him every last detail she had noticed about the man who came to the Masterton's doors, Rob Roughouse's murderer.

She realised then that the phone on the little table beside her was ringing, had possibly been ringing for some time. Charity seemed, equally, not to have taken notice of it.

She put down her still brimful mug.

'Shall I?' she said, her hand on the receiver.

Charity did not respond.

Harriet picked up, gave the number, and waited to see who this was. Charity's trainer saying she was late? Somebody selling something? Someone, at last, ringing with the appalling news?

'Is — Is that Charity?' a voice said.

A voice Harriet thought she recognised. Knew she had, despite its unexpectedness.

'Tonelle?'

'Yeah? That's me. But that ain't Charity.'

'No, it's Detective Superintendent Martens. Harriet Martens. Tonelle, were you ringing to tell Charity what's happened?'

'Yeah, yeah. 'Course I was. Didn't think it'd be clever to do it with the Bill all around. But you must've gone a long time ago, if you're down in London now.'

'Yes, I went off with DS Woodcock as soon as I'd finished talking to Nurse Smithson, just leaving the Scene of Crime people with you. I needed to come down here pronto to see various people.'

'Check alibis, that it?'

Smart girl.

'Yes, something of that sort. But I thought no one might have told Charity, and it'd be better if she didn't hear the news on the radio or something.'

'That figures. Always thought there was a kind heart somewhere under those new-every-morning shirts of yours. Yeah, an' that reminds me. You do buy some funny things.'

'Buy?' she asked, momentarily baffled.

'That shopping-list on the back of your note.'

So Bolshy had handed it over after all.

'Oh, that. Yes, John has a particular liking for semolina pudding. The shopping-list happened to be the only bit of paper I could find when I sent DS Woodcock to ask if anyone called at the Clinic last evening. Anyone with questions.'

'Yeah. An' I told him. There was this bloke who said he wanted to know if our rooms were *suitable* for a friend of his. Friend he didn't happen to say anything else about. But, soon as I told that to old DS What's-his-name, he just said *Thank you* — almost polite for once — and took himself off.'

'Did he indeed?' Harriet said sharply. 'Didn't he ask you for a full description of this caller?'

'Not really. Not everything about the full outfit the guy was wearing. Suit-and-tie type, even though he didn't have the tie. Open-neck shirt, white I think. Yes, white definitely, may have had a bit of a blue stripe in it. Couldn't see much else. He was a big feller, in a big coat, sort of riding-mac, pockets stuffed with stuff. Oh, an' I forgot. Most noticeable bit. He wore one of them brown felt hats, like you see at the races on telly.'

'Yes, DS Woodcock did tell me about that.'

Another example of de rigueur dress, she thought. But no one ever actually laid down a law that hats like that had to be worn at the races. Why were they then? Answer, of course, copycatting, nothing more.

'Hey,' Tonelle breezed on, 'thank you for what you wrote on the other side of that shopping-list. I was still worrying over it, all that east and zero business. See now what it meant. Can sleep o' nights. But, listen. Charity, is she all right? I mean . . .'

'Well, no. No, she isn't all right. How could she be just after hearing what I had to tell her? She's stunned. Yes, that's it. Stunned.'

'Should I come to her, down to London? I could. Tell old Fishface, stuff her job and just come.'

'No. No, honestly, I don't feel there's any need for that. If I'm right in thinking Charity is —' She looked down at the crouching, balled-up figure in the small chair. 'That she's a pretty tough lady?'

'Yeah. Yeah, she's tough all right. You should've seen her battling her way through when she was down here.'

Harriet jerked her head up in surprise.

And at once made herself think coolly and rationally.

Is this suddenly the answer to that niggle of doubt I had when I was here before? The tiny fly-spot on the open surface of Charity's personality, that unaccountably long silence when I asked why she had been at the Masterton? Yes, the one dark spot on the shining exterior of that on-and-on, up-and-up life.

'Tonelle,' she said, turning her back on Charity's lost-in-grief figure and keeping her voice low, 'Tonelle, tell me exactly why Charity was in the clinic.'

No immediate answer. But one came soon enough.

'She told you it was a sports injury, did she? Generally does if anyone asks. But she shouldn't have tried to hide that from you, not when you were there to find out if she knew anything about Rob Roughouse that might get you to who shot that thing at him. No, believe me, in this place they wouldn't know a tendon from a toenail.'

'So, why was she with you?' Harriet almost breathed into the phone.

'Drugging. Used to give herself a little extra when she had a race to win.'

The implications began to go clicking through Harriet's head. She turned and glanced at Charity. She was already beginning to look up.

'OK,' she said to Tonelle. 'Listen, I ought to be looking after Charity. I'll speak to you later, all right?'

'Yeah. OK.'

The sound of a replaced receiver at the far end.

Yes, a very bright girl, Tonelle. Catching on quickly as can be. But what to do about Charity now? Now that I know her secret. For a possible future Olympic medallist to have a record as having run races with a drug in her bloodstream, it would be a storm shadow almost impossible to survive. All right, at some time in the past, before any random drugs test had caught her, she must have realised she was hooked. And, yes, she would have confided in Rob Roughouse, and she had been lucky. Not only would a man taught from his schooldays to be entrenchedly loyal have at once decided to keep her secret come what may, but, as someone with a house not far from Birchester, he must have known about the Masterton, refuge of rich idiots with drink or drugs problems, and got her in there to be cured. Which is how she came to be friends with her fellow black, Tonelle.

But Charity, should I tell her what I've learnt, this very minute? With the state she's in she won't be able to hide anything from me now. I'll have the truth about that drug out of her in no time, and then I may go on to learn from her things about the man she loved that she's felt it would be disloyal to him, lying unconscious, to tell me.

Disloyal. The word sent up in her a picture of Robert, just recovered from unconsciousness, and muttering that word, almost impossible to make out, *loyal.*

Yes, it must have been that. Not royal, or spoil, but loyal. I see it now, now that I've learnt what Kailash Gokhale told me, that Robert's loyalties to the other members of the Cabal he founded were under strain.

'Charity,' she said, her mind having in an instant made itself up. 'Charity, it's up to you now, despite this horrible thing that's happened, not to slip back into — into the way you were when you had to go into the Masterton.'

Charity's eyes suddenly flashed into terrified life.

'How — How do you know that?'

Harriet looked at her.

'That was Tonelle on the phone just now,' she said.

'She told you? Tonelle?'

'Yes, she did, and she told me, too, that she wished you hadn't tried to hide it from me when I saw you before. You know, truth's best. It almost always is, in the end.'

A long silence.

'Yeah. Yeah, I suppose that's right. Not

telling you probably put all sorts of ideas in your mind.'

'It did. And they got in the way of me finding out enough about Robert to get a line on why someone shot that thing at him. On why, now, he's been murdered.'

'All right, yes. Yes, I'll tell you anything more I can.' She looked up suddenly from her little chair. 'But there's one thing I'd like to say straightaway. It's this. Once I'd got out of that mess I was in — And it was easy enough to slide into it in the days when I just had to win every race I'd entered for — I swore I'd never touch anything like that ever again. And I haven't. I haven't.'

'I believe you, Charity. I really do. But, listen, is there anything you didn't think I should be told when I was here last? It's time you told me everything you possibly can. You owe that much to Robert.'

She leant intently over Charity, willing her to sift her memory, to speak.

And she did.

'Yes,' she said. 'Yes, there is something. Something I thought was private between me and Rob. Rob when he was alive. When I thought, with time, he was going to be OK.'

'Yes?'

'Yes, it's a bit stupid really. It didn't seem

to matter then, when you were here last, and Rob . . . Rob was going to be well again.'

'But tell me now, Charity. Whatever it was, tell me. All right, it may be, as you said *stupid.* But you should let me be the judge of that. You really should.'

'Yeah. Well, OK. OK, it was just this. It was something he said when we were in bed together the night before he went down to that place, Gralethorpe. To make that speech, about how fox-hunting was part of the great tradition of being British. How it meant much more than it seemed to. He believed in that, you know. It was . . . it was somehow what made him the man he was.'

For a moment Harriet saw again Roughouse, dressed in his full hunting kit, brick-red coat, white stock at the neck, white breeches above gleaming brown boots, as he put all the effort he was capable of into convincing that angry crowd that hunting was worth preserving. Into showing them *the man he was.*

'Tell me, Charity. Whatever it was, tell me.'

'It was just this. It wasn't really much. But some time in the night, God knows when, it was still dark, pitch-dark, something woke Rob. Or it didn't quite wake him. But he stirred and moaned. I think that was what must have brought me to the surface, too.

210

Because I don't think I was awake before . . .'

She lapsed into reminiscent silence.

Harriet waited. Until her patience came to its end.

'Yes, what happened then?'

A weak, wavering smile appeared on the boot-polish brown face in front of her.

'Yeah, this is what was stupid about it. And Rob wasn't silly. Dead serious Rob was. I used to think I'd try and cure him of that. When we were married. Because we'd agreed that one day, one day soon, we would —'

And the tears sprung from her eyes, coursed down those shining brown cheeks, made the wide-lipped mouth gulp and gulp.

Harriet stood there, waiting. Nothing else that could be done.

Then, at last, Charity lifted up her head.

'Sorry. Sorry, shouldn't have . . . No use crying, isn't that what they say, over spilt mil— over spilt blood. Spilt blood. But I . . . I couldn't help it when it all came back.'

'Of course, you couldn't, love. Of course, you couldn't.'

'But it's over now. That's over now. Let me tell you what he, what Rob, said then.'

'Yes. If you can.'

'It wasn't so much said as, I dunno, murmured, muttered.'

'Yes? What was it?'

'This. This. He muttered, kept muttering *I don't want to go, I don't want to go to that place.*'

'Just that? No more?'

'Yeah, just that. But you should have heard the — the agony. Yes, that's what it was. The agony in his voice when those words sort of came out of him. You know, even at the time, I thought he's saying more, something more, than just that he didn't want to go down to that demo, try to convince a lot of idiots there's some good in hunting. But in the morning, when he said nothing at all about having woken up, and when he seemed to be his usual — No, might as well say it. When he made love to me again. Then I thought that must after all have been what he'd been trying to say. That it was just going up to — what's it? Gralethorpe — to make his speech that he didn't want to have to do. This was when I was lying beside him after . . . afterwards, you know, like you do if it's been good . . .'

'Yes,' Harriet put in quietly. 'I know what you mean. And it was then, when you were relaxed, dreamily relaxed, that you thought Rob must have simply been worried about going up to Gralethorpe, that he had a sort of uncharacteristic reluctance to face — well, the enemy. Some enemy.'

'Yeah, that was it. That was exactly it. But, when you were here before, I thought I couldn't tell you anything about it. It — It sort of showed Rob as weak. What's it they call them? Yes, a weakling. I thought it showed Rob as being a weakling, and he wasn't. He wasn't at all. He was strong. He wouldn't knuckle under. He never would knuckle under to anything.'

'Yes, I can believe that. Just in the little I saw of him there in Gralethorpe that night he certainly wasn't knuckling under. But, tell me, where was it, do you think now, that he was so reluctant to go to? Can you put your finger on it?'

Charity was silent for a few moments. And when she spoke she sounded more than a little unsure of herself.

'It's hard to say. I mean, you notice things, just little things sometimes. And then, because they don't seem to amount to much, you sort of forget all about them. But . . . but, yes. Yes, here's one thing. He — He had a row once, not all that long before that night, with one of that Zeal School lot, the ones that call themselves the Cobbles. Is it?'

213

'Well, I think it's actually the Cabal. Cabal's a not very common word for a secret club. I seem to remember it was originally made up of the initial letters of the five members of a group of politicians, though I've not the remotest idea who they were or even when they existed.'

'Yeah. Yeah, that was it. The Cabal. Rob didn't ever talk much about it, so I never really cottoned on. But that was what he said: the Cabal.'

'And he had a row with one of the members? A bad row, when he wouldn't knuckle under about something?'

'Yeah. Yeah, it was with a man called Fledge. Morris Fledge, I think. I only met him once, just for a few minutes, so I don't know all that much about him.'

'I do, as a matter of fact,' Harriet put in by way of encouragement. 'If we're talking about the same man, and I think we are. He's actually called Sir Marcus Fledge and he's chairman of that huge firm, Pettifer's, very rich, even by the standard of the rich guys who've been at the Zeal School. He's richer than any of them, I got the impression. Rich, but dull, someone called him. A dull fellow.'

'Yeah, that's him. Didn't seem to have a word to say for himself when we met for those few minutes. Just stared at me when Rob introduced us, sort of like a big fat red-faced pig, and just muttered the one word *Pleased* . . . And a *Goodbye then* when he went.'

'But Robert, Rob, he had some sort of row with him? Was it about him having to go somewhere? Not to Gralethorpe, but to somewhere quite different?'

'Yeah, I think it was. Or it may have been. When we came back here after, Rob was blazing. I've never seen him so angry. And he does get — oh God, he did get angry at times. Even with me, though we made it up quickly enough. But with — what's-it? — Sir Marcus Fledge, he wasn't going to make it up, not at all. And that's when I knew he hadn't knuckled under to something which that great big fat pig-face wanted him to do.'

'Something? Did Rob give you any idea, even a hint, about what that something was? Was it that Sir Marcus Fledge wanted him to go somewhere and he was determined not to?'

'I don't know. I don't know at all. I asked. I asked Rob, though I knew he wasn't going to say anything. But he was so angry about it all that I really wanted to know why. But, no. No, he just said there were things he was bound not to say a word about, and that this was one of them.'

'So you never got to know?'

'No.'

'And do you think, now do you think, that the way Rob muttered the night before he went to Gralethorpe was because he was badly worried about this, whatever it was?'

'Oh God, I don't know. It might have — oh, it might have been anything, anything. But, yes. Yes, I suppose I do think it was to do with pig-face Fledge. It was the agony behind Rob's voice that made me feel what was troubling him was more, much more, than that stupid — brave all right, but stupid — idea of confronting those — were they miners? It was as if he had some awful decision to make. Yes, that was it. A decision that was tearing him apart.'

'But you don't know what that actually was? If it was that at all, those muttered words in the middle of the night?'

'No. No, I don't know. Oh God, I wish I did. I wish Rob had told me about whatever it was. I could have — I could, sort of perhaps, helped him.'

CHAPTER FIFTEEN

Harriet would not let herself immediately consider the fact — no, the tantalising half-fact — that Rob Roughouse had been desperately unwilling to respond to some demand made on him, possibly by the chairman of the world-ranking Pettifer heavy machinery company. If this really was at the root of the nightmare Roughouse had before he went to Gralethorpe, it would affect the whole direction of her investigation. But, until she had time and space to work out its every last implication, she was not even going to think about it. One thing, however, she did know. Sooner or later she was going to have to confront the pig-faced — Charity's word — chairman of mighty Pettifer's.

As she made her way out, after contacting a Romanian girl athlete two floors below who, Charity had said, was 'a sort of friend', there came back into her mind that one almost incomprehensible word Robert

Roughouse had managed to mutter as she had sat beside his bed at the Masterton. *Loyal.* Yes, I see now he must have been caught between two loyalties. Loyalty — was it? — to his fellow members of the Cabal, which he had himself brought into being, and loyalty to — to what? To his duty even to uphold the laws of his country?

Yes, it's certainly beginning to look possible that, for some unknown reason, the Cabal, as it now is, may have wanted to ensure Roughouse's silence about something they are planning. But can that really be? That a little group of ex-public schoolboys actually hired a hitman to use that grenade-throwing device? And, after the failed attempt, has the Cabal hired another paid killer, or used the first one again, finally to put an end to Roughouse's life? Or . . . ? Or has one of the group perhaps taken the matter into his own hands and committed murder? And, yes, from Tonelle's description of the man who had come to the Masterton asking questions, he could really have been someone who might belong to that rich men's secretive club.

So, yes, right or wrong, it's imperative now to see every member of the Cabal I know about, or can find out about, and make sure where they were last night.

Bolshy, she found, had moved the car to double yellow lines a little further along the street from where he had been parked. No doubt for the simple pleasure of telling a traffic warden to bugger off. She got in beside him and snorted out the cheroot smoke that had immediately begun to invade her throat.

'All right,' she said. 'We'll go the rounds now of Roughouse's London friends. You've got the list I gave you?'

'Told me to keep it, didn't you?'

'I did. So, who lives nearest to where we are now?'

Bolshy peered at the copy Harriet had made of what she had written down from Kailash Gokhale's Zealots Register, tobacco-stained finger moving slowly from name to name. Then he looked up.

'Hey,' he said. 'Marcus Fledge? He's a suspect? Ain't he the boss of — what's it? — you see the stuff all over the place, heavy machinery. Pettifer's. Read about him the other day. Paper said he'd been begged to buy up Birchester Rovers — worst club in the country, ask me — and he'd given them the correct bloody answer. Two fingers. Just that. You going to see him first?'

'No,' she said. 'I will see him. But not just yet.'

'Don't want to get your backside booted? That it?'

Harriet let an exasperated sigh escape her lips.

Yes, she thought, that probably is it, if I'm honest. Sir Marcus Fledge doesn't sound like a man who's going to pat me on the head and answer any sharp questions I may ask. Not that I won't ask them, if necessary. And, if it comes to it, I'll insist on getting more by way of answer than the two fingers he held up to poor old Birchester Rovers.

'No, DS,' she said. 'I am not delaying seeing Sir Marcus Fledge because of whatever attitude he may have to those who come begging. What I am going to do is make sure that, when I do see him, I'll know all there is to know about him. So, I asked: who's nearest to us now?'

Bolshy, subdued, went back to the list.

'Feller called Cookbury. Lives bit north of here. St John's Wood.'

'All right. But, no. Better give him a buzz. May well be out, Sunday afternoon.'

She waited, too impatient to think whether Martin Cookbury was really the best one to see, while Bolshy with infuriating leisureliness made his call.

'Out, all right,' he said at last. 'But you'll never guess where.'

'I don't intend to guess, DS. Where is he?'

'Working, if what the wifey says is true. *In conference.* 'Course we may find, when it comes to it, what sort of work he's doing. Nice Sunday afternoon activity.'

'Just look at my list, DS, and tell me where his place of work is.'

'Hey, see at the address you've got. Cookbury Parsons Iliff Underwood, all in one great streel.'

'It's an advertising firm. Martin Cookbury runs it.'

'So what do they want to call themselves all that for?'

'You may well ask. But it's the fashion in the advertising world, has been for years. Makes a firm look as if they've got it all.'

'Makes 'em look they're chancing their arm, ask me.'

'I dare say you're right. But let's just go there and see, Cookbury Parsons —'

'OK, OK. I can remember a few names, can't I? No need to give me all the tra-la-la.'

Tra-la-la or no tra-la-la, their long, trafficky drive to the firm's offices in Putney brought them no more than the simple discovery that Martin Cookbury could not have been the man who had come to the Masterton's doors on the evening before

221

the murder. He had been there at work, as he was now, Sunday or no Sunday. Half a dozen eager-beaver colleagues were ready to state that this was where he had been all Saturday evening from six till close on midnight, however cagey they were about whatever big campaign it was that they were planning.

Nor was the next visit they made any more productive. The stockbroker, Reginald Brown, turned out to be at home, in bed with a cold.

'Or that's what they tell me,' Bolshy said.

'So where is his home?'

'Don't you remember? Easy. *The Myrtles, Church Lane, Virginia Water.* The Myrtles, poncy bloody name like that, hard to forget. You really want to go off there?'

'Yes,' Harriet said.

But the stockbroker — very useful to the Cabal, Kailash Gokhale had commented — proved to have been every bit as much of a victim of the common cold as Bolshy had been told. Sneezes came resounding out of his bedroom as Harriet climbed the stairs at The Myrtles, followed by a wife twittering at every step 'Dear, oh dear. Dear, oh dear.'

The stricken man answered all Harriet's questions circumstantially, though in fact there was only one that called for an unequivocal response. *Where were you yesterday from about six onwards?* Answer: 'Here (sneeze) in bed (sneeze). Where else could (sneeze) I be, bloody (sneeze) cold like this?' A reply borne out by a waste-bin half filled with sodden tissues, and the remains of a hot toddy on the bedside table.

Back in London, Bolshy picked as next easiest to get to 'some silly bugger called Drummond, Tigger Drummond, God's sake.'

'It's actually Valentine Drummond. Use that mobile of yours to give him a call.'

Yes, she thought, while Bolshy was busy thumbing at his mobile's buttons, Tigger Drummond, the third man in the party who whisked Roughouse away from St Ozzie's. Him, Matthew Jessop and the surgeon, Jackson Edgeworth. Ask Tigger, when we're there, about that 'kidnap' as well? All right, I may do that. See how it goes.

After a minute Bolshy began shoving the mobile back into the gaping pocket of his seamy black-and-white dogstooth jacket.

'Not in, answer-phone says,' he announced eventually, delighted to report a set-back.

Harriet reacted sharply.

'Then we'll go there, wherever it is. Go there, and see what we can find out.'

'All right, all right. No need to bite my

head off. I was only telling you what you wanted to know.'

Drummond's flat, they found, was in a tall, distinctly antiquated building in Great George Street, on the corner of traffic-encircled Parliament Square. Toiling up its many bare-carpeted stairs to the very top — no lift to be found — Harriet rang the bell of the eyrie-like flat. The door was opened almost at once by a youngish woman with a bush of wild black hair above a deeply tanned face, a voluminous flowered apron doing little to hide feminine lushness below. Presumably, a foreign help.

With an incomprehensible muttered word and a nod of her head, she indicated that her employer was at home.

At home, yes, Harriet thought, but hiding behind that message on his answer-phone? Like a school kid concealing himself behind some flimsy curtain from a searching teacher. But to be found, if you came looking.

Tigger, tall, well-built, dressed in weekend yellow-striped rugby shirt and khaki shorts, with looks as boyish as when he had been at the Zeal School, gave Harriet a prompt reply to the one question she wanted answered.

'Last night? Where I was? Where else but

at that big party of Lady Margaret Tredannick's, down on the coast in Kent. You may have read about it in the Sundays. Gossip people there by the dozen.'

'No. No, I don't know anything about it, I'm afraid,' Harriet answered, carefully polite.

'Well, if you don't, you don't. But the fact of the matter is Margaret's a very old friend, and this was a huge coming-of-age party for her Toby. If I'd missed it, she'd never have forgiven me.'

All right, Harriet thought, I've asked my question, got his answer. Casually enough given, but I see Tigger, however successful as a toy manufacturer, as totally casual in all everyday circumstances. Amoral, perhaps the right word for someone who seems not to take any note of the conventions. At a guess, that lush young woman who let us in probably spends the nights in his bed.

So, go on to ask about that first-light dash up to St Ozzie's? No, don't think I will, after all. I'd get nothing but some off-hand half-explanation, and I had more than enough of those when I asked Matthew Jessop about that private ambulance.

All right, I suppose for the time being I'll accept Tigger's word, however carelessly provided. But if, when I've talked to the others on my list, I find I've got a full set of incontrovertible alibis, I'll get the Kent police to make inquiries about the guests at that big party and then, if they draw blank, come back to my feckless friend. What he said is quite likely the truth, but as an alibi it's by no means hundred per cent.

Right, who on my list is the next nearest? Have to ask Bolshy, when I've got all the way down to street level again.

But only one flight down the interminable stairs — no doubt bouncy Tigger takes them in his stride — she saw thump-thumping ahead of her the curvaceous foreign help, basket in hand evidently on her way to the nearest Sunday-open food shop. At once it occurred to her that, if the woman knew as much as she might about Drummond's everyday life, it might be worth finding out how well she did actually speak English. There could, if Tigger eventually bounces into the picture, be things she would know that I would want to know.

She ran on down until she was at the same level.

'Good afternoon again,' she said, with one of her broadest smiles.

'Yes. Afternoon good.'

Well, not exactly perfect communication. But something.

'Where are you from? Have you been here in England long?'

At once an evasive look in her eyes.

Of course, illegal immigrant. Should have taken that into account, asked something less direct.

'Well, never mind how long you've been here. It means nothing to me. Nothing at all.'

And it was plain she had found the right reassuring words. Head lifted in relief.

'But, tell me, what's your name? Your first name? It's good to know.'

'Is Maria.'

'So have you been working for Mr Drummond for long, Maria?'

'Two — three year.'

'And he's a good employer?'

'Employer, what is?'

Right, that tells me something.

'I mean, is he good to work for? Kind? Helpful?'

'He was bringing from my home where all-all was bad. Now is not bad, but he is knowing about me.'

The cautious and convoluted reply told Harriet a little more. Plainly, Tigger had got hold of his Maria in some wretched country in Europe or from somewhere even in remote Turkey, and had seen that, if he smuggled her into Britain, she would be in his debt, a useful servant to do the cleaning, go marketing, cook his breakfast before he set off happily for his toy-making factory, and be bed-fodder as well.

'So where is your home, Maria?' she asked with a pretence of idle curiosity.

'Is Transabistan.'

Transabistan. Right, I know about Transabistan. It came in *Marching Through Georgia,* and Matthew Jessop had those striking blown-up photographs of the place, made when he went there to film for the book.

For once those often quoted words from Lewis Carroll, *curiouser and curiouser,* seem appropriate. Two members of the secretive Cabal, marching through that little dictator-ruled country. And two of them in the three who snatched Roughouse from St Ozzie's.

Right, now what? Better pick up on the ambiguous answer Maria gave to my *Is he good to work for?*

'So you don't always find Mr Drummond kind and helpful?'

'He not have me in his bed no more. He put me in little room with so many luggages.'

So, yes, I was right. A useful servant and a night-time plaything, but now discarded.

She produced for rejected Maria an understanding smile of sorts, and turned to go on down the stairs. Down and down.

But then a thought checked her.

All right, Maria is afraid Tigger could, at any time he likes, give her away as an illegal immigrant. So she must stick there, relegated to the box-room, to clean and cook as long as he wants. But can I go one better, use Maria as a spy in his camp?

Can I actually plant a toy on the toymaker? Equip Maria with my own little toy-like mobile? Be able to contact her on it whenever I like? Keep an eye, or an ear, on at least one of the Cabal members, if perhaps a party-goer not altogether likely as the man who suffocated sleeping Robert Roughhouse?

No. Come on. Is someone like slap-happy bouncy Tigger the sort to have so determinedly forced his way into the Masterton and ruthlessly put an end to Robert Roughouse's life? Isn't it much more likely, a whole lot more likely, that last night Tigger was cheerfully dancing away down in remote Kent? Surely I don't need to hand over my last physical tie with dead Graham because of him?

But . . . But, yes, John, however affected he still is by Graham's death himself, plainly thinks that I shouldn't keep on cherishing the toy as I do. And he's probably right. I mustn't become like one of those mothers of a killed-in-action soldier who make a shrine of the room they once had, every old schoolbook, every stuck-together model aeroplane, never touched, never moved.

She turned decisively round and marched back up to where Maria was still standing watching her.

'Maria, listen. Pay attention. I am a police officer.' Warrant card flicked open. 'And you, you are here in England illegally. You know what *illegally* means?'

'Please no . . .'

The desperate note of appeal was answer enough, even apart from the look of appalled dismay in the deep-brown eyes.

'All right, now listen again. It might — what shall I say? — it might suit me not to report you. If you will do what I ask.'

'Yes, please?'

Abject willingness.

'Maria, I may need to know things about Mr Drummond. That's why I came to see him. Do you understand what I'm saying?'

'Yes-yes.'

From her handbag Harriet, forcing herself not to think what it was she was doing, extracted the bright toy-like mobile, and fixed it to call nobody but herself while able either to chirp its presence aloud or, a switch flicked, simply to give a quiet rattle in a pocket.

'Do you know what this is?' she asked.

'Yes-yes. Ev'body know. Mobile, mobile.'

'If I teach you how to —'

'Know. Know. Ev'body know.'

All right, I'll do it. Hand it over. Some risk involved if Tigger ever gets to see it, but surely not much, now there are no more bed times.

Laboriously she explained the little machine's use, and the importance of keeping it hidden. Then she impressed on Maria that, if she thought it necessary, she could use it to call, day or night.

And that was all. With reason, or not, an ally installed.

Down at the car, Harriet got Bolshy to find where they could get hold of the one remaining man on her list — since Matthew Jessop, no doubt, was away filming — the surgeon, Jackson Edgeworth.

'You know where he is, Old Slice-'em-up?' Bolshy said eventually, stuffing his mobile back into the pocket of his appalling jacket.

Harriet, still fighting away thoughts of what she had just done, fell for it.

'I've not the least idea.'

'Bloody golf course,' Bolshy brought out. 'Along with half the consultants in the book.'

'When I want your views on the medical profession, DS, I'll ask for them.'

'OK, OK. Thought you'd like a joke, bloody terrible day we're having. But, if you must know, old Edgeworth's busy earning himself yet more dosh. Private nursing home, out Hampstead way.'

'Then get me there, if you please,' Harriet said.

So it was in sullen silence that Bolshy drove back across London to Hampstead. Drawn up in the road outside the nursing home, they saw just coming out a tall well-dressed man and heard a female voice from inside eagerly calling 'Goodnight, Mr Edgeworth.' Bolshy, at once ran to intercept, striding straight over the nursing home's low surrounding garden wall.

'Not exactly the best of times for me,' Jackson Edgeworth said, when Harriet having walked the long way round by the double driveway, had told him who she was and that she wanted to speak to him about anything he might know concerning Robert Roughouse's recent activities, the excuse she had in the course of the day grown all too used to producing.

'I don't suppose you realise, Superintendent,' he replied, 'what a strain an emergency gynaecological operation puts upon a surgeon, even on one who is well-accustomed to performing it. If you've ever sat a major exam, the procedure is in that class of arduousness. You mustn't expect me to be entirely coherent at this moment.'

Sob stuff, Harriet found herself thinking. Whatever *procedure* he's just undertaken can hardly have been that hazardous if it took place in the nursing home here. And what about that nasty little put-down of *if you've ever sat a major exam,* as if it was totally unlikely that any police officer, even a senior one, would have done so.

But why is he being so immediately hostile? And at the same time — the too handsome bugger — so quick to seek womanly sympathy?

Can this possibly be my man? He's the right type. A surgeon, and a successful one, used to taking instant decisions, knife in hand. And, yes, damn him, hasn't he been, right from the first moment, busy creating a swirl of fog about what he was actually doing at the time that up in Birrshire a man was asking Tonelle those stupid questions?

Is this why I've taken an immediate dislike to him, the arbitrator of life and death?

Wait, no. No, mustn't let an upsurge of prejudice affect me. If he's going to lie to me, as I think he may be preparing to do, I must weigh altogether disinterestedly what he says, and how he looks when he says it. Or I'll get it wrong.

So put my real question to him straight-away, point-blank? Why not? Catch him, possibly, wrong-footed?

'Mr Edgeworth, where exactly were you last night from, say, six or seven o'clock onwards?'

No look of surprise. And there should have been. Because I wasn't asking about what I'd told him I'd come here to find out.

'Seven o'clock? Last night? Let me see. Well, I suppose I would have just arrived at the Royal Society of Medicine about that time. I often dine there after a hard day in the theatre. I was alone, of course. But I dare say one of the waiters in the dining room will remember me.'

Harriet took out her notebook and pretended to jot this down.

A witness's behaviour, believing one's eye is off them, more than once has enabled me to jump on a falsehood.

But on this occasion the ruse failed. Jackson Edgeworth stood there just looking, exaggeratedly or not, drained of energy.

Which may mean he has simply given me the facts. Or, equally, could he be still preparing to present me with a complex lie?

'So you dined at the Royal Society of Medicine . . . ?'

'Ah well, it may have been there. Or it may have been at one of my clubs. I belong to several, of course. I really was so bushed last night — my operation had been within an ace of going desperately wrong — that really I can't tell you where it was I found myself sitting all alone at a table, wondering whether I had the strength to eat whatever I'd ordered.'

'I understand,' Harriet said, laying on the overt sympathy.

Or do I understand something quite different? That all this stuff means you're looking for a nicely imprecise alibi?

'But I'm afraid,' she went on, 'this will make checking your statement — something we have, of course, to do — fairly difficult. I mean, can you tell me, here and now, what clubs you actually belong to?'

A pale smile. The wounded warrior?

'I'm sorry. But if I'm to do that without mistake, I will have to leave it to tomorrow. I really will.'

By which time, Harriet thought sourly, you'll have been able to persuade a club waiter somewhere that you and he had a nice little chat last night at seven, or eight, or nine o'clock.

A wave of irritated weariness lapped over her.

Really, to have to catch hold of a slithering fellow like this, it's too much. And he'll be bloody hard to pin down, too. Happy to go on inventing reason after reason not to be explicit about just where he was. And, worse, isn't it possible he has some other object altogether in not being willing to give me a simple answer. A woman? Very likely. Look at the way that female voice just now called out her goodnight to him.

Turn it in then? No. No, damn it, I'm a police officer, a detective, I don't get weary. But, on the other hand, this 'exhausted' surgeon is obviously quite ready to go on and on with his little game. So, why not catch him out at another time? He won't run away. Total admission of guilt if he were to.

'Then I'll expect to hear from you,' she said. 'Here's my card, ring me as soon as you've sorted yourself out.'

She made her way off to the car.

Bolshy, she saw with irritation, had, once more, gone straight to the garden's pretty little surrounding wall and crossed it in a single stride. He was standing impertinently holding the car's door wide.

The slob, he's quite wrong to go over the wall like that. If a wall's there, however low it is, it's meant to be an obstacle you don't ignore. It's a taboo.

'Back to Birchester,' she said.

And for all the journey she remained furiously silent.

CHAPTER SIXTEEN

Early though Harriet was at her office next morning, as she opened the door she heard her phone ring. It was the ACC.

'Superintendent Martens, I'd be obliged if you would come over directly.'

Oho, Harriet thought, in ordinary circumstances he calls me simply Mrs Martens, technically incorrect though that is. But now *Superintendent?* And wanted in his office this early? Bad weather ahead.

Reluctantly she drove across to Headquarters.

'Superintendent — at last,' the ACC greeted her. 'Now, will you tell me, please, why it was only thanks to the media, the media, that I learnt that Robert Roughouse, the victim of the bomb attack at Gralethorpe which I tasked you with investigating, has been murdered in his bed at the Masterton Clinic.'

Oh God, I never even thought to inform

him. And I know why. It's because I didn't want him sticking his bloody finger into my pie.

She took a deep breath.

'I learnt of Roughouse's death barely twenty-four hours ago, sir. I went immediately to the Masterton where I was able to ascertain that the man who smothered him had made some inquiries there the evening before. Since I had come to the provisional conclusion that the attack in Gralethorpe may have been instigated by a secret group of ex-Zeal School pupils, I considered it imperative to ask, before news of the murder was broadcast, such members of the group whose names I knew where they had been at the time.'

'Did you indeed? And could you not, despite that commendably rapid reaction, have picked up a telephone and kept me informed?'

Harriet chose to take that question, sharply put though it was, as being rhetorical.

Still, nothing for it now, she thought, but to produce everything I've discovered about the Cabal.

With scarcely any pause for breath she embarked on her account, finishing at last with what yesterday's inquiries in London had brought to light.

'So, sir, I am left with two people whose alibis for that night are, you may say, open to doubt. There's Valentine Drummond, who told me he was at a large coming-of-age party down in Kent, something difficult to check on, and there's Jackson Edgeworth, the surgeon, who went so far as to claim he was unable to tell me exactly where he ate dinner that evening.'

She took a deep breath.

Something more she had to say.

'And, sir, there is, as well, someone also known to me as a member of the Cabal, perhaps even its head, whom I have not yet been able to contact. Sir, he is Sir Marcus Fledge, the chairman of Pettifer's.'

Now the ACC, who had settled down to hear her account with at least his full attention, jack-in-a-boxed up in his chair.

'Sir Marcus Fledge? Superintendent, are you telling me you have taken it into your head to think that the chairman of a firm of the repute of Pettifer's — good God, it accounts on its own for a substantial part of the country's exports — to think that a man of his standing can be involved in some petty, just possibly illegal, activity of some sort. An activity about which you have given me no details whatsoever?'

Yes, I do think he could be involved, Harriet said to herself. Nothing I've heard about the man has told me he's incapable of being an active participant in whatever it is the Cabal is planning. Once someone gathers up as many millions as they can possibly want, all too often they come to think they have a right — yes, a positive right — to acquire more and more and more. There are examples enough, for God's sake.

The expression on the ACC's face was growing more disapproving by the second.

'Superintendent,' he said at last, 'I am not going to order you no longer to pursue this line of inquiry. If you have even the slightest reason to think that one member or another of this group is involved in a conspiracy that has led to murder, then you must at least do what you can to see that each member accounts for where they were when Roughouse was killed. But, as for your claiming Sir Marcus Fledge is involved, at that I will draw the line.'

'But, sir,' Harriet felt bound to answer, 'if, as I understand is the case, Sir Marcus is a member of this group, the Cabal, possibly at the head of it, and I am to question all the other members, how can I leave him out?'

The ACC's eyes glittered like those of an

241

enraged cat.

Harriet well knew that he was a man whose bad books it was easy to get into, and very hard to get out of. But she could not stop herself now.

'Sir,' she repeated, 'you must see that if you insist on me obeying your instruction, I will have no other course open to me other than to abandon the inquiry and state my reasons for doing so.'

'Superintendent, are you threatening me?'

'No, sir. No. I am just attempting to put to you the logic of the matter.'

A long pause.

'Very well, Superintendent, then do as you think fit. And I hope for your sake, and for the sake of your career in the Greater Birchester Police, that you are not making an utter fool of yourself.'

And so I may be, she thought. All very well for me to be determined to go down to London again and interview the chairman of Pettifer's, to question him about where he was and who was with him at the time an unknown man came to the door of the Masterton and asked ridiculous questions. Yet, when all's said and done, have I really got all that much to go on? All right, Charity told me Rob Roughouse had been so deeply disturbed by some demand Sir Marcus, apparently, had made to him that he had woken, almost gibbering, from a nightmare.

But, understandably the ACC will hardly want to hear that I am relying on the evidence of a young athlete from distant Kenya when I claim Sir Marcus Fledge, prominent industrialist, is involved in some business that has eventually made Roughouse's death imperative. But it's what I've come to believe, damn it, and I'm going to test that belief to the end.

Pettifer House, Harriet saw as Bolshy brought their car to a halt outside it, was one of the many toweringly triumphal buildings put up in the City during the last quarter of the twentieth century. But now, looking up at it, she saw it as doing no more than reflect 'rather dull' Sir Marcus Fledge. Big-built and indefinably menacing.

It was more than an hour after she had marched past the two — two — heavily uniformed commissionaires outside and reached an immensely long reception desk, dead on the dot for her appointment, that she got confirmation, of a sort, for her picture of Pettifer House's owner. From the moment she had reached the long desk she had experienced, simply, unexplained and inexplicable delays. Shunted from one more-than-smartly dressed receptionist to another, her sense of being seen as an irritating chip of something or other interfering with the mighty stream of Pettifer business grew and grew.

Am I, she asked herself, to sit here on my own, sunk into this long, soft, grey leather sofa, looking at those huge wall-to-wall photographs of giant earth-moving machines, *unmatched world over* — words not just displayed but inscribed above them — until at last I am spat out into the world of little people going about their little businesses and am seen no more?

At last, however, her presence reached, apparently, the sole receptionist empowered to have contact with Pettifer's mighty chairman.

A marble smile was directed towards her.

'Sir Marcus is still at lunch, Superintendent. But, no doubt, he will be able to see you as soon as he returns.'

A stream of sarcastic answers entered Harriet's head. *Does Sir Marcus always give appointments he has no intention of honouring? Yes, of course, I realise that the chairman of Pettifer's cannot see a Detective Superintendent of Police until he has fortified himself . . .*

She suppressed them. What would be the

use? It's *Power, infinity: Police nil.*

And even after the generous allowance of time she gave the lunching giant, and the several inquiries she had made to the marble figure of the receptionist at Sir Marcus's sole disposal she still had a long wait on her barge of a sofa, staring ever more glassily at the huge photographs on the walls beside her. But at last she got her signal. A mere inclination of a queenly head.

A speed-lift, entirely dedicated she saw to the firm's chairman, shot her up twenty or more floors. Only for her to have to wait another 'few minutes' since, his secretary said, Sir Marcus 'is taking a call from the States'.

Then at last a discreet buzz, and it was 'Sir Marcus will see you now'.

She found him seated at the far side of a bare glass-topped desk, so big it made her think of a never-swum-in pool in some huge garden. There he was, a bulky shape in businessman's standard dark suit, and de rigueur white shirt, with, implacable across it, a richly silk necktie in broad red-and-white stripes. The Zealots tie.

From two small, red-rimmed eyes she received an unblinking stare, fully justifying Charity's *pig-faced.* And not a word uttered.

Ignoring that, Harriet went straight in.

'Sir Marcus, I am making inquiries in connection with the murder of Mr Robert Roughhouse at the Masterton Clinic in Birrshire between the hours of 10 p.m. and 8.30 a.m. the night before last. I understand Mr Roughhouse was an associate of yours in an informal group of ex-Zeal School pupils called the Cabal, and I would —'

Sir Marcus exploded, one feather-light touch setting off a devastating magnetic mine.

'What do you know about any so-called Cabal? Who told you anything about it? A purely private affair. You have no business whatsoever to call to account anyone who is, or might be, a member.'

Harriet made herself pay no attention to the illogical farrago.

'I would like, Sir Marcus,' she said, 'to be told where you were at the time in question.'

'You have no right — Listen to me, a man in my position does not have to answer questions from any police officer whatsoever, unless he has, if he so wishes, the protection of his legal advisers.'

'Very good, sir. Can we, here and now, make an appointment for me to interview you in the presence of your solicitor, at whatever time in the immediate future is convenient to us both?'

'No,' came the single cannon-shot from the weight-heavy figure on the far side of the desk's glassy pool.

'Then I must tell you, Sir Marcus, that if you are adamant in failing to respond to a request from a police officer conducting an investigation into a serious crime — the most serious crime on the statute book — it may become my duty to arrest you and take you into custody.'

A long glowering silence spread out to fill the softly carpeted room like an oppressive, nose-pricking mist of gas. At last to be broken.

'Very well, if only to put an end to all this bureaucratic nonsense, I was — let me see — yes, I was at home that evening. My house, Cherrytrees Court, is in Surrey, just outside Chertsey, more than a hundred miles from Birrshire, as you can easily ascertain if you are able to consult a map. I was there from about half-past six, and all that night. Most of it in bed, if you must know, beside my wife of twelve years.'

'Thank you, sir, for your cooperation. I will, of course, have to confirm your statement, but I can assure you I will be completely tactful when speaking to your wife.'

She turned away — she had never been asked to take a chair — and began to walk

247

towards the distant door.

Almost there, she turned and, by no means wholly satisfied with the extent of her victory, tried a last shot.

'Oh, and by the way, Sir Marcus, may I ask, do you own racehorses? Do you go to race meetings on occasion?'

For a moment she tried to picture his big, plainly balding head under the sort of brown felt hat worn by so many people in the paddock, the kind Tonelle had said her inquisitive six o'clock visitor had drawn down over the upper part of his face.

'Superintendent, or whatever you call yourself, let me tell you that you have asked me the last impertinent question I am prepared to hear.'

Down at the car Bolshy asked his own impertinent question. 'You were a hell of a long time, guv. Get nowhere, did you?'

Harriet decided she would reply, little though she was inclined to.

'Get anywhere with Sir Marcus Fledge, chairman of Pettifer's? Well, yes, I did get somewhere. In the end. He produced an alibi for the time of Roughouse's murder. One culminating in his being in bed beside his loving wife.'

'As per usual with alibis. I'll believe his

when we've seen the lady. And probably not then.'

'You're right, DS. But we can be quicker about it than that. Just use your mobile to get on to the police in Chertsey, Surrey. My compliments, and could they send, as soon as possible, an officer of some seniority to Sir Marcus Fledge's house, Cherrytrees Court, somewhere in their area, and ask his wife whether he was there last night? And from what time onwards. With luck they'll get to her before Fledge thinks of ringing the lady and telling her what to say.'

OK, she thought, anything more to do now that I'm down in London again? There's Matthew Jessop, of course. Should ask his whereabouts like all the rest, and I haven't yet managed to find out why he told Charity without any explanation not to visit Robert Roughouse at the Masterton. But . . . but I don't know. Think of what he was like crouching over the horribly wounded body of the man who was his best friend. I thought then, when the light of my torch shone on his face for an instant, that I glimpsed the diamond sparkle of a tear. Is it conceivable that he was the man who held a pillow over Roughouse's head? All right, I will see him eventually, but not until I've exhausted every other possibility.

So what now?

Yes, Tigger Drummond's hardly perfect alibi. Time to make a check, I think. Get him dealt with one way or another.

She set Bolshy to finding a number for Lady Margaret Tredannick. A call to her wherever it is down in Kent that she has her big house and I may learn she spent half the evening actually talking with Tigger or I may get the name of a reliable witness who did that.

It took Bolshy more than a little time to do what she had asked. But when at last he pushed his mobile away he had good news.

'You know what? Turns out Lady Whatsit's got a little pad right here in the Smoke. Belgrave Square. And she's there now.'

'Is she indeed? Then I think I'll pay a call straightaway. If you can find Belgrave Square.'

'Dare say I can manage,' he said, flipping at the pages of his *A-Z* guide. 'Anybody's lived in London knows where that is.'

'Then go.'

But it was almost four o'clock when, after a swing round Belsize Square somewhere north of Swiss Cottage, Bolshy pulled the car up outside Lady Margaret Tredannick's house. And, no sooner had he done so —

squeal of brakes — than the mobile in the pocket of his appalling jacket sang out its little tune, one that Harriet immediately recognised, the ribald *Roll me over in the clover. Roll me over, lay me down and do it again,* all too familiar from her nights of patrolling as a constable.

And now, she thought, it will repeat and repeat itself in my head for the rest of the day. Damn the man.

'For you, boss,' Bolshy said, holding out the mobile with an ironic sketch of a bow.

It was the Surrey Police DI who had gone out to Sir Marcus Fledge's Cherrytrees Court. Mrs Fledge — 'bit of a stunner, actually' — had precisely confirmed what her husband had said. 'Got the impression, though, that the lady might have had a chat with hubby on the mobile.'

'Yes, I was afraid of that, DI. But thank you all the same.'

'Pipped to the post,' she said to Bolshy. 'Seems the wife's a stunner, and a liar.'

'Old Fledge our prime then?'

'Not necessarily. There could be a dozen other reasons why he didn't want to tell me the truth. A reason, for instance, even more stunner-like than his wife.'

'As per usual.'

'If you like.'

■ ■ ■ ■

Lady Margaret Tredannick was all that her two distinguished addresses indicated she might be. Pale face, cool on its frame of 'good bones' — Harriet felt a dart of envy — well adapted to looking down a Roman nose from a considerable height even as she sat there in her high-backed chair.

'Really, I cannot see how my private entertainment can possibly be any business of the police from — where was it, Birchester?' she said as soon as Harriet had told her she wanted to establish whether Mr Valentine Drummond had been down in Kent at the party for her son's coming-of-age.

'However, I am afraid that Mr Drummond's presence there is a matter for us.'

'Then can't you come back at some other time? I have just rung for my tea.'

'Lady Margaret, I have come down from Birchester in furtherance of inquiries into the murder of Mr Robert Roughouse, which you may have heard about, and all I need from you is an answer to a simple question. Was Mr Drummond present at your party?'

'Oh, yes, Robert. Poor, poor Robert. I knew him, of course. A good friend from the younger set. It seems no one is safe nowadays.'

None of which answers my question.

'That is as may be,' Harriet said. 'But I need to ascertain Mr Drummond's whereabouts that evening, together with, let me say, the whereabouts of a number of other people.'

'Frankly, I cannot see that Tigger Drummond's presence or not at my party at Ravenham can have anything to do with Robert's death.'

Harriet suppressed a sigh of frustration.

'The particular reason for my inquiry is, as you will appreciate, a confidential police matter. But I can assure you that what you can tell me is of vital importance.'

'Of vital importance?' Lady Margaret allowed the finely traced eyebrows on her frost-pale face to rise a little. 'Superintendent, do you know how many people there were at my party?'

'No, madam, I do not. But, may I say, if you cannot give me your personal assurance that you spoke to, or even simply saw, Mr Drummond that evening, I shall have to ask for the complete list of your guests.'

'Indeed? And you believe you are entitled, somehow, to make such a request?'

'If you cannot prove to me by any other

means that Mr Drummond was at Ravenham House that evening, then, yes, I will
ask you for that list.'

'Suppose there isn't a copy of it? A private
person does not necessarily indulge in the
filling-in in triplicate nonsense that seems
to be the way the police investigate crime
these days.'

Too much of a wriggle, surely.

'Lady Margaret, I am formally requesting
a copy of your guest list for the party that
took place at your address, Ravenham
House, last Saturday.'

She was rewarded by a plain, unaristo-
cratic look of fury. But an answer came.

'Very well, Superintendent, I will let you
have that list. But let me tell you: your
request may be within your powers as a
police officer, though I shall consult my
legal friends as to that, but it is, beyond
doubt, a violation of the accepted rules of
hospitality.'

'That may be so. But, if it is, then I must
violate those undefined rules.'

She almost held out her hand for the list.
But Lady Margaret had more to say.

'Now that I remember, Superintendent,'
she went on, with an angry little breath of a
sigh. 'I believe I did see Valentine during
the course of the evening, or rather of the

night, because the party went on, naturally for an occasion of such importance, until almost dawn. I cannot say that I particularly spoke to him — there were so many other people it was one's duty to pay some attention to — but I can assure you Valentine was definitely present.'

Then an obviously sudden new thought.

'Oh, and, if you are not satisfied, there is someone else who could quite simply confirm his presence. She's the writer of a column in that rather new magazine everybody is talking about, whatever it's called. The daughter of an old friend from my time at Roedean, who married one of the Morgan-Woods. Daphne the girl's name is, though of course she doesn't use it in the magazine. She's Debra Delaville there. I suppose you could talk to her, if you want.'

But Harriet, during the lengthy explanation, had had ample opportunity to fasten her attention on Lady Margaret from top to toe. And she had seen, not any tightening of long-fingered hands but a small wave pass across the shimmering material of the silken skirt of her white dress that told of the tension in the legs below. A lie had been uttered.

But nothing to be gained from directly accusing Lady Margaret without any real evidence. A woman with *legal* friends, as Lady Margaret had been at pains to make clear she had, could at the least make a noisy fuss.

'Then let me say that you have been of considerable assistance to our investigation. If you would send me that list — here's my card — I won't need to trouble you any further. Thank you.'

Oh, yes, she thought as she left the house, you have 'been of assistance' all right, Lady Margaret. I rather think now Tigger Drummond, though invited to your party, may never have shown up.

And I think I can see a way to prove that.

CHAPTER SEVENTEEN

In the car, Bolshy threw onto the pavement the end of the cheroot he had been sloppily smoking. Harriet did nothing to rebuke him. She had fixed on her next necessary move.

If Lady Margaret has put herself out to feed me the name of 'Debra Delaville', she must have meant me to contact the young lady to be told by her that, yes, Tigger Drummond was there at the party.

'Get on the Net fast,' she snapped to Bolshy, 'and find out the name of a classy women's magazine with a lady called Debra Delaville on its staff.'

How many times, she asked herself as she waited boiling with impatience, have I met with vagueness and mystification in the course of this now-you-see-it now-you-don't investigation? Quite enough anyhow to make me determined this time to push my way through to the truth of at least something.

It took Bolshy scarcely longer than she had hoped to produce the information that 'Debra Delaville' had her column in a magazine called *All the Way Round,* its address in a street just north of Piccadilly.

'Right, get there,' she said. 'And to hell with the thirty miles-an-hour rule, just like every other driver on the road. A rule no one holds to is no rule at all.'

'Law's an arse, right?' Bolshy shouted, as the car already went over that limit.

'The word's *ass.* Charles Dickens' rules.'

Barely ten minutes later Harriet entered the smarter-than-paint premises of *All the Way Round.*

'Yes, Debra's in. Who shall I say wants to see her?'

Blessing the fact that she was not in uniform and that Bolshy had not parked the evident police car directly in front of the building, Harriet simply replied 'I've just got a message for her, from Lady Margaret Tredannick. But it's rather a complicated one I'm afraid, so I'd better see her.'

She listened hard for the words she heard then coming from the phone the receptionist had picked up. If they indicated in any way that 'Debra Delaville' had already spoken to Lady Margaret, then, however fast Bolshy had driven, she would be too late. But, it seemed, thank goodness, that Lady Margaret's afternoon tea had taken priority over phoning her old schoolfriend's daughter.

In a moment the receptionist said she could go up. She rapidly made for the lift — was the teacup being finally put down on its saucer? — and in its narrow, wardrobe-like interior was whirred up to the fourth floor.

In the three minutes since entering Debra Delaville's office and being waved to a chair while she took a call Harriet had had an excellent opportunity to assess a witness she hoped would give a plain account of Lady Margaret's party. Daphne Morgan-Woods, as Harriet soon began to think of the blonde blue-eyed columnist, was an impressive young woman. No doubt she must have been helped into her bizarrely influential job through some old-boy, or old-girl, network, but the longer the conversation had gone on the plainer it had become that she was no simpering fool.

So Harriet was quick — that phone might ring again at any moment — to speak as soon as the receiver was put back down.

'Miss Morgan-Woods, I am here to ask

you something about the party at Raven-ham House on Saturday which, I understand, you attended.'

'A duty, and a pleasure. I used to date Toby Tredannick once. A nice boy. But, for God's sake, not *Miss Morgan-Woods*. It's Daphne, if not Daff.'

'Daphne, then. And what I've come to find out from you — I should say I'm inquiring into the murder of Robert Rough-ouse at the Masterton Clinic in Birrshire on Saturday-Sunday night — is how much you saw of Val Drummond, or Tigger as I believe his friends call him, when you were at the party?'

She got a sharply inquiring look from those wide blue eyes.

'Yes, Tigger. Well, I must —'

The phone rang. And another pouncing conversation followed, lasting to Harriet's fury, rather longer than three minutes, although she had to concede Daphne seemed to have used the extra time well.

But at last she put the receiver down.

'Sorry, bloody thing keeps ringing. Mostly people eventually calling back, I'm afraid. They do that for me. But you were asking about Tigger.'

And, yes, Harriet registered, all the while you were listening to that call, interrupting and questioning whoever you were talking to, you've had ample time to decide that if I'm inquiring about Tigger Drummond you may have to be guarded in your answers.

'Yes, Mr Valentine Drummond,' she said. 'I want to know if you saw him, or, better, if you spoke with him during that evening.'

'Tigger. Yes. OK, I don't want to —'

The phone once more. But this conversation was very short.

'Aunty M? Look, sorry but I'm desperately busy just now. Got a —' Voice dropped to an exaggeratedly confidential tone. 'Got none other than a royal's equerry here with me. Can't . . .'

And, despite a squawking sound from the far end, the receiver gently replaced.

Right, no doubt about who that call was from, even if 'Aunty M' was the name mentioned. Lady Margaret Tredannick must have finished her tea and had now attempted to make the call she had planned.

But, hey, who had Daphne claimed was actually in this room with her? A royal equerry. Very clever, very quick. No other visitor would have taken precedence. So in an instant did Daphne guess — perhaps Lady Margaret had just said something that gave her a clue — why she was being called? And has she realised there's something this police officer from Birchester is not meant to be told?

So, what now?

The answer, which came straightaway, was extremely surprising.

'No,' Daphne said, 'I never did see Tigger Drummond at the party, let alone did I talk to him.'

She gave Harriet an unblinking look from those dazzling blue eyes.

'I think you can take it, Superintendent,' she said, 'that he absolutely wasn't at Ravenham House on Saturday night. I was there from start to finish, doing my journalistic duty, and I keep my eyes very well open at a do like that.'

Harriet sat there, hardly daring to believe that she had heard a plain and unequivocal declaration that Tigger Drummond, member of the Cabal, off-hand tosser-out of an alibi for the time of Robert Roughouse's murder, had been telling a plain lie when he had said he was down in Kent. It came to her then — in a topsy-turvying fresh look — that the nickname Tigger, which from the moment of first hearing it she had thought must be that of someone from the world of Pooh Bear, Piglet and pessimistic Eeyore was nothing of the kind. Bouncy, yes bouncy, ever-active and ready-to-go Tigger was a man who had made a great deal of money from manufacturing the enormously successful Tiger Man toy. He was the boy at the Zeal School who had shown his friends the original, homemade tiger toy he had cleverly constructed. He was a man who surely would have been capable of making with his own hands a contrivance to send an egg-sized grenade flying over a distance as long as that from Gralethorpe's Methodist chapel to its dingy old town hall.

Was it him even who had fired the shot Percival Pidgeon had said sounded like *a fowling-piece?*

No, she thought. No, no reason at that time for anyone in the Cabal to have risked their life when, with all the money they seemed to have they could have found a man to hire.

'I'm glad, very glad, you've told me what you have,' she said to Daphne. 'I think the end of all this is not so far off now.'

'Yes, I can see it might be.' A pause, well-glossed cherry-red lips pushed forward in an O of churning thought. 'And I think I've got more information you ought to have.'

But then nothing followed.

Is she still in a quandary over what to tell me? Or how much?

All right, let her sit thinking for a few moments more. At a point like this one over-insistent question can dry up a source for ever.

Almost a minute passed.

'Superintendent, have you ever heard of something called the Cabal?'

The Cabal. Harriet's heart gave a leap. So right to the centre of it. Surely I've been correct all along in my suspicions, half-suspicions, floating-away suspicions, insistently recurring suspicions, on little evidence or none.

'Yes,' she said, 'I have indeed —'

And the phone rang again.

Daphne picked it up, barked 'Call back' and plunged it on to its rest.

'I think it might be better,' she said, as if there had been no break in the conversation, 'if you told me, first, all you yourself know about the Cabal.'

'Right. To begin with, it's a group, a small group and, I think, getting smaller, of men who were all at the Zeal School at much the same time, with perhaps one older new-comer. In fact, I gather from what I've been told, that it started out as just an informal arrangement to meet — to dine and no more — every now and again. I think Rob-ert Roughouse himself put forward the idea.'

'A typically Rob thing to do,' Daphne said,

in a touched-in aside. 'Starting something up, and then finding it's too much for him.'

'And, if I'm not mistaken, it then grew, perhaps over some years, into something more? Something distinctly businesslike. And now . . .'

She hesitated, looked at Daphne to see if they were still travelling on the same line.

'Now,' she went on, reassured, 'I believe the Cabal has some project in hand that goes rather beyond the boundaries of everyday business.'

'Not to say that it's probably highly illegal,' Daphne put in. 'OK. You're in the picture.'

'I'm encouraged to find you think so. But now let me hear what you know.'

'With some names, I think. You know a girl — OK, an attractive girl — who keeps her eyes and ears open can learn a lot of things she isn't supposed to know. So, how about Sir Marcus Fledge, chairman of Pettifer's?'

'And, from what I gathered, more or less, when I went to see him a man perfectly willing to break the rules, provided he can cover up doing so. Something not as difficult as one might expect if you've almost unlimited money to play with.'

'All right. But do you know anything

about Pettifer's as a concern?'

Harriet was about to say that she hardly did when a recollection from her long wait in the lobby of Pettifer House came back to her.

'They make earth-shifting machinery,' she said. 'It seems to be the big thing with them.'

'You're near the nub of it there, I think. If what I've sort of had at the back of my mind is true, my sort of wondering whether I was just indulging in some hare-brained fantasy —'

'No,' Harriet broke in sharply. 'No, Robert Roughouse, once the leading spirit in the Cabal, has been murdered. Murdered at a second attempt.'

'Yes, and there was that first extraordinary business. Where was it? Near your part of the world, I think.'

'In Gralethorpe. And, yes, extraordinary enough. So extraordinary, so odd, that it actually points, in a way, to something almost childishly conspiratorial. Like the Cabal.'

'You're right. But, yes, there's nothing at all childish about what happened to Rob Roughouse. When, of course, Tigger Drummond was not, definitely not, at the party for Toby Tredannick.'

CHAPTER EIGHTEEN

About to step into *All the Way Round*'s wardrobe-like lift again, Harriet abruptly changed her mind. The last thing I want now, she thought, is to find myself sitting in a swirl of cheroot smoke next to grumbling Bolshy. No, what I want is somewhere quiet where I can sit and think. So, a back-exit. Must be one.

She glanced round.

Yes, stairs. Unlit. Just what I want.

She took them at full speed, clatter, clatter, clatter. And there in the basement she saw in the dim light what she was looking for. A heavy door with a push-bar to open it.

Out into a narrow area. A flight of gritty iron steps leading up to street-level. Up, up.

At the top, breathing hard, she looked to left and right. No street-name to be seen, though a *One Way* sign stood out. Never mind what the street's called, must run parallel to where Bolshy's waiting for me. As good a spot as any. And, yes, there at the far end what looks like a coffee shop.

Seated in a narrow mustard-coloured leather armchair next to the window, a cup of something-or-other on the low table in front of her, she pulled out her notebook and began haphazardly jotting.

Tigger not at the party. The Number One fact. So does that prove he's the man in the race-goers' brown felt hat who talked to Tonelle? No. But it certainly can have been him. Tall, well-built, right accent, if what Bolshy said about *pooftahs* wasn't one of his undirected baseless jibes. And, at that one brief meeting I had with Drummond I was conscious, I realise now, of a vague dislike he had for the police, the way he simply dismissed my saying I knew nothing about the party down in Kent with that casual *if you don't, you don't.* Or perhaps it was his deep-seated disdain for the conventions which I unconsciously noted. Amoral, that was the word that came to me there in that flat high up above Parliament Square.

So, yes, Tigger, bouncy amoral Tigger, whom I came when Daphne Morgan-Woods was talking about him to see as care-for-nothing Valentine Drummond, has clearly the capability of eliminating Robert Roughouse if he'd become a threat to some scheme of the Cabal's. A scheme, it must be, of more than a little weight. So, acting at once, and quite possibly on his own initiative, did he block for ever the one gap through which the whole scheme might come pouring into the light of day?

For a moment she saw Robert Roughouse, once in line to be a Master of Foxhounds, as a fox himself, baying hounds in close pursuit, scrabbling at last to his earth. Only soon to find it brutally dug up.

Why did I start thinking all that? OK, the murder attempt on Roughouse, defiant supporter of hunting, was where, so to speak, I came in. A crime to be resolved, and myself by sheer chance witnessing it. So fair enough to think of Roughouse, who, as Charity suggested to me, was desperately asking himself when he had that nightmare whether he should abandon some long-held loyalty. Because, yes, would it have been because Sir Marcus Fledge had wanted him, ordered him, to go, not of course to Gralethorpe, but to Transabistan to help seize the buried wealth that lies in its huge deposit of pitchblende.

Yes, he had been a fox, dipping and dodging its way to — not the darkness of its earth but to the light of day. The truth made plain to see.

And what else did I learn from clever Daphne, truth-seeking even in the gossip columns of glossy *All the Way Round*?

Just this. That she had no hesitation in agreeing with me when I tentatively put it to her that the Cabal had grown from a group of friends dining together and indulging in a little gossip into something altogether more actively directed to a particular end. And finally she had spoken that crucial word *illegal.* The notion of the Cabal as involved in something illegal was what cautious Kailash Gokhale had also hinted at in his deserted Lincoln's Inn chambers. He pointed me, with that seemingly far-fetched story of his being locked in at the big Bristol library, to Roughouse's *Marching Through Georgia,* with its references to Transabistan and pitchblende. He had wanted to plant in my mind his own faint suspicion. But, with lawyer's caution, he did not want to speak about it directly. Yes, he wanted me to think about those words I read, and even paused over. *Little boys black-faced and shiny as niggers because of the pitchblende pebbles they kept throwing at each other.*

And, yet more. Daphne, just by asking how much I knew about Pettifer's, brought me to recall those enormous photographs of earth-shifting machines in the entrance lobby at Pettifer House, machines *unmatched world over,* perhaps then the only ones that could be used for rapidly extracting pitchblende from the earth, eventually, as John actually told me, to yield death-dealing uranium.

It's all beginning to hang together. Yes, it's as if a murderer's features are slowly emerging from the come-and-go shadows. A murderer infuriated to discover that Roughouse, that man with his own code of honour, had rebelled at last and might be on the point of discarding a long-held loyalty.

How right I was to take the half-concealed advice that *Marching Through Georgia* might be worth reading. I was right to make all that effort to get hold of it, even if in the end it was John's copy, overdue at the library, that I read. Yes, that all-night trudge in those dull footsteps has paid off.

What that single mention of pitchblende means is that Roughouse could have worked out that underneath an obscure village in Transabistan there lies a huge deposit of rare pitchblende, now immensely valuable. No doubt, when Matthew Jessop went to Transabistan, ostensibly to make a film of Robert's adventures, he had been able to ascertain that the pitchblende under that village was there in quantity enough to make mining worthwhile. No wonder he had looked disturbed when he saw me staring at those two photographs.

Yes. Oh, yes. Everything is coming together. And it's plain now why Valentine Drummond took advantage of his invitation to that big party down on the Kentish coast. It was in order to come quietly up to Birchester and, with those unlikely inquiries about 'a friend', explore the possibilities of getting into the Masterton. Then, when he was baulked by Tonelle, under cover of the darkness of that rainy night he had explored the outside of the old converted mansion. He had found the window that Bolshy in his turn had located. He had forced it, wriggled through and, shoes sodden by that night's rain, had left a trail of footsteps ending where a card in a little brass holder made plain *Mr Robert Roughouse* was asleep on the other side of the door. And he had blotted out that dangerous existence.

So what to do?

Not, plainly, go rushing round to that flat high above Parliament Square to tackle Drummond, should he even be there. But worthwhile perhaps to test if my inside informant really can use Graham's mobile.

All very well her saying *Ev'body can,* but that may have been no more than trying to establish her so-to-speak citizenship of the mobiles-mad UK.

'Maria, is that you?'

'Is Maria. You are police lady.'

'Yes, yes, I am. And I'm glad you're able to answer.'

'Ev'body can.'

'So it seems. But tell me, Maria. Is Mr Drummond at home?'

'Out. Very much out-out now. Here only when he is seeing those bad men.'

Bad men? What the hell is she talking about?

'What bad men, Maria? He's having men come to the flat? But why do you say they're bad?'

'Guns.'

'They're men with guns? Is that what you're saying?'

'Said. They are showing what guns they have. Mr Drummond telling what to do.'

God, they must be mercenaries. He's been hiring mercenaries. He's going to take them to Transabistan. Gung-ho characters have fought their way to power in other parts of the world. Yes, that's what bouncy Tigger has in mind. And that back-to-camera photo of a gun-toting exhibitionist in Jessop's drawing-room was probably not of poor Rob Roughouse but of Tigger himself. And, yes, now he's got full backing for this expedition of his. From the Cabal.

But what else did Maria just say? *Very much out-out.* Don't like that. Is he preparing to get abroad at a moment's notice? Worse, is the Cabal almost ready to put their Transabistan plan into immediate action? No, don't like this at all.

'You mean,' she asked, to make sure beyond doubt, 'that Mr Drummond's been out a lot these past few days?'

'Yes, not-not here most of day.'

'All right. Thank you. But, Maria, could you ring me and let me know, at whatever time of day it is, that he's back?'

God, will she understand all that?

'Yes, yes.'

So has she understood? Really? I'll have to assume she has. And hope.

Back at last at the car, she found it, of course, thickly grey with slowly eddying stale smoke. No time, however, for a prolonged holding open of the door. She got in, half-holding her breath, and found her mind already made up about what to do next.

'Lincoln's Inn, New Square,' she said.

Without a word Bolshy, perhaps grateful that she had made no fuss about the fug, started up.

She found, as somehow she knew she would, that Kailash Gokhale was in and willing to see her.

'You know,' she said, shaking hands, 'I envisage you here, all day and well into the evening, as it is now, head bowed over papers and books. The embodiment of the Law, that huge net supporting us all.'

The Bengali QC smiled.

'Extremely gratifying. But, alas, something of an exaggeration.'

'Yes,' Harriet agreed, with a wry smile of her own, 'there's always the law of nature, or physics, or whatever, exerting even more pressure on us all than every one of your statutes.'

'There's more. There's the law of God, whichever God you believe in. There's a sharp quotation from Robert Louis Stevenson's *Jekyll and Hyde* that I like to remind myself of, as well as reminding the occasional client. It's this: *In the law of God there is no statute of limitations.*'

'Yes,' Harriet said. 'Yes, that's something to remember, whichever God, as you say, is there not to be bound by any statutes.'

Kailash Gokhale gave her a tight little smile.

'So what has brought you here now?' he asked. 'The weight of the law or the weight of atmospheric pressure? Or the weight of the Almighty?'

'You're quite right. I haven't come just for conversation, however philosophical. I've come, in fact, for something right at the other end of the scale. I want the low-down on a number of people whom I've begun to suspect of some seriously illegal activity.'

'The Cabal. Yes, I thought the moment our Clerk rang through to say you were here that it would be the Cabal you wanted me to tell you more about. So, what have you found out yourself?' Another quick glint of a smile. 'Without prejudice.'

'All right then. A lot of guesses and suppositions, and a few hard facts.'

'Let's hear, especially the suppositions.'

'Very well. One way and another I have learnt that a prominent member of the Cabal was supposed to be down in Kent on the night that Robert Roughouse was smothered to death in the Masterton Clinic in far-off Birrshire, and that he was definitely not there.' An abrupt hesitation. 'Or, rather, that there is good evidence that he was not.'

'Yes, exactly. Valentine Drummond — for the moment let's imagine it's him we're talking about — is a great friend of Lady Margaret Tredannick. And Lady Margaret, as the whole world knows, or at least those people who glance from time to time at the gossip pages certainly know, was giving a very large party that night at Ravenham House in Kent for her son's coming-of-age. But, among all the guests there, anybody, any police officer even, would have had considerable difficulty in proving beyond reasonable doubt that any particular person was not present. I hardly need tell you how hard it is to prove a negative.'

'But I have had an assurance,' Harriet ploughed on, resolutely ignoring the legal niceties, 'a very definite assurance, from someone who knows Valentine Drummond well, that he was not at the party.'

'Very well. Evidence coming, as it must have done, from a person who's a friend of whoever it is we are discussing —' A quick smile of complicity, '. . . will carry a certain weight. But, make no mistake, only evidence gathered from everybody who was at the party stating that they never saw our friend there would in law be enough to make it likely, I say no more, that he was not present.'

Harriet felt as if, in the delightful heat of a fine summer's day, she had found herself standing under a chilly waterfall.

OK, she thought, I really knew all that he's been saying. However intelligent and truth-telling Daphne Morgan-Woods is, she could not possibly have been absolutely certain Drummond was not at the party. But somehow, because other circumstances seemed to fit, I let myself believe he was not there. All right, it was fair enough as a working hypothesis. But, no. No, I was running ahead of myself.

So what now? All right, Kailash Gokhale has, in fact, told me what's next. It's that I need hard evidence now that Drummond was at or near the scene of the crime at the relevant times.

'Well, thank you for your advice,' she said to her stern legal mentor. 'You may have pointed out to me what the law will and will not accept. But you have, as well, suggested where I should go next. To the Masterton Clinic, where it's possible I've got a reliable witness who may be able to identify Val —'

'No, no. I really don't think I ought to be hearing the name of anyone I may at some point — it's not impossible — be asked to defend. A brief which, I have to tell you, I would have little trouble in bringing to a successful conclusion. The inexorable law would simply demand it of me.'

That same sweet, and knowing, smile.

CHAPTER NINETEEN

Even though it was dark by the time they had reached Birchester, Harriet told Bolshy to go on to the Masterton. She needed to question Tonelle a lot harder about the man who had come to the clinic's door. She urgently wanted now to compare Tonelle's description with the image, vivid in her mind, of Tigger in his high-perched flat producing that half-alibi of his. Or, better still, she had to ask if Tonelle would be able, in a courtroom, to point a finger at the man in the dock and say: *That's him.*

All right, 'Debra Delaville', or Daphne Morgan-Woods, seemed to have exploded that attempted alibi. But if what Kailash Gokhale gently hinted about proving a negative holds good when it comes to the crunch — a fleeting vision of him, bewigged in court as Defence counsel — my case will require better evidence than a simple challengeable declaration.

Telling Bolshy, once more, to wait at the gates — 'As per usual' came the mutter — she went quickly up to the house. She found she had forgotten that the heavy glass doors would be locked. But by dint of ringing and ringing at the bell, plus a bout of useless thumping on the solid glass itself, she did at last see a figure emerge through the gloom of the big, dimly lit entrance hall and go to the semi-circular reception desk.

Tonelle? It could be.

'What you want, this time of the evening?' a voice came from the phone grille beside her.

Yes, Tonelle.

'It's me, Harriet Martens.'

'East, not zero, leads to dug-out,' Tonelle said with a grin as she heaved open one half of the heavy doors. 'Though, if you're here to talk to Fishface, you're out of luck. Gone into Birchester, see an old film, club cinema. *Brief Encounter,* or something. Said she *just had to see it again.* God knows what it is.'

'I could tell you. But it's not her I'm here for. It's you. I have got questions for you to answer, if you can.'

Tonelle swept the doors wide, and led Harriet, heels clicking, across the decorative tiled floor back to the reception desk.

'If this is going to take time, sit yourself in

281

my chair,' Tonelle said, hopping up on the desk itself and swinging her legs round.

'Thanks. And I think I may take up a fair bit of your time. You see, I want to hear more, a lot more, about that mysterious man who wanted to know if the Masterton was — didn't you say this? — *suitable* for a friend of his.'

'Yeah, he said that. The exact words, now you remind me. And, yeah, suppose there may be more to tell about him. Anyhow, much more than I told that DS of yours, couldn't wait to be on his way.'

'Sorry about him. I was too caught up with the Scene of Crime people this morning to be able to see you myself.'

'But wanting to ask me about that bloke means you're getting somewhere? Going to nick the bastard who broke in here?'

'Well, I can't tell you, not just yet. But learning as much as I can about that man is what may well help. Would you be able to point him out, for a certainty, in an identity parade?'

Tonelle thought for a moment, her ebony-black face totally lacking its habitual full-lipped smile.

'No,' she said at last. 'No, I couldn't ever swear to him. It was dark, you know, dark-ish, an' he kept his face sort of — yeah, crossword word, *averted.*'

'Ah, well. Can't have everything. But let's see what we can have.'

'OK. You said you had questions for me. Shoot, then.'

'No,' Harriet said, at that moment seeing her way forward. 'No, this is what I want to do. I want you to go back to the minute that man rang at the bell, just in the way I did a moment ago. And then I want you to imagine it's all happening again, and tell me every detail that comes to your mind.'

'OK then.'

Tonelle took in a long breath and closed her eyes.

'I'm sitting here, where you are now. In my chair. Thinking it'll be only five minutes till I can close the doors, tidy up, finish for the day. And I'd done the crossword, every clue in it, so I'm feeling pretty chuffed. First time ever. An' you know what? I was thinking of your old man, what a clever bugger he must be.'

Harriet stopped herself, with some effort, from endorsing Tonelle's assessment. The flow was not on any account to be interrupted.

'An' it was then I heard the bell. No. No, wait. It was a bit after. I'd been so far away thinking about the clues I'd solved all by my own self an' what a brilliant bitch I'd become that the bell must've been rung for quite a bit before I noticed. Anyway, soon as I realised, I jumped up from where I was still sitting here at the desk, went over an' pulled one half of the doors open. And there was this bloke standing there. Big bloke, like he was a boxer or something, broad shoulders. First thing I really noticed about him, though, was that hat of his, like what guys have at the races. Seen 'em on telly. Brim pulled down so you couldn't hardly see his eyes.'

For a moment she fell silent, sitting up on the desk in a deep dream.

'And . . . ?' Harriet softly prompted.

'And he asked me if the clinic had any vacancies. An' it was then he said *suitable,* an' I thought *poncy cunt.* So I looked him up an' down, much as to say *Who are you then?* But he just went on with his stupid questions, 'bout how many rooms there were, did they look out on the grounds — That's what he said *the grounds* — on an' on. And I thought *What the hell you up to, matey?* So I took a better look at him. Sort of riding mac he had on, all stiff like, and trousers, what I could see of 'em, from a tweedy brown suit. An' shoes, brown polished brogues. Hundred per-cent the country gent. 'Cept for them pockets of his mac. Bulging with stuff crammed in there. Could 'ave had tools of some sort in one of 'em.'

Tools. Harriet thought at once of Bolshy's description of the forced window.

'What do you mean *tools?*' she asked. 'A jemmy? You know what a jemmy is? Something weighty enough to break open a door. Was this a professional you were talking to?'

What if this man was not Tigger Drummond, but the hitman who sent that egg-bomb flying across the square at Gralethorpe?

'Nah,' Tonelle answered. 'That pocket was just weighed down, like. Didn't have no major stuff in it. I'd 'ave seen if it had. An' the other pocket looked pretty stuffed too, with gloves, maybe. Real thick ones, though, enough to make a big bulge. Oh, an' there was a bit of something dangling out, too. Hey, yes, I'd forgotten all about that till this minute. Let me just think.'

She lapsed into her envisioning world again, eyes unfocussed, plainly looking once more at the crammed pockets of the man who had come to the door, had stood there asking his duff questions.

'What? What did you see?' Harriet asked at last, unable to contain her excitement.

Tonelle came back from her dream-state.

'Yeah. You know what? There was, there really was, something poking out of that pocket. I'm right. An', just at the moment I took it in, all of a sudden he swung round an' went striding off. Must've thought he'd learnt all he could from this black bint at the door, got fed up of me an' the little I'd told him. As if I'd go gabbing to any stranger come asking stupid questions.'

'But what you remembered just now? Was that all? Did you see anything more?'

'Yeah. I'll tell you. You see, he, that feller, took the wrong way rushing off in the dark like that. Went straight into the shrubbery there. And — An' this was the last I saw of 'im. There's some brambles there in among the proper bushes, an' whatever it was sticking out of that pocket of his caught on one of 'em, on the thorns, got pulled right out. Saw it. An' old Felt Hat didn't notice nothing, went shooting out of the bushes, looked up an' down, saw where he was, an' belted off down the drive, heck of a lick.'

Harriet looked at Tonelle perched on the desk, her back just brushing the chrysanthemums in their bowl at the far end, bright yellow these ones instead of bronze.

'You're a marvel,' she said. 'But, listen, could whatever it was that caught on those brambles still be there?'

286

'Don't see why not. Gardeners never ever bother with the shrubbery. Why there's so many brambles.'

'Right then. There's a torch in the car, I'll go and get it, meet you here again.'

'No need,' Tonelle said brightly. 'Always got a big torch on the shelf underneath where I am. Fishface's strict orders, case of a power cut. Which we ain't never had.'

She slid down, groped under the desk, came up with a long powerful torch and switched it on. Its white beam cut across the dimness of the hall.

'Come on,' she said. 'Race you there.'

Tonelle won easily. Harriet, half-blinded by the torch beam, could only stumble after her.

Then, half a minute later, less, came the triumphant shout.

'Got it. It's a tie. Bloody posh one, too.'

But Harriet, when she had reached the spot a yard or two inside the shrubbery, felt shooting-up in her a yet bigger triumph. The tie Tonelle was holding up to the light of the torch was one she instantly recognised. Fellow to the tie she had taken particular notice of when she had first called on Matthew Jessop at his Rutland Place house. Carefully knotted, with its dignified broad stripes in white and soft earth-red running smoothly down the length of his ultra-white shirt, she had thought of it then as being a club one.

But now she knew it was not. It was the tie worn by the old boys of the Zeal School, the tie she had seen poor flurried Judge Cotmore wearing. And pig-faced Sir Marcus Fledge. No proof, of course, that Valentine Drummond, the Zeal School former pupil, was the man who had asked Tonelle those questions. It could, as easily, indicate that spruce Matthew Jessop had been there, were he tall enough.

Then, as Tonelle moved the torch a little, she thought she glimpsed something else about the long rain-wetted strip.

'Just a moment,' she said. 'Let me have the torch for a second. There's something I'd like to get a better look at on that tie.'

Tonelle handed the torch over and held the tie out to its full length.

Harriet stepped nearer, pushing aside the rain-damped bushes, twisting her head to benefit to the maximum from the light of the torch. And, distinctly, there was a little circle in black on each of the broad red stripes.

In Matthew Jessop's smart house, she recalled with clarity, she had, making conversation, paid his tie a compliment. He had then betrayed some embarrassment, and, had gabbled out a half-explanation about the small black circles on its broad red stripes indicating membership of *a sort of little club.* He must have thought, guiltily perhaps, that I'd particularly noticed them, though I hadn't at all, and had felt bound to explain, or half-explain.

But what matters now is that the lank strip Tonelle is holding up to the light must mean the tie belonged to a member of the Cabal, and Tonelle's first description of the inquisitive visitor, broad-shouldered *like a boxer,* fits, really, only one of the Cabal members I've seen. It's all but a certainty now that it was Tigger Drummond. So, won't Kailash Gokhale, in the event he is actually briefed to defend Drummond, have more than *a little trouble* in bringing his task to a successful conclusion?

But, abruptly overcome with fatigue, all she could do then was to murmur to herself *Tomorrow to fresh woods . . . ,* say goodnight to Tonelle and get waiting Bolshy to drive her home.

CHAPTER TWENTY

'What is it about this case of yours?' John asked.

Harriet was sitting at the dining-table tense with tiredness. The freezer fish-pie John had left too long in the low oven was heavy on her stomach. She took her time to answer him.

Indifferent and unimaginative cook though John is, she thought, he has the one great necessary talent. He can judge my mood to a nicety. He knows unerringly the right thing to say at just the right moment.

'What is it about the case?' she said at last. 'I'm not sure I even know myself. It's just that I've been feeling all the time as if I'm fighting ghosts. Or, no, not that. More it's that everyone I question feels like a phantom figure, people never quite what they seem to be. Or who seem to be what I think they cannot be.'

'You're leaving me baffled.'

'Well, I'm pretty much baffled myself. Or at least I was till an hour or so ago. Now I think things are beginning to come clearer. I think. Because I can hardly believe it. But — all right, perhaps I can give you a taste of it. I mean, when you said, or implied, there was something about the case somehow wrong, my mind went straight back, not to my actual discoveries just now but to first thing this morning. It seems ages ago. The ACC had summoned me to report on progress, and I knew I wasn't really ready to. You can't properly report on a mishmash of suppositions. And, for another thing, he'd called me over when I'd hardly set foot in my own office.'

'You don't actually get on with the chap, do you?' John said.

'No, I don't. I don't know why exactly. It's probably because I did get on very well with his predecessor, bless his dour Scots heart. But . . . Well, this chap has a very different way of going about things. I mean, what he says, his appreciations of whatever I have to tell him, are perfectly fine, and even fair. But —'

John ventured a small laugh.

'*But.* By which you mean they're unfair?'

'Oh, all right. I do think he's unfair. On me. I mean, what he says is generally reasonably well thought-out. But it's almost always not what I happen to believe about whatever it is we're discussing. Or, rather, about what he's giving me his view of.'

She stopped for a moment to get her thoughts into order.

'All right, a case in point. At the very beginning of this, when all that had happened was that someone in the darkness there in the square in Gralethorpe had shot some sort of missile at Robert Roughouse as he was haranguing those anti-hunting protesters, the ACC simply announced to me that an off-shoot group of the Animal Rights people was responsible. He said he was going to hand over the inquiry to the Met task force set up to deal with such extremists. OK, it was a possible answer. And, yes, maybe I was hostile to it because I had thought this was going to be my own case. After all, as you've good reason to know, that bomb had been hurled right in front of my eyes.'

'So, in fact you were probably every bit as much entrenched in your view as the ACC was in his.'

'No. Not fair. Certainly, I wanted the case, and felt I had a right to it. But I wasn't totally — your word — entrenched. I know I wasn't. I'd have accepted any reasonable, well thought-out theory for the inquiry going to whoever was best equipped to have it. But it was — Oh, right, it was the way that man just laid down the law that got to me. ACC's law. And you'd better obey it.'

'All right, but look at it this way. He's newly appointed. From another force, didn't you tell me? Used to different ways. But he'll adapt. You know he will. Sooner or later you'll find yourself getting on with him just as well as you did with his predecessor.'

Harriet sat thinking.

'No,' she said at last. 'I don't believe you're right. It isn't as if that's the only thing he's been bloody bull-headed about.'

She saw John's sharply raised eyebrows.

'Oh, all right. I'll find some other word than bull-headed,' she said. 'Adamant? How about that? More classy, more smoothly academic.'

'Let you have it. Just.'

'OK. But here's another instance of his bull— of his adamancy. And I don't believe there is such a word as that.'

'In the dictionary,' John stated.

'Well, you're the dictionary-monger. But it oughtn't to be there. It's not a proper word. It's something some pedant made up once. To make himself — it would be a him — look important, one of the ones who tell the lesser breeds what's right and what's not. And his fellow pedants all jumped on it as making them look important in their turn. But why should a mere dictionary, even one written by Dr Johnson, be able to create laws?'

'I think, if I may say so, you're straying somewhat from the point.'

The mild rebuke brought her up short.

'I am. You're right. What I was saying . . . What I wanted to tell you is that just a day or so ago that man wanted to stop me interviewing a possible suspect because it was someone with a high position in the world. But my man's also a member of a sort of secret club about which I have some evidence — not perhaps court-of-law stuff, but evidence — that it's behind both the attack at Gralethorpe and the murder at the Masterton. A group of ex-pupils of the Zeal School who —'

'I know about the Zeal School. They insure with the Majestic. I went down there once. A very odd place. And very, very expensive.'

'You would know. OK, I've got some evidence that this group — they're very secretive, they're all rich as rich — is up to something. And — you're not to pass this on to anybody — one of the people in it is the industrialist, Sir Marcus Fledge.'

'Pettifer's. Chairman of almighty Pettifer's. You're on dangerous ground, my girl.'

'Well, so I am. It's where a police officer has to be sometimes. But what a police officer of my seniority does not expect is to have it suggested — it was all but given as an order — that Sir Marcus should not be interviewed.'

'So you've interviewed him.'

'I have, though not until I dragged out of that man a sort of grudging permission to do so.'

'Then what are you worrying about? Your ACC was amenable to reason, yes?'

Harriet sat thinking.

'But I am worrying,' she said eventually. 'I'm worrying because, not only is this case such a phantom-like affair, but because I find I'm totally out of sympathy with the officer I have to report to. And, what's more, I've a pretty firm idea that he's going to be where he is for a long time to come. You know what a place like Headquarters is, gossip-ridden from head to foot. Especially, in fact, at the foot. You'd be surprised at the things that are well-known to the bottom-of-the-barrel people, the clerks, the PCs, the lab assistants, even the catering staff. There's a whole bubbling, boiling layer of

— if you like — sludge down there. And it's all animated by rumours, true or false, slithering about from one end to another.'

'A fearsome picture. Actually much the same at Majestic House.'

'Right. So, from things that rise up from that bottom layer, I've a fairly good idea that our friend wants to see out his days in Birchester. He's made remarks that indicate as much, and they've been heard, overheard, passed down, and floated upwards again.'

'Yes. I see why you feel disheartened.'

'I do, John. I've told you — I think it was actually in the car at Gralethorpe while we were wondering how to get past the crowd blocking the square — sometimes I feel disheartened to the point of wondering whether to chuck the job in altogether. But now I'm beginning to think the moment may have come. What if, when I report on my newest evidence about what's actually happening — and, true enough, it does take some believing — our friend simply declines to accept it.'

'Darling, all this isn't like you. Really it's not.'

She sighed.

'I know what you mean. And I know, too, that it's really not, as you say, like me to indulge in conspiracy theories. If that's what

I am doing. But I know, as well, that this is what I feel at this moment. In fact it's, more or less, what I've been feeling almost from the start of the whole business. And there it is.'

John looked steadily at her across the smeared remains of fish-pie and frozen peas.

'Look,' he said at last. 'Let's put all this in suspense until the case is over, one way or another. You may find you feel completely different when you have made an arrest, or a dozen arrests come to that.'

Now Harriet managed a laugh, of a sort.

'It won't be a dozen arrests,' she said. 'Or at least I'll be very surprised if it is. From what I've learnt about this group of middle-aged, money-flush ex-public schoolboys, the Cabal as they call themselves, it probably runs to no more than eight or nine merry souls. With one or two of those beginning to ease themselves out. Robert Roughouse, I believe, was among them.'

'And you think that's possibly why he was murdered, twice murdered if you like?'

'Yes,' Harriet said with decision, 'I do look at it that way. There's no other reason, as far as I've been able to make out, for anyone else to want him permanently out of the way.'

'Not even dear old sex? Lies at the back

of a lot of seemingly mysterious deaths.'

'No, not even that. Roughouse had a lover, a mistress if you want to put it that way. She's a star athlete, a long-distance runner from Kenya. I've seen her, talked to her at length, great length, and there's no doubt in my mind that sex doesn't lie at the bottom of this.'

'All right. So, let's accept that you're on the right lines with your Cabal. You know the history of that word? It's —'

'John, stop. Stop at once.'

'Oh, all right. If a fellow can't have a bit of a ride on his hobbyhorse, I suppose he can't. OK then, accepting you're on the right lines, shouldn't we leave it like this: one, you're contemplating taking early retirement, partly because you're frustrated over your current inquiry and partly because you think you're at variance with your stuck-in-place boss. And, two: whatever difficulties you're experiencing in investigating the case, in the end, judging by your track-record, you're going to arrive at the right answer. So, let's leave it till you succeed, or not. And then, if you're still of a mind to quit, we'll talk about it. And you, ultimately, will decide.'

'Please, sir, can I go to bed now?'

'You may.'

CHAPTER
TWENTY-ONE

Harriet, coming at her own request to report to the ACC next morning that she might be nearing the end of her inquiry, found him producing something resembling a smile.

'So, you've got a case against somebody? Why don't you take a seat and tell me about it?'

Big folder of statements from the Incident Room clasped to herself, Harriet took the chair in front of the desk, notorious for being so hard that no one sat there a minute longer than they had to.

'Yes, sir,' she said. 'In my estimation we have an excellent case against one Valentine Drummond for the murder of Robert Roughouse. You may remember me telling you that a man went to the door of the Masterton Clinic in the evening of the night Roughouse was smothered and asked the receptionist there, Tonelle Danbury —'

'Black girl? Sounds like it.'

'Yes, sir, she is black, and, incidentally pretty bright.'

The ACC grunted.

'Yes, sir. And, as I was saying, this man who appeared at the Masterton asked Miss Danbury a number of questions about the clinic. In the interests, so he said, of a friend who might need to become a patient there. The man, whom Miss Danbury cannot, unfortunately, be absolutely sure of identifying — he wore a hat with the brim pulled well down — eventually turned away, apparently in a bad temper because he had learnt so little. But in the gloom — it was latish — he strode straight into a shrubbery.'

'Is there much more of this, Superintendent? Shrubberies and bad temper and hats pulled well down?'

'Yes, sir. There is more. But not a great deal.'

'Very well then.'

A sigh.

'Inside the shrubbery, sir, there are a good many bramble bushes, and, on one of these a necktie, the end of which was jutting out from the pocket of the visitor's mackintosh, caught on their thorns and was pulled out. The visitor, not noticing this, crashed his way out of the shrubbery, found again the drive leading from the house and left at a fast walk.'

'A dramatic picture, Superintendent.'

'However, sir, the point is that the tie he lost was a very unusual one. Basically it was the tie of the old boys association of the Zeal School, that rather unconventional establishment on the edge of Dartmoor that I've mentioned before. But it had been modified to indicate membership of a group called the Cabal, a club within the club of all the ex-Zeal School pupils.'

'Yes, you have mentioned the Zeal School, Superintendent. And you also took it into your head to inform me that Sir Marcus Fledge, chairman of Pettifer's, had been a pupil there. Something which in your eyes, it seemed, labelled him as some sort of criminal.'

As she sat there battling, there came suddenly into her mind one of John's quotations — almost bound to be Trollope — about everyday rules being *packthread to a giant.* Yes, Sir Marcus Fledge was very likely a giant such as Trollope had had in mind, ready to snap any packthread that hindered him. Whatever exactly *packthread* was.

'I don't think I went as far as calling Sir Marcus a criminal, sir, though I did say that I understood he was a member of the

301

Cabal, and I suspect, strongly suspect, that the Cabal is planning some illegal activity on a very considerable scale.'

'And have you now interviewed Sir Marcus, Superintendent, contrary to my advice?'

'I thought it necessary, sir, though I have to tell you I learnt nothing directly from him that indicated his involvement.'

'You don't altogether surprise me.'

'However, sir, I ought perhaps to tell you that when I checked his account of his whereabouts at the time Roughouse was murdered, I found he had taken pains, shortly after he had told me he was at home at his house in Surrey for the whole of the night, to instruct his wife to confirm the statement.'

'If nevertheless that statement happened to be true, you don't surprise me.'

'Very well, sir. But let me go on to tell you what is indicated by that tie that I found in the shrubbery near the doors of the Masterton.'

'Will I have to hear more about this — what did you call it — club within a club?'

'I'm afraid it's necessary, sir. You see, finding this particular tie where we did — Tonelle Danbury witnessed it — is strong evidence that the six o'clock visitor to the clinic was a Cabal member. That makes it

more than likely that a Cabal member suffocated Roughouse.'

'A supposition, Superintendent, that I am
not at present willing to grant.'

'There is more evidence, sir.'

'Very well, let's hear it. Time is getting
on.'

'Apart from the fact that, although Tonelle
— although Miss Danbury cannot be certain of identifying Valentine Drummond as
that visitor, she did mention to me two
things that indicated who he was. There was
his voice, which she described as that of a
poncy cunt, which I take to mean possessed
of a markedly public-school accent. And
there was his build, again clearly described
as being like a boxer's with noticeably broad
shoulders. Now, sir, I have interviewed all
the members of the Cabal whom I have had
named to me, and, except perhaps for Sir
Marcus and a surgeon called Jackson Edgeworth who is at least distinctly tall, only
Drummond answers to that description.'

'Your mere impressions, Superintendent,
will hardly stand up in court. If you can do
no better than that, I think —'

'But I can do better, sir. To a certain
extent at least. Miss Danbury described the
shoes the visitor was wearing. A pair of well-
polished brown brogues. And, of course, sir,

Scene of Crime photographed at least one rain-dampened footstep inside Roughouse's room. I have seen the photo, and it looks very like the sole of something like a brogue.'

'But you've made no definite match?'

'No, sir, to find that I would have to conduct a search of Drummond's London flat.'

'For which you will need a warrant. Do you really think you have grounds to ask a magistrate to grant one?'

Faced with the hardly concealed contempt of the question, Harriet was on the point of flatly contradicting him. But then she realised that, quite possibly, she had no need to search Drummond's flat. She had, already in place, a searcher she could rely on. Maria.

'You're perfectly right, sir. I have to admit,' she said to the ACC. 'Yes, I would have more than a little difficulty in persuading a magistrate to give me a warrant.'

As soon as she was out of the Headquarters building, Harriet found a quiet corner, pulled out her mobile and jabbed into it the number for Graham's toy.

No immediate response.

God, has she gone back on our agreement? Come to see Drummond as having more power over her than I have? Surely not. Plainly she'd realised, even before I gave her the mobile, that a police officer could get her detained as an illegal immigrant much more easily than an ordinary citizen, which after all is what Drummond is. So what's happened? Has Drummond discovered what I've done? Somehow spotted that mobile? And then what . . . ? Beaten Maria into submission? Or worse even? Has he —

'Yes-yes.'

The words came, breathily quiet, into the ear she had glued to her own mobile.

'Maria? You're there? Tell me —'

'No. No. Later. Soon.'

Drummond nearby? Hopefully not close.

She stood there, mobile still pressed too tightly to her ear.

A minute went by. Two.

'Yes, now I am on stairs with basket for shopping.'

'Well done. Clever Maria. Now, listen. I want you to look at all his shoes. His shoes, yes? Yes?'

'Shoes. He has many, many. Too many he is needing.'

For a flash of time Harriet saw in her mind's eye the row on row of shoes a

wealthy man like Drummond could possess.
Yes, Maria might well say *Too many.*

'Can you get to see them? All of them?'

'Yes, yes. Have to polish, all.'

'Good. Excellent. Now, I want you to get
hold of, if they're there, a pair of brown
brogues.'

Oh, God, how can I explain what brogues
are.

'Many little holes for pretty?'

'Yes, yes. You've got it. Now do you
remember if he wore that pair — But is
there only one of that sort?'

'Is. He was wearing, came back Sunday
morning in the night. Late, late. I hear door.
Then kick off shoes. Monday I clean. Much
of mud, grass also. Was rain, I think.'

So, yes. Yes, surely I've got my evidence.
Maria in court will — Oh, God. Maria
won't let herself appear in court. Any
contact with the law and she'll disappear altogether, like hundreds of other illegal im-
migrants before her.

Well, have to deal with that somehow
when the time comes. And in the meanwhile . . .

'Maria?'

'Yes. What is?'

'Maria, do you think you could take those
shoes, those brogues, and give them to me

if I come down to London?'

'No. Not possible.'

'But why, Maria? You said Mr Drummond has lots of shoes. Surely he won't miss one pair.'

'Gone.'

'What do you mean gone?'

'He take. When I am going to cupboard again not at all seeing.'

'You're sure? It's not simply that he's put them on for some reason?'

But she knew it was a hopeless question. There could be no doubt that Drummond, reading in the paper, seeing on TV, details of Roughhouse's dramatic murder, has realised the shoes he wore that night might be traced to him. And . . . and, no doubt, now they've been disposed of. Damn it, the Thames is there, only a few hundred yards from where he lives. Its swirling waters will have carried my evidence clean away.

Foiled again, she thought with wryly humorous bitterness.

But, no. No, surely the very fact of Drummond's disposing of his brogues is evidence against him. Inadmissible negative evidence perhaps, but evidence good enough for me.

'Maria, thank you,' she mouthed into her mobile. 'Always ring if . . . if you have anything to tell me.'

For a few moments, as she stood there still clutching her own mobile, she thought of how Maria might, after all, have to appear in court and testify to the shoes she had cleaned of all their mud and grass being suddenly made to disappear. Will she be a witness, if she doesn't succeed in making herself scarce, worth having? Think what a Defence counsel, not half as sharp as Kailash Gokhale, would make of an illegal immigrant's honesty. Well, we'll have to see. Drummond's a long way from the dock at this moment.

But . . .

What if I go to him, now, at once, and put some pointed questions about a pair of good brogues that suddenly were no longer there in his shoe cupboard?

Why not? Why not indeed? I could do it. I could. Jab at him question after question. About the brogues. About Lady Tredannick's party, and the guest list she eventually sent me which indicated no more than that Mr Valentine Drummond had been among those invited? About the manufacture even of that ingenious device which sent the egg-bomb flying through the dusk of Gralethorpe's town square to smash into a wall only inches away from Roughouse's head? About the Cabal?

Yes, he's vulnerable. And haven't I, a dozen times at least, had a vulnerable suspect in front of me across an interview-room table and reduced them to admitting to whatever crime it was they had committed. Even to murder.

Right, yes, I'll —

The mobile in her hand emitted its warble.

For an instant, still wrapped up in her bout of optimistic thoughts, she just looked at it, hardly able to remember what it was, why she was holding it.

Then she answered.

'Yes?'

'Superintendent Martens?'

The unmistakable voice of the ACC, little knowing what a short distance away he was.

'Yes, sir? Yes. Harriet Martens here.'

'Very good. Now, I've been thinking about our recent conversation, and I've come to the conclusion that your case against Valentine Drummond may have more substance to it, a little more, than I was inclined to believe.'

'Yes, sir?'

What's this? Did I convert him after all? Is he going to back me in seeking a warrant to search Drummond's flat? And, how bloody ironic. If I do get a warrant, what am I going to find in that flat? Certainly not a pair of brogues with one of their soles corresponding exactly to the ribbed stitching on the photograph of the wet footprint Montague-James was so proud of having had made.

But the ACC was ploughing on.

'Yes, some more substance. Enough, I think, to make it worth putting what we've got to the Crown Prosecution people. Let the CPS decide if there really is evidence to make a prosecution tenable. In the little you've managed to find.'

The cunning old bugger. If the CPS agree enough evidence is there, he can claim the credit. If they shoot the whole thing down, then guess who'll be landed with the blame? Detective Superintendent Martens, that's who.

And what happens to my decision, just a minute ago, to drive down to London and question Drummond till his very teeth drop out? It's off. That's what. If I were to tackle him unsuccessfully — as, admit it, might very well be the case — then he'd be warned, and quite likely jump on the first plane to Rio, or wherever. But, perhaps worse — no, certainly worse — the Cabal would be warned that their scheme, whatever it is, is in danger. Then all they'll have to do is batten down the hatches. Not one

of them in any danger of being hauled into
the nearest police station.

CHAPTER
TWENTY-TWO

The conference to discuss the case against
Valentine Drummond was to be held at one
of the Crown Prosecution Service's London
offices, since the arrest, if there was to be
one, was likely to take place in the capital.
It had been convened for the afternoon of
the following Friday. Even this much of a
delay had given Harriet little enough time,
working all hours in the incident room, to
select all the necessary documents and other
evidence.

As she arrived at the designated CPS office, after speeding down to the capital
alongside the ACC, both of them stiff in
uniform, Harriet realised they had sat, like
sworn enemies, deep in silence for virtually
the whole way.

She found, swept into the conference
suite, that the other participants were not
already seated, as she had expected, at the
long table in the centre of the functionally

arid room. Instead they were standing about, coffee cups (good china) in hand.

'Coffee,' she was unable to prevent herself murmuring indignantly. 'And, look, biscuits.'

There, laid out in a row along the table, were three plates of them, chocolate digestives, shortcakes and round sandwich ones with, jewel-like at their centres sticky red jam. Despite those being her childhood favourites, her indignation soared.

The done thing. The trivial rigidly adhered to. Biscuits will be offered, in regulation order. Whatever the circumstances.

A police cadet, borrowed from somewhere, came up to the ACC and asked if he would like coffee.

'Yes, please,' he said with every sign of eagerness.

'With milk? And sugar, sir?'

'Yes, yes. Both please. Two lumps.'

'There are biscuits on the table, sir.'

The cadet turned to Harriet.

'And for you, ma'am?'

'Nothing, thank you.'

So it was with an unexpected extra of reluctance that, when at last she saw the table cleared of the scarcely disturbed plates, she made her way to her place — name on a printed card in a clear plastic holder. Then abruptly she recognised, seated alone at the opposite end of the table, the Deputy Crown Prosecutor who was to conduct the proceedings. He was Mr Peregrine Smith QC, known, for his obdurate opposition to letting any case go to court unless there was total certainty of a guilty verdict, as Stonewall Smith.

She took a quick glance at the ACC taking his place beside her. Was he, picking up her dismayed reaction, now doing his best to conceal a glint of triumph? Had he been able to fix things — the grapevine always there — so that Stonewall Smith would preside? If so, no telling what branches of that grapevine had been tugged at. And certainly nothing to be done about it.

Unless, she added to herself, I can make the case for bringing Drummond to court so solid that even Stonewall Smith will have to accept it. But, out of the wisps of straw that are all I have managed to collect, will I be able, somehow, to build a structure nothing can sweep away?

And now, after a little attention-calling cough, Stonewall Smith, note-taking secretary, pencil poised, at his elbow, was ready to address the meeting.

'Gentleman, ladies. I would like first to lay down the ground rules under which this inquiry should be conducted, despite the slightly unorthodox decision that we are to consider here in London a crime committed in Birchester. In this way we will all know where we stand.'

Harriet perked up a little.

If he's going to conduct this by his own ground rules, she thought, there is perhaps a chance my admittedly flimsy case may in the end meet with his approval. Have I misjudged him? Paid too much heed to the gossip?

But he was going steadily on.

'I have always found, however, that there is no better way of conducting matters than by following the commonly accepted procedure used in all our inquiries in order to make sure we have every piece of the material necessary, the compelling evidence. So let us begin by considering, as is customary, the most basic requirement of a successful prosecution, the plans of the locations involved.'

Harriet's just risen hopes began to crumble. The rigmarole all bureaucrats are so attached to. How, in face of that frothy surge of rules and regulations, can my possibly unorthodox case stay upright?

'We shall have to bear in mind,' Stonewall Smith went on, 'the possibility that, if there should be a trial, the Judge and the jury may need to visit the scene itself. So, Mr Richards, will you give us your opinion of the plans as the necessary basis without which it will be impossible to go forward.'

Oh God, Harriet thought. What was the point of thinking his ground rules would be at least similar to any I might have set myself? No, ground rules of their nature apply differently in different circumstances. Different societies work often in quite different ways. Even the generation below John's and mine has a different code of behaviour, let alone that of a generation one step further down.

So Stonewall is as stony-walled as ever. Will he, even here, find some error in what we've done that will bring the whole process of assessment to an abrupt end before it's properly started? Will I, in half an hour or less, be going back to Birchester, speeding along in a new silence beside the secretly triumphant ACC? And then what? A transfer to some plodding desk job? Traffic Branch perhaps?

Well, it won't be that I promise. I'll quit. No question.

Near her, at the side of the long table, a podgy man in an ill-fitting blue suit shuffled the thick pile of documents in front of him.

Harriet glimpsed plans of the various sites inside the Masterton which, in consultation with infinitely fussy Mr Montague-James, she had decided would be needed. They ranged from the whole lay-out of the house down to Roughouse's room itself, to which Valentine Drummond — surely it could not have been anyone else — had made his way, brogues squelching from the steady rain that he had walked through, to where his victim lay in deep healing sleep.

But will they be enough, she asked herself in sudden panic. Will Stonewall Smith declare in just a few minutes that something vital is missing? And terminate the whole conference there and then?

Laboriously the expert went, item by item, over the heaped pile beside him. But, as he turned each plan face-down, no comment he made appeared to damn any of them, bar perhaps a little tut-tutting over some smudge or other. At last he finished.

Harriet waited to hear Stonewall Smith's verdict.

'Very well,' he said at last. 'That much out of what will eventually have to be produced in evidence appears to be satisfactory.'

Harriet's hopes rose by half an inch.

'So, can we now proceed to the photographic evidence? Miss Parker?'

317

'Mrs, actually,' the youngish woman in grey-striped, mannish shirt and neat grey suit jacket, dared to put in.

'I'm sorry. Mrs Parker then.'

Harriet could feel, almost as if it were real, the black mark being ticked against the impudent name *Parker* on some internal list.

Mrs Parker, conscious of that mark or not, went laboriously through the photographs. Scores of them of the room where Roughouse's body had lain, starch-white pillow over his face. Others of all the places inside the clinic which Monty-tonty and Harriet between them had seen as providing possible evidence. The drying wet footmarks, the forced window of the disused storeroom, a door with a trace of mud on it.

And, at last, came Stonewall Smith's comment.

'Very well. That seems in order. Now, eyewitnesses. Superintendent Martens, perhaps you should enlighten us here?'

Harriet braced herself.

Tonelle was the only eye-witness she had offered, if in fact the man who had come to the clinic door at dusk with those duff questions was Drummond. If it was Drummond who had turned away, defeated, and plunged in the darkness into the bramble-infested shrubbery and there lost the Zealot tie that, modified, indicated membership of the Cabal.

Now, how can I present Tonelle as a witness who will convince a jury she is rock-solid in everything she says?

'Yes, sir,' she said, looking Stonewall Smith straight in the eye. 'We have, as you will know from the summary in front of you, only one eye-witness, since extensive house-to-house inquiries in the barely inhabited farmland round the Masterton Clinic failed to produce any reliable evidence. She is Miss Tonelle Danbury, receptionist at the much respected Masterton Clinic.'

'Much respected?' Stonewall Smith interrupted sharply. 'How is the respectability or otherwise of the Masterton Clinic relevant to the case you are presenting, Superintendent?'

Harriet gave herself a second to think.

'Sir,' she said. 'I believe that it is. It will be important, should the case come to trial, to show the jury that Miss Danbury is an absolutely reliable witness. But she is, as it happens, black, and her speech is liable to veer into the language she was brought up with in a black area of London. You will appreciate, sir, that both those factors, though it is perhaps a sad thing to have to acknowledge, may adversely affect some members of the public among the jurors. Unless, of course, they themselves are black.'

'So, how do you propose to present Miss — er — Danbury as being reliable in the witness-box?'

'I don't think, from what I know of her, sir, that it will be possible to coach her into using the best middle-class language. She is not a person to accede to the conventions. But emphasising the respectability of the Masterton Clinic will, as it were, endorse her own.'

'Indeed? So, in what way do you propose to make it clear to a jury how very respectable the Masterton Clinic is?'

Another second or two to think. But not now to any avail.

How *respectable* in fact is the Masterton, she had asked herself. And, in that fraction of time the answer had come clearly into her head. A clinic could hardly be described as thoroughly respectable when, she knew from her own discoveries, it had taken Charity Nyambura in to be detoxed but whose authorities — Mrs Fishlock, in all probability — had allowed it to be given out she was there because of a leg injury.

'Well, sir,' she said, unable to keep the tinge of doubt out of her voice, 'the Masterton is known for the film stars and the top footballers and — and — and, yes, cricket-ers who have been patients there. The facts have been recorded in the press.'

'In the press, Superintendent? I take it by that you mean in the gossip columns?'

'Yes, sir, I suppose, many of the mentions would have been of that sort.'

'Then I think we need pursue this line no further. Shall we put, let us say, a large question mark against Miss Danbury's name? And, since apparently your inquiries have failed to produce a single other person who saw the man at the clinic's doors, I fear we shall have to discount the whole of that episode.'

'Very well, sir.'

Harriet fought against a wave of depres-sion that threatened to topple down on her.

'So we come,' Stonewall Smith went steam-rollering on, 'to the officers who interviewed the suspect. And they are?'

'Only myself, sir.'

And will I, she thought, be able to produce from that one occasion on which I spoke to Drummond anything that will convince this uncompromising sceptic that there is a case against him, now that he has demolished Tonelle, the best witness I thought I had?

'I conducted a short interview with Drummond,' she said, 'in the course of checking the alibis for the time of the murder of all the persons I saw as possible suspects. I asked him, as soon as I had been admitted to his flat at the top of a building near Parliament Square, if he could tell me where he had been during the evening of Saturday, September the twenty-fifth, and he replied, without hesitation, that he had been at a party given by a certain Lady Margaret Tredannick at her house, Ravenham Court, on the Kent coast. I decided, however, that I should see Lady Margaret and ask her to confirm Drummond's presence there.'

'Which she did or did not?'

'Lady Margaret was unable to state to my satisfaction that Drummond was definitely at that party, though she indicated that there were witnesses in plenty, herself among them, who would say he was there.'

'You did not accept Lady Margaret's word on its own?'

'No, sir. I thought it possible she might be protecting Drummond, whom I understood to be a friend of long standing. So I went directly to the one person she had claimed could say with certainty he was among the party guests, one Miss Daphne Morgan-Woods, a columnist on the magazine *All the Way Round*.'

'And from this journalist, on a woman's magazine, you learnt what, Superintendent?'

'I received from her,' Harriet replied, a little beat of triumph throwing light over the gloom increasing in her mind, 'an unequivocal statement that Valentine Drummond, whom she knows well, had not been a fellow-guest with her as she made her way backwards and forwards all evening in pursuit of her business at the party.'

'One witness to an absence, Superintendent? I cannot see a Defence counsel, any Defence counsel, allowing that to go unchallenged.'

'No, sir. And on that account I secured from Lady Margaret, not without difficulty, a full list of those invited. However, since that comprises some two hundred persons the process of checking their recollections has not yet been completed.'

'And when will it be, Superintendent? By next July?'

'I am unable to say, sir. You will realise it could take a great deal of time. But, unless it produces reliable evidence from more than one witness that Drummond was present, I am happy to rely on Miss Morgan-Woods in the box.'

'So was it that assertion of hers that led you to see Drummond as the most likely suspect for the murder of Robert Roughouse?'

'It confirmed to the hilt, if I may put it this way, sir, my suspicions of Drummond.'

'An assertion by a gossip columnist, Superintendent? One who makes a living, and no doubt a good one, by exaggerating any scraps of fact she may have learnt. Or, indeed, by inventing semi-likely stories when no such scraps come to hand?'

'Yes, sir. I accept that claim as a description of gossip columnists, though I suppose it is possible that there are those to whom it does not apply. However, when I interviewed Miss Morgan-Woods, at some length, I was perfectly satisfied she was telling me the truth about her time at that party. I believe she will make an excellent witness in court.'

'Very well then,' Stonewall Smith said, with the faintest of sighs. 'I suppose we had better proceed with the remaining items which we customarily examine. I gather that Detective Sergeant William Woodcock also questioned Miss Tonelle Danbury about the visitor she encountered at the door of the Masterton Clinic on the evening of the murder. I understand you do not think it necessary to have him here today. But we must certainly hear a report on his notebook, which is among the documents submitted to us. Mr Hastings, I believe you have conducted that examination.'

'I did, sir,' said a hunched, grey-suited heavily bespectacled figure.

As soon as he began to go through the pages of Bolshy's notebook, Harriet's disquiet grew. She could guess that whatever words Bolshy had written would be at best scanty and at worst totally incoherent.

Looking down the table she saw, with fresh dismay but no surprise at all, that even the cover of the notebook appeared to have been subjected to considerable mistreatment. Had Bolshy stubbed out cheroots on it? Very likely. So what would the contents be like?

The document examiner's report at once confirmed her fears. Bolshy was about to be shown up as one of the worst notebook keepers in, possibly, all the forces in England. The examiner began with a loud sniff.

'I have not been able to make out a great deal of what was written — *scrawled* would be the better word — concerning DS Woodcock's interview with Tonelle Danbury. I have noted, however, that her name is misspelt throughout as *T-o-n-e-l*. But the gist of what Detective Sergeant Woodcock wrote is that Miss Danbury told him only that a man, he added two words I made out as possibly being *brown hat,* had come to the clinic's door. But he noted no other description of that individual. I was able to decipher only that the individual at the door had asked some questions about, I quote, *what rooms, what else.* That, in fact, was all.'

'Thank you, Mr Hastings. I note that the inquiries into Mr Roughouse's death have not all been carried out with that degree of efficiency one might expect.'

Then Harriet burst in, unable to help herself.

'I am sorry, sir, that, since you dismissed Tonelle Danbury as a witness worth putting forward, you have not heard anything of her account to me of the visitor DS Woodcock described so briefly, and, I will admit, incompetently. Sir, Miss Danbury can offer a much fuller account, one which you will find fully written up in my own notebook.'

'I think we have dealt with that matter sufficiently already, Superintendent,' Stonewall Smith snapped back. 'If you are to put to a jury the account in your notebook, it would be necessary to have it corroborated by Miss Danbury, and we have already decided she would be a witness altogether unlikely to impress a jury.'

'Sir, nevertheless I must insist the inquiry

hears my notebook account.'

Is this the moment, she asked herself, when somehow I see one of those half-exceptions which any iron structure of rules and regulations seems of necessity to create?

The silence that followed hung in the air of the arid room, tense as waiting thunder.

Boats burnt, Harriet thought. So will it be resignation? Well, if it is, it is. A lifetime's work in the waste basket.

Then Stonewall Smith produced a long sigh which Harriet, at the far end of the table, heard as clearly as if he had breathed it in her ear.

'Oh, very well then, Superintendent, let us hear your account. Never let it be said that a CPS inquiry omitted to consider even the least likely shred of evidence.'

Yes, the half-exception, the wriggle in the iron structure that lets something go through.

So, reading from the notebook she had taken from her uniform pocket, she gave the inquiry a full account of her own interview with Tonelle and of what they both had discovered in the brambly shrubbery outside the Masterton's glass doors, the barely visible little black circles on the regulation Zealot tie indicating membership of the secret Cabal.

And, bit by bit as she contrived to read her notes about the Cabal, she sensed the others round the table — she dared not look at Stonewall Smith at the far end — had begun to see a different case from the one that had been put so far. Even, next to her, she recognised that the ACC himself, from his occasional shufflings and in-taken breaths, was beginning to see the case might be sound.

She brought her account to an end, filled with a certain pleasure that, after all, Tonelle, the bright crossword lover, despite her irredeemably colloquial speech, had had her influence on the proceedings.

It had been more than she had dared to hope for.

'We come next,' Stonewall Smith said, blandly as if nothing new had been brought to light, 'to considering the evidence that will be offered by the SOCO team which investigated the murder, and then, in accordance with our laid-down rules, finally to considering the evidence of the expert witnesses, Dr Edwards, of the Forensic Science Service, and the duty forensic physician. When we have heard them our deliberations will be over.'

He slapped his papers together with a

crack of finality.

But what is he saying, Harriet asked herself? Isn't he going to comment in any way? He's been quick enough to do so all along, dismissing as worthless almost every aspect of my inquiries. So why isn't he dismissing the whole case I presented?

And the answer came to her. Because he has changed his mind. Because he now believes Valentine Drummond does have a case to answer.

CHAPTER
TWENTY-THREE

Events moved swiftly once Stonewall Smith had indicated, in however roundabout a way, that any further evidence they heard would not affect his eventual decision that Valentine Drummond should be prosecuted for the murder of Robert Roughouse. It had been too late, when the conference was at last brought to a formal end, to do anything about making arrangements for the arrest. But, outside, Harriet managed to seize an opportunity to contact Maria's softly rattling toy mobile.

'He here,' came a whispered answer, from somewhere in Drummond's eyrie flat.

'He's there with you?'

'I saying. Here.'

The voice was plainly angry, and frightened.

'Yes, I heard you. I just wanted to make doubly sure.'

'What *doubly*, please?'

'Never mind, never mind. Tell me, has he said anything about going? About leaving the flat?'

'Not ready. But he say tomorrow I must go out all morning. Keep out of bloody way. Busy tacking. What is *tacking*?'

Tacking? Tacking? Then suddenly the penny dropped.

'No, not *tacking,* Maria. Packing. Wasn't that what he said? Packing? That tomorrow he is going to be packing up his things? Putting them in his cases, and boxes? Before he leaves the country?'

'Is packing, yes. Now I knowing.'

'Very good, Maria. You do what he's asked you to. Stay out, stay well away all morning.'

'But is bad day for out.'

'What do you mean, *bad day*?'

'Much people in street.'

'Oh, I don't expect there'll be many more than usual. Why do you think that there will be?'

'Is hunting day.'

Heck, what does she mean now? Hunting? Is this something to do with the attack on Roughouse in Gralethorpe? Can't be. No, some fantastic misunderstanding of some sort. Forget about it.

'OK, Maria, But tomorrow you stay out of the flat. All right?'

331

'If you tell.'

It was only, late that night back in Birchester, summoned by the ACC to discuss the best way to effect Drummond's arrest, that Maria's babbled out words *hunting day* became suddenly clear.

'You say Drummond's flat is in a building at the edge of Parliament Square?' the ACC had asked, his voice prickling with unexpressed objections.

'Yes, sir. As a matter of fact it is. The building's rather odd, and pretty old. I imagine in a few years at the most it will come tumbling down under the demolition men's sledgehammers. You have to climb interminable stairs to get to Drummond's flat, which I suppose is why he lives there. The eagle safe in its eyrie, safe and watchful.'

'Very romantic, Superintendent. But what you've evidently managed somehow totally to ignore is that tomorrow there's going to be a vast protest meeting outside the House of Commons because of this Bill to ban hunting. People are disgusted at the way the countryside is being trampled all over just to please townee voters. There'll be thousands there, thousands, making themselves heard. How can you have seen nothing about it, in the newspapers, on every TV news?'

'Oh, yes, I did of course, sir. But just in the days up to the CPS meeting I'm afraid I ignored everything except getting together the evidence against Drummond. I just wasn't able to think of anything else. But thank you for pointing out the scale of the protest, sir. You've alerted me just in time. I suppose it's possible Drummond's building could become almost totally surrounded.'

'You had better check with the Met, Superintendent. But I suggest you bear in mind what people say about the early bird and the worm. I strongly recommend it to you.'

When Harriet contacted the Met she learnt, to her dismay, they were taking an even more apprehensive view of the Houses of Parliament demo than the ACC.

'Superintendent,' her senior officer contact had said. 'I really think you should consider postponing your operation. There are going to be, so far as our intelligence goes, a greater number of demonstrators involved than ever before. To tell you the truth, it's damn scary. So to come up almost to Parliament Square itself and to try to effect an arrest — I don't ask who your target is, I'd much rather not know — is, what shall I say? An utterly foolish thing to do.'

Harriet thought.

No, it's not simply a question of arresting Drummond for the murder of Robert Roughouse. No, there's a great deal more involved. The Cabal must be on the point of putting into operation their whole plan to send those mercenaries to Transabistan, and topple President Olengovili. Then they'll replace him with some dummy of theirs so they can exploit that huge mass of pitchblende and sell its uranium to the highest bidder. The only way it can be stopped is to arrest Drummond. It's only if he's suddenly removed from the scene tomorrow, that Fledge will be prevented from cancelling the whole operation, destroying all evidence of it.

'Thank you for being as frank as you have,' she said to her contact. 'And, all right, I accept your *utterly foolish thing to do.* But there are considerations involved which I cannot tell you about. Absolutely cannot. So, well, I'm going to have to risk coming down to London. No way round it.'

A sigh, loud down the line.

'Your decision, Superintendent. No, wait. Wait. Yes, let me at least give you a mobile number that'll get you our central control tomorrow. You've got such a thing as a simple pencil?'

'Ballpoint in my hand.'

She finished scribbling and put the phone down, unable not to feel she had been right in insisting on making the arrest. But full of apprehension.

So it was a very disgruntled Bolshy Bill who, at 6 a.m. next morning, settled himself in Harriet's own car, her newish Honda Jazz. No point in risking that Drummond might spot from high up in his eyrie a vehicle marked *Birchester Police*.

'Haven't had an early start at a god-damn hour like this since I was a PC,' he complained. 'Can't see why you say we've got to be there arresting the feller this early. Be wrapped up cosy in bed till gone ten, toff like him.'

'Not this morning he won't be, DS. He'll be the one making an early start if, as I suspect, he's just about ready to go off to a place called Transabistan to lead a bunch of mercenaries to start a revolution.'

'First I heard of that. Nobody tells me nothing.'

'Well, you've heard now. And put your foot down, for heaven's sake. I want to get there.'

But they reached the neighbourhood of Parliament Square much later than Harriet had hoped. Her calculations had not allowed for the huge number of protesters making their way along the London streets, eventually fully in the roadway.

'God's sake, look at 'em,' Bolshy muttered. 'What the hell do they think they're doing? An', look at all the wooden tops called out to keep 'em in order. Poor sods.'

'They're objecting, the protesters — I took a look at *News 24* before I went to bed last night — to what they see as an unjust law that's about to be put on the statute books. Though whether any law passed by a democratically elected House of Commons can really be described as *unjust* is something that could be argued over till doomsday.'

'Law's the law,' DS Woodcock, firm upholder of the British constitution, complacently agreed. Simultaneously priding himself on ignoring all the rules.

The British constitution, Harriet found herself dreamily thinking as they slowly pushed their way through the crowds — Bolshy jab-jabbing at the horn — that's a wonderful concept for you. Not a word of it ever written down, but people swearing by it year upon year. Look at Dickens' Mr Podsnap teaching his French visitor that the *Constitution Britannique* was Bestowed Upon Us By Providence. One of John's favourites among all his quotations. And how when he produces it he bops out each of those capital letters.

'God knows where I can put the vehicle.'

Bolshy's grumble brought her back to reality.

We've arrived. At last. Parliament Square just in front of us. And, goodness, everybody who warned me was right. There's a solid mass of protesters here even as early as this, well before the time I'd thought we might bring off the arrest.

Better get in contact with Maria before she does what Drummond told her to do and keeps *out of bloody way.* Should find out if she's prepared for all this.

She pulled out her mobile.

Her buzz was answered immediately.

'Maria?'

'Yes, is OK. He busy, bedroom.'

'And are you ready to leave?'

'Ten minute.'

'Good. Now, Maria, have you seen the crowds down here below? Will you be able to get through them?'

'Yes-yes. Ev'body can.'

All right, if she thinks so.

'Now, Maria. listen. Can you leave the flat's door on the snib? You know what I mean by that? The little knob on the lock that you push down so that the tongue of the bolt stays where you put it, either in or out?'

'Yes, yes. Very good knowing. Push down little knob. But when I do, how I get out?'

Why the hell can't Drummond have taught her to use reasonable English while he's had her here? No, I suppose the less she understood the better, considering the sort of visitors he's been having recently.

She turned back to the mobile.

'No, Maria,' she said, calmly as she could. 'I want you to turn the big knob the way you do whenever you want to open the door, and then push the little knob down so that the door can't be shut fast.'

'Why you no say at start? Maria not damn idiot.'

'No. No, of course you're not. It's Mr Drummond who sometimes calls you that, I suppose. So, now you know what it is I want. I want to find the flat's door not locked when I come, so that I can go straight in. All right?'

'Is all right.'

'Hey, here's a space,' Bolshy broke in. 'Nice double yellow line right up outside Drummond's building. He'll never see us there, not from any window at the top, and no one ain't going to complain about yellow lines, day like this.'

He laughed then.

' 'Course, some of these protesters may turn the car upside-down or try an' throw it over the railings into bloody Parliament. But who cares?'

Harriet, who did care about her Jazz, said nothing.

They sat there in silence. After only a few minutes Maria emerged from the building, big shopping-bag flapping at her side. Protected by the windscreen's reflection, Harriet kept quite still, and Maria actually went hurrying straight past, peering anxiously at the noisily shouting crowd beyond.

Harriet, in her turn, began to look at them, though without any of Maria's stranger-in-a-strange-land fears.

Groups of police were going marching by, clad in cumbersome yellow jackets, riot shields on their arms.

'Could do with a bit of rain,' Bolshy commented. 'Cool down the wooden tops, poor buggers. But don't suppose we'll get any. Not when it's wanted.'

'Yes. And it won't be only them who need cooling down,' Harriet replied. 'Look at that banner there. *Kill Cops.* All right, they may feel they've got grievances that need remedying, the protestors. But that's just not on.'

'Human nature,' Bolshy said. 'You got a chance to smash up some nice policemen, you're going to take it.'

'It may be a law of nature but it's certainly not the law of any civilised country.'

'An' how many civilised countries are there? Lot of blacks slitting each others throats.'

'That's enough,' Harriet said.

Bolshy contented himself with a smirk.

The crowd beside them was thickening by the minute. Banners were waving in violent, if unreadable, defiance. The shouting had become one unceasing tumult, with emerging every now and again a single continuous chant *Unjust law — Unjust law — Unjust law.* On and on. Against the far side windows of the car the mass of people had pushed a couple in full hunting regalia right up to them. Harriet found in a swirl of *déja vu* that the vibrant red of the man's coat, only inches away from her face, had put into her mind Robert Roughhouse outside Gralethorpe's town hall. The hunting gentleman pounding out to the sullen faces in front of him his *You cannot end four hundred years of history.*

Shaking the vision out of her head, she leant towards Bolshy.

'At this rate,' she said into his ear, 'we're not even going to be able to get to that doorway just over there.'

'You're right. Gonna wait till tomorrow then?'

'I certainly am not. I've no intention, either, of just sitting here in the car with those people butting up against us. Look, you should be able to get your door open. Nip out, go round and clear those two away.'

'Want me to risk me life, is it?'

'Nonsense. No one's going to do anything to you, however many *Kill Cops* banners there are. You're in plain clothes, aren't you? If you can call that horrible jacket plain clothes. Off you go.'

Bolshy, pleased perhaps with her acknowledgement that his appearance was a continuing act of defiance against the directive that officers should *at all times dress with due respect for public standards,* eased the door beside him open, and slid out.

Harriet, in the time it took him to work his way round to her side of the car, found a new source of anxiety. It was a ridiculous one she knew, yet she could do nothing but let it rip.

The real danger, she kept telling herself, is that, at any second, Drummond's going to come out. What if he's been looking down from one of his windows at the crowd along there in Parliament Square itself, heaving and thrusting a thousand times more violently than the miners in the square at Gralethorpe. He could decide he had to leave now before it gets impossible. If he comes out into the street just behind me, pushing and shoving with those broad shoulders of his, he could be out of my sight in minutes. And even if he's not I could never arrest him here amid all the yelling and chanting.

Oh God, where's Bolshy got to? He's not going to desert me, is he? Skive off under pretence of not being able to get back here? It'd be all one with his general conduct.

There came a rapid tattoo on the window just beside her.

Bolshy. Purple-faced and sweaty. Pushing the pair in hunting gear vigorously out of the way.

Harriet swiftly leant over and released the door she had locked.

'Cripes, worse than I thought,' Bolshy shouted into her ear. 'You should just see

342

'em in the square. They're already trying to pull down those railings. The lads there going at it with their sticks 'ammer an' tongs. Wouldn't mind being there with 'em, matter o' fact. Always liked having a bash at the great British public. 'Cept I think they'd get a better bash at me, way they are today. Talk about mad dogs. An' they've got dogs too, some of 'em. Bloody what you call hounds, like in fox-hunting. Square's full of that sort, all dressed up in their red coats and little black hats.'

'Pink —' Harriet began, correctively. And abandoned the attempt.

She allowed what Bolshy had told her, for all its exaggerations and digs at herself as the senior officer, to enter her consideration.

Yes, the huge protest was already going far beyond what the excited midnight reporter on *News 24* had promised, as far or further than her contact in the Met had expected. Heaven knows, what's got into these people. They're meant to be from the so-called solid backbone of England, decent law-abiding folk. And look at them. Mad dogs, Bolshy's not wrong. They've succumbed to some form of mass hysteria. God knows what'll have happened before the day's done.

So, what am I going to do?

Only one answer. Abandon my nice shiny almost new Jazz. And push our way as best we can over to that doorway, get in, climb those stairs — Bolshy won't like that — and then at last quietly thrust open the flat's front door. Unless . . .

Oh God, don't let that have happened.

Unless Drummond, passing by that door for some reason or other, noticed it's a bare quarter of an inch open and freed the tongue of the lock to click back into place.

'Right,' she said to Bolshy. 'We're going in. Now. Get in front of me and make for that doorway.'

CHAPTER
TWENTY-FOUR

As they neared the tall building they experienced one final delay. Pushing past the dozen or so protesters on the narrow pavement, Harriet had been unable to prevent herself jostling a jodhpurs-clad young woman.

'Look what you've done,' the girl screeched. 'You bloody knocked my basket of eggs right out of my hand.'

Harriet looked back over her shoulder.

True enough, on the ground beside the angry young harridan there was a plastic fruit basket and spilling out from it a cluster of eggs, two or three of them smashed.

'Sorry,' she called back, intent on the doorway just within stepping distance.

'Cow! Fucking cow!' the young woman yelled at her. 'Those were specially rotten eggs, you pig.'

Eggs 'specially rotten', brought for throwing, Harriet realised. And at any moment one of them may be hurled at me in place of any passing uniformed officer.

But Bolshy, now just beside her, gave her a sharp tug that sent her staggering into the protection of the doorway ahead. And, steadying herself there against the grimy wall, into her mind came, with sudden vividness, the recollection of the supermarket-fresh eggs that back in Gralethorpe she and John had watched being flung at Robert Roughouse. And then of the purple egg that had been shot from that deadly device.

Bolshy broke into her flashback recall.

'Good job she didn't get you with one of them eggs,' he said. 'Wouldn't never have done up at the top there, you spieling out *I am arresting you on suspicion of murder* and him reeling back from the stink.'

'Thank you, DS,' she said, 'for keeping unblemished the majesty of the law.'

She began to climb the long haul of the stairs.

'And now no talking, please. I want to take Mr Valentine Drummond totally by surprise.'

Bolshy pointedly put a finger to his lips as he thumped his way up behind her.

On and up they went, Harriet pausing near the top only to rebuke Bolshy, still clumping onwards, with a sharp look at the shoes on his feet.

A moment afterwards she was able to see that the flat's door was, after all, just a crack open. So the caged tiger inside had failed to notice what Maria had done.

Revenge for all the bullying she'd suffered. Good.

Taking in a breath, she held her hand out flat and gave the door in front of her a single push.

No sign of Drummond in the living room that was immediately revealed. But, beyond, as she knew from her previous visit, must lie the flat's bedroom, with Maria's box-room somewhere to the side.

Almost on tiptoe she walked towards the closed bedroom door, Bolshy a couple of paces behind her.

She reached for the knob, turned it and thrust the door wide.

Drummond, from where he had been stooping over an opened suitcase on the bed, rose to his full height.

'What the hell . . . ?'

'Mr Drummond, you may remember me. Detective Superintendent Martens, Greater Birchester Police.'

'What the devil do you mean, barging in here? There's a buzzer at the door.'

Harriet ignored him.

'Valentine Drummond,' she said, beginning the spiel Bolshy had parodied just a few minutes earlier, 'I am arresting you on suspicion of the murder of Rob—'

But Drummond at the word *murder* had hurled himself forwards, right fist thrusting out.

Harriet felt as if some heavy lump of metal propelled by an explosion had struck her full on the point of the chin.

There was a moment when she was conscious of her whole body being lifted from the floor. Then she fell back, her head striking the doorpost behind her.

Was there a wild flurry of dark bodies somewhere above her? Not until much later did she know whether she had seen this or half-guessed it. Total obscurity had overcome her, the screen showing a smooth descent of blankness as the cursor had homed in on *Exit.*

It can have been only a few minutes, she worked out eventually, two, perhaps three, before she had regained consciousness. Into her mind then had come the incongruous thought *It's the unwritten rule: a man does not strike a woman.* Almost at once, as her full senses came back, she added wryly and aloud, 'Not that the rule isn't flouted often enough.'

The sound of her own voice completed the process of her recovery. She realised she had been left slumped against the doorpost, half-upright. And, yes, isn't that, coming through the wide-open front door, the sound of banging steps on the hard stairs below?

Bolshy, she thought. Good old Bolshy, he may have been thrust aside but he's there now, in pursuit.

Carefully she heaved herself to her feet, feeling a thumping pain at the back of her head as a wave of nausea overtook her.

But should I set off following Bolshy?

Pointless. It'd be utterly pointless. At any second they'll both be out in the open. If Drummond hasn't got there already.

For a groggy moment, she imagined him pounding away along Great George Street towards St James's Park and the offer of freedom that lay in its wide spaces.

But, no, she thought. No, Drummond'll be too cunning to try that. There've been police helicopters circling overhead almost ever since we arrived. In the open he'd be in full view. No, if he's half as clever as I think he is, he'll have gone the other way. Taken the unorthodox route. Into that huge mêlée of Parliament Square.

Among all those protesters, intent on pressing towards the Commons, he'll be able to disappear like a fox weaving its way through a bushy covert.

Lost him. Lost the bugger, perhaps for ever.

She looked wildly round, as if to find written on Drummond's walls some secret instructions that would lead a pursuit to find him. Across the sitting-room she saw the bright daylight coming through the window. The window that must look out, she realised, as clearly as if Drummond himself or Maria had told her, down on Parliament Square below.

Four or five staggering steps towards it. And then she was watching the turbulent shouting mob beneath.

For perhaps half a minute she just stood there, leaning over the sill. But then . . .

Then she made out — surely it's that — a twisting little snake of blackness parting the multi-coloured mass of the crowd.

Yes, it is. It's Drummond, pushing his way through the press of jumbled bodies, leaving that small black snake of emptiness behind him.

No, wait. The black snake wouldn't be so visible if it was just Drummond carving his way through. No, it must be, long as it is, because there's another person pushing against the mass of the crowd not far behind. Bolshy. Bolshy really is there in close pursuit.

She stared downwards, engrossed as if a TV showing breaking news was hypnotising her.

And then she realised that Bolshy had actually caught Drummond up.

Is he repeating those statutory words *I am arresting you on suspicion . . . ?*

The next moment she saw she was right. Bolshy was making the arrest. But it was immediately evident he was not making it the success it should have been. No, he was a police officer attempting to effect an arrest in the middle of a crowd of inflamed countryside protesters, anti-Parliament, anti-city dwellers, anti-police.

Then Bolshy went down. She saw it. Where he had been facing Drummond a moment before there was now a little angry whirlpool in the multi-coloured sea of protest.

God, I hope they're not going to go for Bolshy. Riding boots slamming into his sides, the poles of placards brought down on his head.

But Drummond? Has he taken advantage . . . ?

He has. He has. The black snake of his wake is there once more, plain to see from this height and moving steadily as before.

What to do? What to —

At that instant she knew. She plunged her hand into her pocket, pulled out her mobile.

What's the number that man at Scotland Yard gave me?

It came into her head, obedient as a foxhound to a horn call. She thumbed hard at the buttons. The officer who answered sounded extremely harassed. But when she gave her name and rank, all in one breath, she got an immediate response.

'Yes, we were given orders about you. I took special notice because another woman officer might be at risk.'

Rapidly Harriet explained the situation.

'All right. I'll get directly on to one of the 'copters. They'll certainly see what they can do. You said you're watching the whole scene from where you are, top of some building?'

'I am.'

'OK, keep the line open, and I'll patch you to the pilot.'

Within a couple of minutes Harriet found herself describing to an officer high above her under thrumming helicopter blades the path which Drummond seemed to be taking.

But it was of no immediate use. Drummond was making less progress now, however powerfully he was using those boxer's shoulders of his. The black wake that was indicating his position had all but vanished away.

Harriet, at the thought of his thrusting shoulders, touched her chin, and caused a spasm of blotting-out pain to run up into her head. But Drummond, she realised as she began to recover, was nowhere near getting to the edge of the huge mass of yelling and shouting protesters. He was far from any point where it might be practical for officers from the police cordon to grab him.

For a long time then she and the helicopter pilot, between them, tracked the new wake Drummond had begun to make as, turning this way and that, he sought for the easiest place to break out. They lost him once, and Harriet had difficulty keeping the tears out of her voice. But then she spotted him again, apparently trying now to make his way back once more to the end of Great George Street. Was he going to try the escape route he had earlier rejected?

But his progress was erratic and infinitely more slow than it had been in his first heady rush through the safe density of the main mass crowding Parliament Square. The black snake was getting shorter by the minute, and much harder to make out.

What if, before long, he lacks the energy to make any progress in any direction? Lets himself simply be carried this way and that by the mass of people around him? Will he come dully to find that when at last the demo peters out and the protesters trudge away he can somehow sneak past the police looking out for more obvious law-breakers?

And then her tireless helicopter came, booming and blasting, low over the forefront of the crowd, now making a frenzied effort to pierce the barrier erected outside the grey walls of Parliament. Suddenly, the pilot's voice shouted 'Got him. He's there. Just on the edge.'

Harriet thrust herself further out of the window, twisted to see where below there raged the ugly, no-holds-barred battle, now separated, it seemed, from the almost innocent shouting and chanting of the main mass.

God, that's war there, open war, she thought. Where have the decent British citizens gone, the Queen's law-abiding subjects?

But then she saw Drummond, clearly as if

she were looking at him across some wide garden.

'Yes,' she shouted to the pilot. 'Yes, I can see him, absolutely.'

'Right then. We're going to do something naughty. We've been talking about it for minutes. It's a manoeuvre strictly reserved for people drowning in the sea. But, if you can give us second-by-second guidance, we're going to send down a one-man snatch squad and pluck your Mr Drummond right up into the sky.'

'No,' Harriet shouted. 'No, listen, you shouldn't do it. You're putting your winchman into danger. Real damn danger. Don't do it. Just don't do it.'

'You'd better look upwards, Super. It's too late now.'

She looked up. Dangling out of the helicopter on the end of a steel cable there was a bulky man in a harness.

'More to the left,' she called into her mobile, abandoning any protest. 'He's more to the left.'

The noise the machine was making all but drowned now the screaming and crashing of the battle directly below.

'No, come a little further back if you can. He's seen there's no hope the way he was going.'

She kept her eyes fixed on the man at the end of the cable, some sort of straitjacket held between his gloved hands.

'Yes. Yes, that's it.'

She calculated hard now, as if she were tapping in vital alterations to some crucial spreadsheet.

'Now. Now, go. Down, down.'

The steel cable lengthened by a few feet. The officer dangling at its end spread his arms wide. And clasped them.

Valentine Drummond was swept up into . . . The arms of the law.

Hunt over.

'Hunt over?' John said. 'That broken rule *Thou shalt not kill* surgically removed from the body politic, that it?'

In the chair opposite, it took Harriet a moment or two to reply.

'Yes,' she said at last, a long sigh escaping her. 'Yes, I suppose, if you like to put it in that philosophical way, that's what has happened. Not that it seemed like it to me at the time. I take it you saw the whole thing on the *News?*'

'Yes, very dramatic, particularly for one of the few people who knew, or guessed, what was actually happening. At first I thought, like every other viewer I suppose, that the person being lifted out of that scrum of protesters was just someone the police particularly wanted, somebody dangerous. But then . . . Well, then I actually caught a glimpse of you leaning out of the window at the top of that tall building, and of course realised what it was all about.'

'Oh God, I never thought some idiot cameraman would think of zooming up to where I was. If the ACC's seen that, he'll be having a fit.'

She laughed then.

'And, do you know,' she said, 'I don't care a damn.'

'Such language. But — But, darling, don't you actually care? Is it, really and truly, that you don't care at all?'

'Really and truly, I don't.' She straightened up in her chair. 'Yes, this is it. I've totally proved to my own satisfaction that I'm every bit as good a detective as I was before —'

But now she choked, if only for an instant.

'I'm as good a detective,' she repeated slowly, 'as I was before Graham, my so-to-speak successor in the Service, was killed on duty. All right, in the months after that terrible moment when we heard about him, I was, I admit, less sharp than in my Hard Detective days. But I deny that I was like that for very long. I was certainly altogether as much on the ball as I have ever been in tracking down Valentine Tigger Drummond.'

'Of course you were.'

'All right, we're agreed. So now, or as soon as Drummond's trial is over and MI5 have dealt with the rest of the Cabal, I can hand in my resignation.'

'No.'

It was, plainly, John's first instinctive reaction. But in the shortest of moments he modified it.

'All right, darling, I'm not going to stand in your way, if that's what you genuinely want. But, as they say, do not act without due reflection. I mean, you've been successful for virtually your whole life in the Service. Do you really want to duck out before your time? Really want to?'

Harriet looked at him. Good, sensible John.

'All right,' she said. 'I will think. I'll give it your due reflection. But I tell you this: however long that I think, I can't at this moment promise anything.'

ABOUT THE AUTHOR

H. R. F. Keating is well versed in the worlds of crime, fiction and non-fiction. He was the crime books reviewer for *The Times* for fifteen years, as well as serving as the chairman of the Crime Writers' Association and the Society of Authors, and for many years as president of the Detection Club. Best known for his Inspector Ghote series, which twice won him the CWA Gold Dagger Award, in 1996 he was awarded the CWA Cartier Diamond Dagger for outstanding service to crime fiction. He lives in London with his wife, the actor Sheila Mitchell.

We hope you have enjoyed this Large Print book. Other Thorndike, Wheeler, and Chivers Press Large Print books are available at your library or directly from the publishers.

For information about current and upcoming titles, please call or write, without obligation, to:

Publisher
Thorndike Press
295 Kennedy Memorial Drive
Waterville, ME 04901
Tel. (800) 223-1244

or visit our Web site at:

http://gale.cengage.com/thorndike

OR

Chivers Large Print
published by BBC Audiobooks Ltd
St James House, The Square
Lower Bristol Road
Bath BA2 3SB
England
Tel. +44(0) 800 136919
email: bbcaudiobooks@bbc.co.uk
www.bbcaudiobooks.co.uk

All our Large Print titles are designed for easy reading, and all our books are made to last.